The
Zorzi
Affair

A Novel of
Galileo's Italy

SYLVIA PRINCE

The Zorzi Affair:
A Novel of Galileo's Italy
(Renaissance Unveiled)
© 2016 by Sylvia Prince
First edition

Visit the author's website at www.sylviaprincebooks.com.

This is a work of fiction. The characters, organizations, and events portrayed in this novel are either products of the author's imagination or are used fictionally. For more, see the Author's Note.

Cover design by BubbaShop

ALSO BY SYLVIA PRINCE

The Barrett Brides Trilogy
Engaged to an Earl
Seduced by a Surgeon
Romanced by a Rake

The Belladonna's Kiss Trilogy
Belladonna's Kiss
Belladonna's Embrace
Belladonna's Revenge

The Stolen Crown Trilogy
The Medici Prize
The Broken Blade
The Stolen Crown

The Lion and the Fox:
A Novel of Machiavelli's Florence

The Zorzi Affair:
A Novel of Galileo's Italy

Salem Mean Girls

A Matter of Glass
Palazzo Galileo Mysteries, Book One

CONTENTS

ONE

Venice, Italy
August 1609

Zaneta Lucia Zorzi ducked under the low doorway separating the kitchen and the alley. As she emerged into the sunlight, a wave of heat and a foul smell knocked her back.

This was a door that most people had forgotten. Only the scullery maid, Gianna, used it to throw out refuse. The narrow *calle* stank of rotting fish, with a mixture of fermenting vegetables and the ever-present tang of salt.

The odor was a selling point. Zaneta Lucia only used the door when she wanted to sneak out without being noticed. The stench drove everyone else in the household away. It was her secret—one of many that would cause significant problems if her father ever found out. Or, God forbid, her mother. A shudder passed through Zaneta Lucia's body as she considered the possibility. No, it wasn't even worth imagining. It was too terrible.

Zaneta Lucia held a cloth over her face to dampen the smell and pushed the tiny wooden door closed behind her.

She slunk down the pungent alley and hopped over a narrow rivulet of water and waste. Now she was behind the neighboring palazzo. For some reason this side smelled better, even in the middle of August. Maybe she would tell Gianna to throw some lemons into the alley. But that might draw undue attention. Why would the daughter of the illustrious Ser Zorzi care about the smell of the alley, where only rats scurried?

She pushed that thought, too, out of her head. Hugging the side of the building, she weaved her way toward the street.

Zaneta Lucia focused on her goal. She had to cross the city, all the way to the other end of the island, without being recognized. She tugged the cloak tight around her face. If anyone saw her, Zaneta Lucia's mother would certainly find out, and she would lose her tiny sliver of independence.

The cloak alone made her stand out in the shimmering heat. No one else was foolish enough to don a cloak in this weather. Drips of sweat were already running down her back, but she refused to disrobe.

Under the cloak, Zaneta Lucia was wearing pants. For the first time, her legs were unencumbered by the thick folds of fabric that Venetian girls wore. It had felt strange, sliding her legs into the pants. And now, on the streets, she could feel the eyes of a thousand strangers trained on her.

But what would they see? Not the daughter of a patrician. No, today she looked more like the son of a middling merchant or a tailor, some artisan boy out running errands.

Or at least she hoped.

Zaneta Lucia wasn't very confident in her disguise. In addition to the pants that had once belonged to her older brother, she'd carefully daubed a little soot around her face to darken her porcelain skin, and tied back her honey-streaked brunette hair in a thick braid that hid its length under the cloak. But she also needed the security of the cloak, even in the heat. It strengthened her resolve to visit the palazzo, in spite of all the risks.

Her heart pounded in her ears as she hurried across a bridge, her thin body bent against the unseen eyes of those around her. She walked through streets familiar to her from birth, hugging the walls of buildings. Zaneta Lucia barely noticed the palazzi that sprung from the canals. She passed the church where she had been baptized, and where her brother Filippo had married.

Filippo was so much older that he probably thought of her as a niece, not a sister. Filippo was practically out of the house for his apprenticeship in long-distance merchant trading by the time Zaneta Lucia was walking. But she had attended his wedding and stood proudly as the entire city watched. Or at least that's how it had felt to her, huddled in the crowded church as the priest joined Filippo and his wife in matrimony.

It had been an elaborate wedding. Her father had cried, "What else can we do? When a Zorzi marries the city expects a day to remember."

Zaneta Lucia had been too young to attend the feast after the wedding. Her mother had deemed it improper for an unmarried girl. So instead of celebrating with her brother, she had returned home under the watchful eye of their housekeeper, Maria. She had begged Maria to let her stand on the balcony overlooking the *campo* where wedding guests danced, but Maria was under strict instructions. So Zaneta Lucia sat, pretending to sew a hem, while the city celebrated.

She shook her head to clear the memories from her mind. If she lost her focus, she might make a mistake, and that would cost her much more than a night of dancing.

Zaneta Lucia reached down to grip her skirt, and found only the thin fabric of pants. She was not wearing the tightly fitted pants of an aristocrat. Instead, these were the pants of a working man, cut straight and in a light fabric that let a breeze pass through to her skin. Or, it would, if the breeze was not as hot as the August sun beating down on her.

She remembered her mother chastising Filippo for owning such clothes. Her mother had shouted that a Zorzi should not be seen in pants fit only for the boat makers at the Arsenale. Filippo had laughed, but he had also set aside the pants so that Gianna could dispose of them. Luckily, his little sister had snatched them up before they could be thrown unceremoniously out with the trash.

The unfamiliar feel of the pant legs brushing her skin made her shiver. She had heard that there were laws against women wearing pants. Gianna had whispered rumors about a woman arrested for impersonating a man, but her mother had overheard and scolded the maid for spreading such tales. Zaneta Lucia had been too afraid to ask about the punishment for a woman caught in pants, but it had consumed her mind ever since.

The church bells began to chime the quarter-hour, and Zaneta Lucia picked up her pace. She was late.

She skirted around the back of the Piazza San Marco. She also avoided the Merzeria, crowded with shops. Instead, she kept to the back streets. In a city like Venice it was possible to run into someone in the least likely places.

The midday sun beat down on the narrow streets, and even the heart of Venice felt empty. But few Venetians were out today. Everyone else was smart enough to avoid the heat, and the foul smells that were inescapable in summer. Zaneta Lucia kept her eyes down, and listened to the water lapping against the sides of the canal next to her. After narrowly avoiding a collision with a young man, she ducked into an alley, wiping sweat from her brow with the back of her hand.

She took a deep breath and pushed forward.

Finally she was at the Rialto. She skipped across the massive marble bridge, without pausing to gaze at the palazzi on the

Grand Canal, the ones she had dreamed about walking through. On one occasion she had even been asked to attend a ball at one of those extravagant palazzi. But her mother had made her turn down the invitation. It was unseemly for an unmarried woman to attend a dance, according to Bartolomea Zorzi.

Zaneta Lucia felt her lips curl back in a sneer at the thought of it. Her mother was so old fashioned when it came to her only daughter. Maybe it was because scandal had destroyed her own sister's marriage prospects. Aunt Ricciarda had be caught in a compromising position with a young man of less noble birth, and now she was in a convent. She seemed happy enough, but that was beside the point. A noble girl's virtue was a prize, one to be safely guarded at all times, especially before marriage. Or, at least, that's what her mother said.

But today Zaneta Lucia was going to walk into one of those palazzi on her own, and ignore everything her mother had taught her. She had snuck out, risking her virtue according to her mother, and broken the law by dressing as a man. She was walking across the city without a chaperone. And now, Zaneta Lucia was standing outside a palazzo, where she planned to interact with numerous unmarried men.

Zaneta Lucia loosened her grip on the cloak, letting it fall at her sides. She let out a breath of air and looked up at the shadowy façade of a massive building, which jutted out of the small campo like an Alpine mountain. Her eyes were fixed on the large painted door, cracked slightly to reveal the dark interior of the palazzo.

She willed her feet to move forward, but something held her back. An overwhelming urge gripped her. She wanted to run home and race up the stairs to her bedroom, where she could close the door and be alone.

Zaneta Lucia took a deep breath and told herself it was just nerves. But it was hard to ignore her instincts, which were telling her to flee.

Zaneta Lucia forced herself to take one step forward, and then another, until she had passed through the open door. The interior of the palazzo was cooler, at least. Her eyes adjusted to the dim light and she saw that she was in the entry hall. A servant standing to the right of the door bowed his head, waiting for her to speak.

"I'm here for the lecture?" she squeaked, and then cleared her throat. She hoped that she had masked any hint of femininity in her voice.

"Yes, right this way," the servant said.

Zaneta Lucia let out another breath. He had not thrown her out of the palazzo, or laughed in her face. The servant had accepted her disguise, and her right to enter the palazzo.

She had pictured this moment a thousand times as she plotted to attend the lecture. Just in case her true identity had been unmasked, Zaneta Lucia had practiced her speech to the angry patrician who owned the palazzo.

But thankfully the servant led her into the house, and pointed up the stairs to the lecture room. He told her to walk through the *portego* on the *piano nobile* until she reached the second door on the right.

And then he turned back to the door, ignoring her. She gave a brief nod of thanks and began climbing the stairs.

In her fantasies, she had never gotten further than the entryway of the palazzo. Her steps echoed on the marble stairs, and she refused to look behind her. She did not want to appear out of place. Even though she had made it into the palazzo, the risks had not vanished. She had to stay on high alert.

At the top of the stairs she almost lost her breath, gazing at the magnificent paintings that hung on the walls of the palazzo's grand hallway. Here, the wealth of the family was on display, in numerous paintings as well as elaborately casted candelabras and mahogany furniture. She saw paintings that looked familiar, perhaps similar to ones she had seen in the city's many churches. The colors, vibrant reds and blues with splashes of bright, pure white, whirled in front of her eyes, conveying the richness and culture of the palazzo's owners. She was, as she was supposed to be, impressed.

It wasn't quite like the Zorzi palazzo. They did have some fine paintings, but most were from her grandfather's era, not in this new style which was more alive. Plus, Zaneta Lucia had grown up with those paintings. The furnishings in their great hall, though certainly done in the nicest woods with elaborate carvings and some beautiful inlaid paintings, were simply not as modern as the ones she saw in this house. It made her family's home feel shabby in comparison, out of date and behind the times.

She was startled out of her rumination by someone walking very close to her, just past her shoulder. It was a young man, she saw, perhaps someone else attending the lecture.

"Nice paintings, right?" he said.

"Yes. I like them very much." She schooled herself to keep her answers short. What if she somehow revealed that she was a trespasser in this house?

"That one sure has some amazing tits." He gestured to a painting of a reclining nude.

Zaneta Lucia's breath caught in her throat. He clearly didn't think she was a woman, or he never would have spoken so crudely.

Was this how men talked amongst themselves?

Then she knew—her disguise worked. When she had gazed into the mirror in her bedroom, the slightly sooty face and pulled-back hair had simply transformed her, in her own eyes, into a dirtier version of herself. At not quite sixteen, she did not have the shape of an adult woman yet, but Zaneta Lucia feared that she looked too much like a girl to pass for anything else.

And yet this stranger believed that she was a boy.

The young man was staring at her, watching as her thoughts flashed across her face.

"Uh, yeah," she said. "Nice."

He shook his head and turned away, muttering something about Castello rubes. Her cheeks flushed and a wave of anger washed over her body. He knew nothing about her—and yet he somehow knew she was from the Castello neighborhood. Was it her clothes? Or did she appear badly out of place in the grand room, wearing her working-class pants and a cloak clearly inappropriate for the season?

Zaneta Lucia forced the anger to leave her body. It couldn't be her clothes, she reassured herself. After all, he did think she was a boy. So what if he guessed her neighborhood? It meant nothing, as long as her disguise had fooled him.

Zaneta Lucia traced his steps to the second door. She peaked inside and saw an impromptu lecture hall, with several rows of seats and a podium at the front of the room. There were already quite a few young men milling about, and even more seated in the chairs.

Her mouth went dry. She had always wanted to attend lectures, but of course her mother would not allow it. When Zaneta Lucia confided her secret wish to her older brother, he had scoffed. Filippo said that lectures were boring and he was glad that he never had to attend another one.

Of course, that was easy for him to say. As a Zorzi man, now established in trade, he was barred from very few places.

Zaneta Lucia started when she realized a man stood near the door watching her.

"Name?" he asked, his tone conveying impatience.

Her mind spun. She had not anticipated the lecture keeping attendance.

"Luca Manetti," she blurted out.

Luca had actually been her nickname when she was a young girl. Or at least, it had until she was old enough that her mother insisted a diminutive boy's name would deform her character in some way. Since then, her mother insisted that she be referred to by her full name: Zaneta Lucia Margherita Zorzi. She missed the simpler moniker.

The man wrote down her fake name in a large, leather-bound book, and looked up at her again. What could he want now?

"School?"

School? Oh, he wanted to know which school she attended. Venice didn't have a university, but it had a network of local schools where boys were educated in writing, Latin, and the book-keeping skills necessary for merchants. She had received something of an education, mainly from the tutor that her mother had hired to train Zaneta Lucia, but that had been primarily in Greek and Roman poetry, music, and dancing. "The sorts of things a young woman needs to know," her mother had said.

But Zaneta Lucia had wanted to learn other things. She had snuck into her brother's old collection of books and devoured them, reading about philosophy, political theory, and especially the study of nature. Science enthralled her. She was enamored with the ideas of Aristotle and the Greek authorities, who said that the world was made up of elements, each of which had a natural place. Earth wanted to be near earth and fire rose because it was in its nature to reach to the fiery sphere of the heavens.

Of course it appealed to her—on most days, she felt like an element removed from its natural place.

She snapped herself out of this daydream. The man was waiting for an answer. Zaneta Lucia quickly racked her brain, and mumbled, "Ser Giorgio Niccolini, Castello."

The man recorded her answer with a nod. Luckily, she remembered the name of her brother's instructor from ten years earlier. But her heart was pounding at how close she had come to ruining her disguise. She took a deep breath, her hands still shaking.

Zaneta Lucia scooted into the room and quietly took a seat in the back row. Hopefully she looked inconspicuous. When her heart stopped racing, she glanced around at the other people in the room. They were mostly boys her own age, dressed like patricians, though she saw a few in threadbare hand-me-downs. She felt out of place in her ill-fitted pants, and tucked her legs under the chair as if she could will herself to vanish.

Luckily she didn't recognize anyone. Not that she knew many boys her own age anyway. It was improper for unmarried men and women to congregate outside of church. Zaneta Lucia was practically living in a convent, like her aunt. A flash of resentment built in her chest as she looked around at the boys, who were allowed to travel the city at their own whim. It was her own bad luck that she'd been born a girl.

Aside from the boys, she saw a few older gentlemen, or at least they dressed like gentlemen, with lacy cuffs sticking out of their black robes. She assumed these were instructors, men who gave private lessons to the sons of Venice's noble families. She hadn't seen many of them herself, since her brother had finished his lessons when she was still a young girl.

A thin, older man with a clean-shaven face stood next to the podium at the front of the room. He was also wearing a black robe, the sign of Venice's republican brotherhood.

He looked intimidating, from her perspective, but then he was a professor and she was simply an uneducated girl who'd snuck into the lecture. Sweat coated her forehead as she pictured what might happen if someone recognized her deception. Would she simply be asked to leave? Would they report her to the city council? Or would one of them escort her home and tell her mother all about it? If Zaneta Lucia was exposed, she'd rather jump into a canal in January than face her mother.

In her mind, she repeated a mantra: I'm Luca, I'm Luca, I'm here to listen to the lecture. If she thought it hard enough, maybe it would start to feel true.

The doors of the room swung shut with a bang and the professor stepped behind the podium. He tapped it a few times to get the attention of the audience. Everyone settled into their seats, and Zaneta Lucia leaned forward in anticipation. She forced her body to relax back into the seat, mimicking the posture of the boy sitting two seats away.

The professor began to speak in a dry voice. "Welcome. I am Professor Cornaro from the University of Padua. Today, we will discuss nature. Whatever we call it—science, natural philosophy—it means the study of our world. Let's begin today with Aristotle. The philosopher states that an arrow shot from a bow will gradually fall back to the earth. And we know this from experience as well."

Zaneta Lucia's eyes widened. The professor was talking about Aristotle's laws of motion. After years of secretly reading books, she was finally listening to a real lecture on natural philosophy.

"But why does this occur? Why does an arrow return to the ground?" The professor paused expectantly, scanning the audience as if he wanted a volunteer to supply the information.

Did professors pose questions to the students? Zaneta Lucia had no idea.

Her eyebrows compressed as she racked her brain for the answer. The words came to her mind in a flash. An arrow is made of earth and wants to return to the earth, so of course it will eventually fall to the ground. She was confident that her answer was correct, but she glanced around to see if anyone else would take up the professor's challenge.

The other boys fidgeted in their seats, avoiding eye contact. Zaneta Lucia's palms were suddenly damp. Was she supposed to raise her hand, or was this some kind of trap? Her neighbor, Nino Romani, had told her some instructors asked trick questions to shame and fool students. Zaneta Lucia felt faint as she pictured the entire room laughing at her.

But the professor continued to stare out at the students, his eyebrows raised. Still, no one volunteered.

Zaneta Lucia took a deep breath and slowly raised her hand. The professor's eyes locked on to her, and with a nod he signaled that she should speak.

Her mouth was bone dry. Why had she raised her hand? "Aristotle says—"

"Speak up, I can't hear you," the professor said gruffly, eliciting a few chuckles from the other boys. They seemed relieved that someone else had volunteered for the professor's scrutiny.

Zaneta Lucia balled her fists and resolved not to back down. She continued in a loud voice. "Aristotle says that an arrow, made of earth, will naturally try to move back toward the earth. The force elicited by the bow will push it forward, but the arrow will eventually seek its natural resting place."

The room was silent for a moment, and her vision wobbled. Had she said something foolish?

"Bravo, young man, you've read your Aristotle," the professor said.

Zaneta Lucia felt her face redden with the praise. She looked down at the floor to cover the unmanly reaction. But in her mind, she was singing. She had longed to discuss natural philosophy, and here, in her first conversation with a professor, she had received confirmation that she was on the right track.

And she had answered his question when none of the boys

had been willing to raise their hands.

Her internal celebration was cut short by the professor's next statement.

"But," the professor asked with his eyes still on her, "Why does the arrow continue to travel forward after the bow is no longer exerting force upon it? How can we predict where the arrow will fall? How long will it travel along that path?"

Zaneta Lucia's mind went blank. Had Aristotle ever addressing these questions? She tried to remember every word she had ever read about Aristotle. But she had not read all of his books.

The professor looked at her expectantly.

Zaneta Lucia opened her mouth and stopped, feeling the blush in her cheeks deepen. The other boys began to chuckle.

Professor Cornaro tapped his podium. "You're all so willing to mock this pupil, but can anyone answer my question?"

That silenced the room.

"I didn't think so," the professor continued. "That is because Aristotle himself could not answer these questions. He tried to claim that an arrow, cutting through the air, creates a vacuum behind it. Since nature abhors a vacuum, the air in front of the arrow would rush behind it to fill the vacuum, propelling the arrow forward. But this is a rather shaky explanation, wouldn't you say?" His eyes swept over the room, daring one of them to speak. No one answered.

"If that were true, why would the arrow ever slow down? It would continue indefinitely. Why would the vacuum cease to exist once it had come into existence? Further, if nature abhors a vacuum, why can simply loosing an arrow create one? That would be outside the laws of nature."

Professor Cornaro's words washed over Zaneta Lucia, poking holes in the great Aristotle's theories. She leaned forward once again, entranced by the question. She had not even considered these problems while reading Aristotle.

Had she read Aristotle incorrectly? Was it obvious to true students that his books, esteemed by all, had flaws?

Zaneta Lucia frowned. What if Aristotle was not correct on every issue? What if she didn't have to accept the views of the classical authorities as truth? Could their ideas be open to questioning? Might they even change one day?

Professor Cornaro was not tearing down Aristotle. He was pointing out that there was still work to be done.

Zaneta Lucia let out a breath of air.

Maybe Aristotle was wrong about other things, too. She had heard whispers about the ideas of the monk Copernicus, who claimed that the earth revolved around the sun. But his writings had been condemned as a fanciful mathematical theory with no basis in reality. What if he was right?

"These are questions we still must answer in natural philosophy," the professor continued, interrupting Zaneta Lucia's internal epiphany. "In fact, one of my colleagues in Padua has been working on the topic of mechanics lately. His most recent work posits a law of inertia which explains the arrow's flight. The arrow will continue to fly because it carries a residual force from the bow. Along the same lines, anyone who has studied military technology knows the importance of mathematics and the ability to plot parabolas and trajectories. My colleague dares to ask, is it possible to trace the arc of an arrow and describe it using mathematics?"

The professor's lecture was interrupted by a voice near the front.

"Mathematics?"

Zaneta Lucia's eyes zeroed in on the student. She realized with a start that it was the boy she had met in the hall, the admirer of art.

"Mathematics is a low-class pursuit. I would rather work

with Aristotle and the classical authorities than run calculations like some sort of menial book keeper."

The boy next to him snickered, but most of the other students looked astonished at the outburst. The professor leaned on his podium, a faint smile on his face.

"And what is your name, young man?" the professor asked.

"Tommaso Mocenigo."

Mocenigo—he was from one of Venice's richest families. As she stared at the back of the boy's head, Zaneta Lucia could almost hear her mother's voice praising the illustrious family.

"Oh, you look down on mathematics, do you?" Professor Cornaro said with a grimace. "I feel sorry for your professors at the university, if you make it that far. Mathematics is the most important skill for a natural philosopher to master, and will define our field for the next hundred years at least."

Zaneta Lucia eyes darted back to the boy. Would he continue to challenge the professor? The back of his head revealed nothing. She doubted that a Mocenigo boy was used to such a dismissive response. The professor must not be from Venice.

And yet Tommaso was silent.

The professor looked back at the audience, effectively ignoring Tommaso's outburst. "Now, returning to the lecture, I want to explain the latest findings in the study of motion. This work has begun to challenge some of Aristotle's ideas. Let me be clear—this may not overthrow Aristotle's laws of nature, but the work will give us a better perspective on how our world operates. And these new ideas, as I mentioned, come from a colleague of mine at the University of Padua, named Professor Galileo."

TWO

After the lecture, Zaneta Lucia practically floated home. She felt alive, practically vibrating with energy. The lecture been like nothing else in her life. Zaneta Lucia replayed Professor Cornaro's words in her mind. She had never heard of this Galileo before, but his new ideas had already revolutionized the way she saw her world.

Professor Cornaro had warned that not everyone agreed with Galileo's conclusions. But Zaneta Lucia was captivated. To think that the world worked in terms of force, and motion, and everything acting according to mathematical rules.

It reminded Zaneta Lucia of the clock in the Piazza San Marco. The hand on the blue and gold clock face turned as if by magic, though she knew it was driven by mechanical gears, invisible to people watching from the piazza. At the top of the tall tower, two bronze men marked the passage of time by striking a bell. As a young girl, she had stared at the clock and marveled at its precision. How did the bronze men come to life, even though they were metal? And how did they know when to hit the bell? Her father had explained the clock to her, revealing its hidden secrets.

The universe must work similarly. It was so perfect that Zaneta Lucia was astonished that no one had thought of it before. Or that Galileo wasn't already famous, with everyone worshipping him for revealing the majesty of God's creation.

Tommaso had not interrupted the lecture again. But as soon as the professor finished speaking, the boy had quickly turned his back on the man, and laughed loudly as the professor walked to the door. Was he pretending that the professor's admonishments had not affected him? Zaneta Lucia was still embarrassed at her own flubbed answer. In comparison, Tommaso's behavior was horrifically rude. The professor was an honored speaker, and to treat him so dismissively was unthinkable.

On top of that, Tommaso Mocenigo had all the advantages of being born into an illustrious Venetian family, and he was treating those gifts as if they were worthless.

It made her shake just to remember his smirk.

Zaneta Lucia climbed the Rialto bridge, the sun bouncing off the bright marble. She turned her thoughts back to the lecture itself. She wanted to remember every word. And how could she get some of Galileo's writings? She had to learn more about his theories.

Soon she was back in her own neighborhood. Zaneta Lucia stopped to pull the cloak closer around her body. She rubbed at the soot on her face and unwound the braid pulling back her hair. As she shed her disguise, she realized with a sigh that she already missed the freedom she had experienced as Luca Manetti.

But she had no choice.

Zaneta Lucia ducked behind the neighbor's palazzo and began weaving back toward her own house. Retracing her steps, she jumped lightly over the thin rivulet separating the two buildings.

The afternoon heat had only magnified the alley's stench, and the sleeve she held in front of her face barely helped. She hurried along the *calle*, suddenly fearful that she might be spotted from one of the upstairs windows.

Finally she was at the back door. She pushed it open and

slipped inside.

"There you are," a voice cried out and Zaneta Lucia jumped, slamming the door behind her. She spun around, her hairs all standing on end.

"Gianna," she gasped, still in shock, when she saw it was just the scullery maid. "You terrified me." Zaneta Lucia clutched the cloak tighter to hide the boy's clothes that she wore underneath. She would have even more to explain if Gianna saw what she was wearing.

Gianna frowned, her hands on her hips. "Terrified? That's nothing compared with what will happen if your mother catches you smelling like that. I told her you were out at church, but dressed in that dirty old cloak and smelling like the wife of a fishmonger? She'll never believe it."

Relief had swept over Zaneta Lucia when she had seen Gianna, but now her anxiety flooded back. She bit her lower lip. Gianna could be fired if her mother found out about the lie.

"But how did you know I had snuck out?"

"No one ever opens this door," Gianna said, hustling Zaneta Lucia to the back staircase in the corner of the kitchen. "But suddenly someone moved my pans out of the way, and stole the cloak Messer Giovanni put in the pile for charity." She gave Zaneta Lucia a scolding glance, which quickly changed into a smile. "There's no time for chatter. Run upstairs, wash your face, and change. Your mother is looking for you."

Zaneta Lucia's throat tightened at the mention of her mother. She ran up the stairs two at a time, silently promising to somehow pay Gianna back. For all her tough words, the maid had always looked out for Zaneta Lucia.

"I hope the boy is worth it," she heard Gianna mutter before she was out of earshot.

Zaneta Lucia nearly stumbled. She wanted to turn around and correct Gianna. Did she really think Zaneta Lucia was foolish enough to risk everything for a boy? Her cheeks reddened at the thought, and she shook it from her head. She had to concede that Gianna's deduction was firmly grounded in practical experience. After all, it was a more common scenario than sneaking out for a lecture on Aristotle. She suppressed a laugh at the thought.

Out of breath, she reached the top of the stairs and raced toward her bedroom, nestled into a back corner on the third floor of the palazzo.

"Zaneta Lucia Margherita Zorzi!" Her mother's voice called from somewhere on the *piano nobile*.

Zaneta Lucia's eyebrows shot up as she looked down at her clothes. If her mother saw her dressed as a boy . . . She could not even imagine what her mother might do.

Zaneta Lucia ran into her room and slammed the door behind her, wincing as the sound echoed through the hall. Pulling off the cloak, she shoved it into the bottom of the chest, burying it under a pile of dresses. Hopefully its smell wouldn't corrupt her other clothes. She hopped out of the pants—much harder to take off than a skirt—and pulled a dress over her head, on top of the loose shirt she had worn to the lecture. No time to put the pants away—she shoved them under the edge of her bed with a foot.

She had only a moment to glance in the looking glass. She smoothed out her hair and splashed some water on her face.

The door flung open.

When her mother walked into the room, Zaneta Lucia was kneeling on the floor in front of her bed, hands clasped in prayer. She tried to look completely innocent, masking her face in surprise as though she hadn't heard her mother. "Oh, mother, what is it?" Zaneta Lucia asked. Hopefully her mother couldn't hear the beating of her heart, which sounded louder than the Sunday church bells.

"Young lady, where have you been?" her mother asked, her hands crossed under her chest. Bartolomea Zorzi stood several inches shorter than her daughter, who had sprouted taller in the past year without gaining the womanly attributes that she would prefer over the inches, but her mother still struck an imposing sight. She glared at her daughter, her eyes narrow.

Bartolomea walked over to the window, casually glancing outside, and then turned back to her daughter. Her hands smoothed down her deep purple brocaded gown. Her mother stared at Zaneta Lucia, lips pursed.

Zaneta Lucia swallowed. "I'm sorry, mother. I walked over to the church because I wanted to pray for all the young children kidnapped and sold into slavery by the Ottoman infidels." She was fumbling with the loose folds of her skirt as she spoke, and willed her fingers to be still. The skirt somehow felt foreign after just a few hours in pants. Had there always been so much fabric?

She watched her mother's face for any sign of disbelief, and thanked her patron saint that a lie came quickly to her lips. Her mother would jump on any sign of weakness or indecision.

Bartolomea narrowed her eyes even further, but then gave a quick nod. "Well. You know that you are not supposed to leave without a chaperone. You're too old to be walking the city by yourself. It is simply not safe. And the Ottoman Turks. You shouldn't think of such things. It will give you wrinkles."

As she spoke, Bartolomea walked from the window over to her daughter's bed, and stood directly in front of Zaneta Lucia.

What could she want now? Oh, she was waiting for an apology. "Yes, mother. I was wrong and I won't do it again."

Bartolomea gave another nod, and reached a hand down to her daughter, pulling her to her feet.

"I trust that it will not happen again," her mother began, and then her voice got lighter. "But that's not why I was looking for you. Your father and I need to tell you something."

Zaneta Lucia let her mother link arms with her and led her toward the sitting room near the front of the house. She racked her brain. What could her parents want to talk with her about? Her mother's foul mood had vanished, replaced by an unsettling cheerfulness. But a conversation with both of her parents could not be good.

After all, it was not like her mother to drop such a serious transgression so quickly. Bartolomea never allowed Zaneta Lucia to leave the house without a chaperone, even to visit the church around the corner. Yet her mother had already forgotten the infraction. What could possibly make her mother neglect proper social decorum?

Was something wrong with her brother Filippo? Was his wife going to have another child? No, that couldn't be it—no one had told her the last time Giulia Maria had fallen pregnant. So what could it be?

Zaneta Lucia's feet dragged in anticipation of bad news. Her mother practically pulled her into the sitting room. Her father stood at the window, his back to the door. He was gazing at the canal that flowed in front of their house.

He turned as they entered, and Zaneta Lucia was struck by how the sunlight highlighted the gray in his hair. He would turn sixty next year, and the age was starting to show in his face. His broad shoulders spoke to the strength of his youth. Though he still cut an imposing figure, he had always been warm and gentle with his only daughter.

"Zaneta Lucia," her father began. He paused, glancing once more out the window before turning his eyes back to his family.

Was it possible that he had seen her sneaking home after the lecture? Did her mother only pretend to accept the story about being at church? Zaneta Lucia's blood pounded in her ears.

"Your mother and I have an exciting announcement for you."

An announcement?

Her heart beat quickly as she waited for him to continue. He pursed his lips, and opened his mouth to speak. Then he closed it, the growing silence only increasing Zaneta Lucia's anxiety.

Her mother sighed and interrupted her father's laborious thought process. "We have arranged a marriage for you."

Zaneta Lucia blinked. Her knees wobbled, and she reached out to steady herself on a nearby chair. A marriage? Her parents wanted her to get married?

"What?" she managed to gasp.

Her father had finally found his words. "Yes, dear, you are the right age, and when the Barbaro family approached us, we thought . . ." Her father trailed off. "You see, we have a dowry, and it's a rather good size, and it's only a boy in a minor branch of the Barbaro family. But, you see, they take a small part in government, just as we do . . ." He again stopped, under the harsh glare of his wife.

Zaneta Lucia released the chair. "A small part in government? You mean, like our family, hanging our name on an ancestor centuries ago who was the doge?" Her voice rose, and she barely recognized the tone that she never used with her father.

Without warning, her mother's hand flashed out and caught Zaneta Lucia across the face in a loud slap. Zaneta Lucia raised both hands to her stinging cheek as the pain reverberated through her body.

"You will not speak of our family that way," her mother warned in a low voice. "You will be an obedient daughter. This is a good union for our family, one which will bring us much prestige. It is very difficult to make an alliance like this."

Zaneta Lucia blinked back tears. She refused to cry.

How was she supposed to know that her parents had been plotting an engagement? Yes, in the past few months her mother had brought up marriage. She had gone on and on about the neighbor girl's favorable engagement. And she kept talking about rising dowry prices. But Zaneta Lucia had ignored those conversations. They had felt so unimportant in comparison with her clandestine intellectual pursuits.

Her stomach sank. What about her studies? What husband would want a wife who read Aristotle? It would be unseemly for a married woman to put herself on a public stage to discuss natural philosophy. Shameful, even. No husband would allow it. The acid in her stomach rolled, and she was overcome with nausea.

"Is she okay?" her father asked her mother. "She looks ill."

Would she have to end her studies? All to please her parents and some man she had never met?

"Ignore it, she's just getting used to the idea. All women go through something like this," her mother said.

After a moment of silence—"Did you?" her father asked.

"Of course not," Bartolomea replied brusquely. "I was thrilled and honored to join an illustrious family like the Zorzi."

Her mother's words pulled Zaneta Lucia out of her nausea. She almost laughed at this obvious lie. What had Filippo told her several years ago? Oh, that their mother had apparently wept when she first saw her future husband. Not that the Zorzi weren't in the upper echelons of Venetian society—their name was in the Golden Book, the original list of ruling families made in the thirteenth century, after all.

But the Zorzi had seen better days. And their mother had been born into the more illustrious Dandolo family. After her sister Ricciarda disgraced the family by sneaking off with a boy who barely had a last name, her parents had quickly arranged a marriage—any marriage—to repair the family's reputation.

Somehow, remembering her mother's engagement did not ease Zaneta Lucia's worries. But was her mother right? Did all girls feel sick when their parents announced an engagement? For Zaneta Lucia, it felt more like a death than any kind of new beginning. It would be the end of the meager freedoms she had carved out, and an end to her dreams of learning natural philosophy.

Both her parents were watching her. Her father looked worried and her mother's eyebrows were raised, as she waited for her daughter to respond appropriately.

Zaneta Lucia drew in a shaky breath. Breaking down would accomplish nothing. She unballed her fists, which had been clenched at her sides, and pushed down her emotions.

"What is the man like?" Her voice sounded cold and distant to her ears.

A smile crept over her father's face. "His father has served in the Senate, and he is an only son, although the family has three daughters. His branch of the family is well regarded, descended from the doge in the early sixteenth century. He is twenty-nine, or maybe thirty."

The details about the family didn't mean much to Zaneta Lucia. But the man was twice her age? She knew it was common for adult men to marry teenage girls. After all, her mother was much younger than her father, and though Filippo was over a decade her elder, his wife Giulia Maria was only a handful of years older than Zaneta Lucia. She must have been sixteen when they married.

Still, Zaneta Lucia had never thought of herself as a bride, even as her own sixteenth birthday drew near. In fact, she'd rarely thought about marriage at all, much to her mother's chagrin.

But had she been fooling herself? Zaneta Lucia ignored marriage, but that did not somehow insulate her from an engagement. She knew that at sixteen most girls from Venice's elite families were either married or engaged. But somehow she had distracted herself from applying the same logic to her own life. Was there no way to avoid the terrible fate?

And what had she been thinking, reading those old books of Aristotle? Why had she snuck out for a lecture? She'd been a fool, denying what was right in front of her face. And now she had to marry some stranger who was older than her brother Filippo, nearly as old as her own mother. Her face crumpled and she hid her tears with her hands, not wanting her parents to see her cry.

Her mother put an arm on Zaneta Lucia's shoulders. She gently pushed her daughter's hands back down to her sides, and waited until Zaneta Lucia met her gaze. But where Zaneta Lucia hoped to find comfort, or at least sympathy, instead she saw only her mother's steely gaze.

"You will marry this Barbaro man," Bartolomea said slowly. "We have arranged an engagement party for next Saturday, and you will find it within yourself to be happy about this union."

"Bartolomea, you're frightening her."

"She needs to get used to the idea sooner rather than later," her mother said, releasing Zaneta Lucia's hands. "And the sooner you realize that, Gino, the better." Her mother turned and left the room without looking back, leaving Zaneta Lucia and her father alone.

Her vision blurred with tears. She quickly brushed them from her face, staring at the carpet. She did not want to see the worry etched on her father's face.

"I understand this might come as a shock," her father said quietly. "But you will be sixteen in a few weeks, and that's old enough . . . that's how old your mother was when we married."

She knew her father wanted to help. He was trying to give her the sympathy she had craved only moments ago from her mother. But instead of feeling grateful, she felt empty. Could her father really expect her to marry some Barbaro stranger who was thirty?

Her life as she knew it would be over if she married.

She would have to leave behind her house, leave Gianna and her parents and her neighborhood. She didn't even know where this man lived. She would have to move in with strangers. She would have to give up everything she knew, and everything she cared about, because . . . Well, why?

In her mind, she heard the answer as if spoken by her mother: Because that's what's done.

Her mother would never let her study natural philosophy and remain unmarried. It would bring shame to her family, and they would be the laughing-stock of the city. In her mother's eyes, it would only be one step down from the dishonor of Aunt Ricciarda.

Her father took a step toward her, his concern wrinkling the skin around his eyes. "Maybe you . . . maybe you would like to go lie down for a little while?" He paused. "I can walk you back to your room if that would help?"

Zaneta Lucia nodded, and allowed him to take her arm and led her out of the room. She barely saw the furnishings, paintings, and pictures on the walls during the short walk back to her room. Had it truly only been a quarter-hour earlier that her mother was leading her in the opposite direction down this same hall? It felt like a lifetime ago.

Her life was whirling out of her control. The whole thing felt like a blur.

Her father let go of her arm outside her door, and gave her a slight pat on the shoulder. "It will be alright, daughter. He really does come from a good family."

Zaneta Lucia stood in the doorway, watching her father's back as he walked away. Was that all her father cared about? That he comes from a good family? As if that somehow made everything fine.

Bile was rising in her throat. Her father knew nothing about what it was like to be a girl. She would be carted off to a new family as if she were simply some commodity to exchange between men.

Of course her father couldn't truly understand. But her mother should know Zaneta Lucia's fears. Why was Bartolomea so cold and brittle? Her mother jumped at every chance to defend the family honor. She cared more about what the neighbors thought than what Zaneta Lucia wanted.

Zaneta Lucia pulled the door closed. Had her mother really expected her only daughter to be thrilled by the prospect of an engagement?

Maybe other girls, in her shoes, would have been happy. Girls like Maria Romani, their neighbor. Her mother kept pushing Zaneta Lucia to befriend the girl. Maria spent all her time bragging about her trousseau and the size of her dowry, and mooning over eligible families. Eligible families, not even eligible men. All she cared about was making a good match and getting married. No wonder Zaneta Lucia had preferred talking with her brother Nino about natural philosophy.

Zaneta Lucia threw herself on the bed. Her anger receded, replaced with a sense of hopelessness. She had no choice—she would have to marry the Barbaro man, because what else could she do? As the daughter of Gino Zorzi, she bore the weight of her familial obligations. Zaneta Lucia could not escape her last name.

But her aunt had avoided an arranged marriage. Was Aunt Ricciarda happy in the convent? Could Zaneta Lucia be happy in one, too?

Nuns were cloistered, kept away from the eyes of the city. They lived behind high walls, never leaving their convents. Zaneta Lucia only visited Aunt Ricciarda a few times a year, even though her convent was five minutes from the Zorzi palazzo.

Her aunt seemed happy enough, but maybe she was simply grateful to see someone from the outside world.

Zaneta Lucia wondered if nuns ever snuck out to attend lectures. Probably not.

She knew, from what she'd overheard from her mother's conversations, that there were convents in the city that catered to girls from wealthy families. With dowry costs skyrocketing, many were forced into convents because their families could not attract prospective husbands. After all, who would marry a girl if her family couldn't offer a substantial dowry? It would be a black mark.

And her mother had gone on and on about the Priuli family, which had six daughters. What had her mother said? "Those girls will be the ruin of their family."

Zaneta Lucia rolled her eyes.

But then she sat up. Were her parents making similar calculations? They had only two children—unusual enough. Most families were larger. But Filippo was an adult, married off and already established in business. He had children of his own. She was the only daughter, so her family could afford a large dowry. They could make a strategic match for their daughter, placing her in an elite family.

They must have been planning this since her birth, saving up so that she could marry up, to make the family look better. She was a tool to improve the status of the Zorzi, born for that purpose alone.

Zaneta Lucia sank back onto the bed. She couldn't join a convent. They'd never allow it. It didn't matter if she would be happy as a nun. Her wishes did not factor into her parents' decision. They only cared about the family's honor, and in that calculation her only value was on the marriage market.

Zaneta Lucia spat out a curse. It was her bad luck to be a girl. How things might have been different if she had been born a boy. She wouldn't have to marry a stranger. She would have at least a decade or longer before anyone would pester her to settle down and start a family.

She would have years and years to devote herself to learning.

Zaneta Lucia rolled over, peaking through the small window next to her bed. It looked out on an interior courtyard where the flowers had wilted in the August heat.

Had she been born Luca Zorzi, she would have received an education. The finest tutors would have visited the palazzo to instruct her. She would not have to sneak around trying to steal books on Aristotle, and she would never have to disguise herself to attend a lecture.

She could attend a university.

It was all too much.

Zaneta Lucia buried her face in her pillow and wept.

THREE

Later that day, Zaneta Lucia pulled out the pair of pants she had stuffed under her bed. She clutched the pants in her hands for a moment, then dropped them to the floor.

She reached into the wooden chest at the foot of her bed and gently removed her small collection of natural philosophy books. She slowly stacked the books on her desk.

Her days of reading books and wearing pants were over.

Zaneta Lucia pictured herself wrapping the books up in the pants and throwing the bundle into a canal.

Then she picked up a slim printed volume of Aristotle's *Physics*. Her neighbor Nino had given it to her. It was only an abridged version, and the pages were worn. Nino's father had bought him a newer edition, so Nino happily sold the older book to her. It was one of her most prized possessions.

The thought of throwing it into a canal made her sick.

Zaneta Lucia had moped around her room all afternoon. She had to come to terms with her future. But she could not let go of her past. She scooped up the book and the pants, gently placing them back in the bottom of the chest.

She would just have to find some way to keep reading even after she became Signora Barbaro.

Zaneta Lucia Margherita Barbaro. It sounded so foreign to

her ears. How could she transform into an entirely different person? "Signora Barbaro" was a stranger to her.

It felt like she should don widow's clothes.

Zaneta Lucia spent most of the next week in her room, gazing out the window at the single lonely tree in the courtyard. Its leaves drooped, even in the shade. Zaneta Lucia watched as a lone breeze ruffled the branches.

She wanted to escape her life.

On those long, hot August days, Zaneta Lucia avoided speaking with her mother as much as possible.

Her father visited her room every few days. Those visits were awkward and short. Her father clearly believed she would cheer up at any minute. Zaneta Lucia overheard her parents whispering about her in the hall, her father's voice strained with worry while her mother remained firm.

Her mother was a constant presence on the third floor. Every time Zaneta Lucia turned around her mother was there, watching and judging. When Zaneta Lucia's appetite disappeared, it was her mother who pushed a clear broth into her hands, insisting that she finish it before bed.

Zaneta Lucia refused to acknowledge her presence.

Her mother seemed to believe Zaneta Lucia would eventually get used to the idea of marrying. She chattered on about Zaneta Lucia's trousseau, and the wealth of the Barbaro family, as if Zaneta Lucia cared.

Then, a few days before the engagement party, Bartolomea burst into the room with a pair of servants. They carried a billowing dress. Her mother ordered her out of bed for a fitting, and practically dragged Zaneta Lucia down the hall.

Zaneta Lucia had to admit that it was a beautiful dress. It was tight though the bodice where she had little to show off, and it flared out at the hips, making them look more impressive than they actually were. The skirt was full, made of deeply layered blue cloth, slashed through with peeks of silver threaded material. Tiny pearls covered the bodice, and the dress shimmered in the light.

It must have cost a fortune.

Bartolomea, Gianna, and another servant pushed, pulled, and prodded her into the dress. Zaneta Lucia gasped when she finally saw her reflection in the mirror. Instead of a scrawny young girl, gawky with age but lacking a feminine body, a beautiful woman stood in the mirror. Zaneta Lucia blinked, half believing the image was a mirage.

Her eyes were drawn to the row of ruffles at the sleeves and collar. The pale lace made her skin glow.

"And with the right necklace," her mother said as she draped a strand of pearls over Zaneta Lucia's head. "Yes. That will do."

Zaneta Lucia took a step back. The dress moved slowly, weighed down by fabric and embellishments. How was she supposed to walk in this outfit? Underneath layers of cloth, the dress was held up by a hidden infrastructure of supports and holds. Zaneta Lucia nearly tripped over the dragging hemline. She had not even tried to stand in the tall heels she was expected to wear. And the dressmaker had promised additional alterations to increase the size of the billowing skirts.

During the fitting her mother had spared no time for compliments. Instead, Zaneta Lucia listened to a lecture on etiquette. She should always consider how she looked to others. She must avoid awkward movements. And, at all times, she would watch her words when she spoke with anyone at the engagement party.

Zaneta Lucia still trembled at the thought of the party. On Saturday, she would meet her future husband for the first time. The thought made her feel faint. Every time Zaneta Lucia imagined the party, her stomach tied up in knots. Not only would it be her formal entrance into Venetian society, she would have to speak with the Barbaro man at the party. She'd finally learned from her mother that his name was Mario. Zaneta Lucia thought it was a stupid name.

But her mother cared little for such concerns. To her, the party was meant to show off the wealth of the Barbaro and the Zorzi families. Everyone attending must be impressed with the quality of the union. Zaneta Lucia's only purpose was to look perfect, which meant she had to look expensive. To her family, she was just a living mannequin.

Zaneta Lucia wiggled out of the dress with a sigh of relief. The tight bodice had cut off her breath, and she ran to the window for a gulp of fresh air. How was she supposed to wear the dress for hours at the engagement party?

Her stomach did another flip. Time was slipping away, and with each second, the engagement party drew closer.

~ ~ ~

The night before the engagement party, Zaneta Lucia lay on her bed, clutching a book to her chest. She threw down the book—then checked to make sure it hadn't been damaged—and sat up. She hurried to the chest and pulled out her cloak.

Before the party, before she came face-to-face with Mario Barbaro, she would sneak out of the house one last time.

Zaneta Lucia tiptoed down the wide staircase at the back of the palazzo, her ears trained to pick up the sound of her parents, or one of the maids. The palazzo was silent, a massive stone tomb carved with the Zorzi family name. Soon she reached the small door in the kitchen that led to the narrow *calle*. A week earlier she had made the same journey. This time, instead of facing blazing sunlight and the smell of rancid fish, she paced through the alley in the dark. She had to find her way by the moonlight and narrow strips of light shining from the windows of the surrounding buildings.

She was not going far.

Instead of heading west, toward the Piazza San Marco, she turned in the opposite direction. Her route took her down the tail of the fish-shaped Venetian islands. Within minutes the palazzi where she had grown up faded into the dark, and she was walking past smaller buildings, packed into streets where multiple families lived on different floors.

Zaneta Lucia had never been to a fortune teller before. Nino had mentioned the woman recently, bragging about her ability to divine the future. The soothsayer had told Nino that he would be rich and happy—not difficult to guess based on the boy's clothes, and easily believed through wishful thinking. The woman might not actually have the gift, but right now, Zaneta Lucia just wanted someone to promise her that she would survive the Barbaro marriage.

She saw the sign at the end of a narrow alley. "Signora Battaglia," it read, in yellow paint on a black background. Zaneta Lucia stopped at the mouth of the alley. She shifted her weight, building up the courage to take the final steps to the woman's small shop. Zaneta Lucia set her jaw and practically stomped up to the door.

Zaneta Lucia knocked lightly, and a voice called for her to enter. She pushed open the door, and immediately her senses were assaulted by all manner of things. The smell of incense coming from the shop was overwhelming, and she winced against the bright light of a dozen candles. When her eyes adjusted to the light, she saw a room full of eclectic goods. One wall contained a row of books, their large, leather-bound spines painted with writing in multiple scripts. Another wall held glass jars competing for space on a wide shelf, in a rainbow of green, blue, and brown. Directly in front of her, an older woman sat wearing rather demur clothes, her graying hair tied at the nape of her neck and her body cloaked in black.

"Welcome," the woman said, gesturing for Zaneta Lucia to sit at the table across from her. "You are here to see the future."

It almost sounded like a question, but there was no mistaking the declaration. Zaneta Lucia nodded as she sat, clutching her cloak tightly.

"First, your coin?" Signora Battaglia thrust out a winkled hand.

"Oh," Zaneta Lucia sputtered, "I wasn't sure how much . . ."

"For you, just one *zecchino*. A steal."

Zaneta Lucia reached into her thin cloth purse and pulled out a single gold coin. She gave it a squeeze, and handed it to Battaglia. Hopefully the woman's prediction would be worth the money.

Signora Battaglia made the gold vanish in a flash, and gave Zaneta Lucia a hard look. "You have many secrets," the woman finally said. "You do not hide them as well as you think."

Zaneta Lucia swallowed hard. Was she so transparent? "I want to know about Mario Barbaro." She tried to keep the tremble out of her voice.

One corner of the woman's mouth rose. "I'm sure you do. He is not the man you hoped for, unless I miss my mark?"

Zaneta Lucia held her tongue. She gave a quick shake of her head.

"You are not the kind of girl who chases after boys, I think. No, you crave a different sort of life. You have many dreams, but you lack the power to grasp them."

Zaneta Lucia leaned forward. "Then how do I get what I want?" she breathed.

The old woman released a long sigh. "We will have to ask the beans to answer your question." She reached to pick up a dark cup from the shelf behind her. It rattled softly as she turned back to Zaneta Lucia.

"The beans?"

"You don't know about the beans? With these beans, I can see the future."

One of Zaneta Lucia's eyebrows dipped.

The woman must have seen the skepticism written on her face. "You doubt the beans? Just watch."

Signora Battaglia shook the cup, the beans jumping wildly against the porcelain. With a flourish, the woman tipped the cup, tossing the beans onto the table between them. They scattered, quickly falling silent on the velvet surface.

"Ah," the soothsayer breathed, gazing at the beans. "See the pattern they make?"

Zaneta Lucia looked down, but all she saw was beans.

"These beans will answer your question: how do you get what you want? But before I tell you what they say, the beans have a warning for you. Soon, very soon, you will have to make a choice. If you choose wisely, you will be happy beyond your dreams. But if you choose unwisely, the beans see only sorrow."

The woman spoke with such conviction. Zaneta Lucia wrapped her arms around her body. She had come looking for reassurance, but she had not found any yet. Instead, she wished that she had stayed home.

"What is the choice?" she pressed the woman. "How will I know when it is time to decide?"

"Not everything in the future can be seen," the woman replied cryptically. "But look," she said with a flourish of her sleeve. "I see a hillside, dotted with houses. At the top, a church. I see a long corridor, flanked by pillars. I see . . ." She fell silent, her eyebrows furrowed with concentration.

The words meant nothing to Zaneta Lucia. A hill? There were none in Venice. Pillars and a corridor? That could be anywhere.

"Wait!" Battaglia threw up her hands. Zaneta Lucia jumped in her seat. "I see the stars. I see the night sky. And I see you, on a boat. Alone."

Zaneta Lucia shivered. "But what does it mean? Am I supposed to leave Venice? Is that the choice?"

The soothsayer slumped back into her seat. She reached down to scoop up the beans, tossing them back in the cup. "You are the only one who can answer those questions."

Her coin was gone, and she did not feel any better about her situation. "But what about Mario Barbaro? Do I have to marry him? Can I still study natural philosophy?" Zaneta Lucia felt the tears welling up in her eyes.

Signora Battaglia reached out to grasp Zaneta Lucia's hand. "Your path will not be an easy one," she said, her eyes boring into Zaneta Lucia's. "You will shed tears before you find happiness. This world is not made for women, it is made for men. But you cannot be a supporting player on someone else's stage. You must write a leading role for yourself."

Zaneta Lucia broke the woman's gaze, suddenly self-conscious about seeking out a fortune teller. She was supposed to create her own role? But how? The beans weren't much help, and neither was Signora Battaglia. Zaneta Lucia felt like a ship without a moor, tossed on a rough sea. Her life did feel out of her control, but what choice did she have?

She gave the soothsayer a nod and stood. "Thank you, Signora, for telling my future."

Zaneta Lucia already had one hand on the door when the woman spoke in a quiet voice. "Signorina Zorzi, do not forget who you are."

Her head jerked around at the sound of her name, but the old woman had vanished into the back of her shop. "How did you . . ." Zaneta Lucia began, trailing off. Had she told the woman her name?

Zaneta Lucia pulled open the door, stepping out into the warm night. The alley felt darker than when she had arrived, if that was possible.

Do not forget who you are. The words echoed in her mind. Did Signora Battaglia mean that she should remember she was a Zorzi, and it was her duty to marry? Or was marriage the choice that would bring her sorrow?

Could she really *choose* not to marry Mario Barbaro?

FOUR

Zaneta Lucia tossed and turned the night before the engagement party. She dreamed of an enormous golden boat that would carry her off into the sunset and save her from Mario Barbaro. And then she dreamed that a galloping horde of evil beans was chasing her through the streets of Venice.

She awoke with a start. The sun was already peeking in through the small window. In hours, she would meet her future husband.

Zaneta Lucia stayed in her room with the door firmly closed until her mother burst in without knocking.

"You didn't forget the engagement party tonight, did you?" her mother scolded.

Zaneta Lucia sighed. She would not get out of bed. "Of course not."

"I trust your attitude will improve by tonight," her mother said coldly. She began to straighten up the pile of clothes at the foot of Zaneta Lucia's armoire.

Zaneta Lucia wanted so badly to roll her eyes, but she restrained herself. "Mother," she said, an idea forming in her mind. "I want to go visit Aunt Ricciarda before the party." She sat up, donning the peaceful face she had practiced for mass.

Her mother stopped, a slip clutched in one hand. "Why would you want to do that?"

Zaneta Lucia knew that her mother did not get along with her disgraced older sister. But if the soothsayer was right, if Zaneta Lucia had a choice, she needed to explore her options. And time was running out.

"Oh, mother, Aunt Ricciarda must be so sad that she cannot attend the engagement party, when everyone else will be there. I just want to tell her about my dress, and about Mario Barbaro."

Her mother shook her head. "If you want to waste your time, go ahead. While you're at the convent, you can pray that your marriage will be blessed with many children."

Zaneta Lucia ignored the comment and jumped off the bed. "Thank you, Mother." She reached for a dress that her mother had just folded.

"Just a minute. I'll have to ask Filippo to escort you."

Zaneta Lucia groaned. "Nothing will happen. I'm going to a *convent.*"

"You are an engaged woman—or nearly engaged, that is. It would be unseemly for you to wander the city without a male escort."

"Fine, I'll go find Filippo."

"No, Zaneta Lucia, I will speak with him." Her mother turned on her heel and left the room.

Zaneta Lucia scowled as she pulled the dress over her head. Her mother would probably tell Filippo not to let her out of his sight—though that would be impossible at the convent, where he was not allowed to enter.

The convent was a short walk from their palazzo, but they rarely made the journey. Strict rules barred even close family members from entering the convent. The church said that nuns needed to focus their attention on prayer, not on the distractions of the sinful world.

Zaneta Lucia looked at her limp brown hair in the mirror. Instead of tying it back, she let it fall down her back. She was still unmarried, and she would wait as long as possible to adopt the style of a married woman.

She stomped down the stairs, her angry mood lingering. Filippo was already standing by the door waiting for her.

"Sister," he called out, a smile on his face. "I hear you need an escort."

Zaneta Lucia returned his smile. "Mother thinks I need an escort, that's all."

"Well, let's get on with it. I only have an hour before Giulia Maria expects me back at our house." Filippo and his wife lived in a smaller Barbaro residence farther from the city center, but Filippo seemed to spend most of him time at his childhood home. Her father was always asking him over to discuss business, and her mother pestered Filippo to bring the grandchildren nearly every day. And Filippo would eventually move his family back into the palazzo when their father died.

Zaneta Lucia took Filippo's arm. They stepped out onto the wide slabs of stone paving the narrow strip between the palazzo and the canal. A gondola was tied outside the building, decorated with fresh flowers and ribbons of brightly colored cloth. Later that night, Zaneta Lucia would have to step into that very gondola, wearing her elaborate engagement party dress.

She shuddered, pushing off the inevitable for a few more hours. As they walked, Filippo asked, "What have you been reading lately? It's so rare to see you without a book."

Zaneta Lucia gave him a shove. "Maybe if you spent more time reading, you wouldn't have to ask Father about what's going on in the world."

"Why would I ask him when I can just ask you?" Filippo shoved her back, gently. In spite of the age gap, they always fell into a familiar rhythm.

"To tell you the truth, I have not been able to read much in the last week." She frowned, her eyes dropping to the stone pavings.

Filippo wrapped an arm around her shoulder. "Cheer up, *Sorellina*. Marriage isn't all bad." He used his nickname for her, which meant little sister.

Zaneta Lucia didn't answer. Maybe it wasn't all bad for Filippo. But she could not even walk outside her house without an escort. Did he have any idea how different things were for her?

They turned into the wide square outside the convent. The tall, white façade of the building glittered in the midday sun. The wooden door looked small surrounded by the rows of arches and pillars that rose up from the *campo*. Zaneta Lucia stopped to take in the view, which always struck her when she walked past the Chiesa San Zaccaria.

Filippo gave her a wave. "Go on then, I'll leave you here. I trust you can make the five minute walk home without falling into disrepute. Just don't tell mother."

Zaneta Lucia grinned. "You think *I'd* tell her?" She gave him a wave and headed around the north side of the church, where an even smaller barred door led to the convent. Zaneta Lucia knocked, and waited for a reply.

A minute later, a narrow wooden slab pulled open and she saw a pair of eyes looking at her. "I'm Zaneta Lucia Zorzi, here to see my aunt, Ricciarda," she began, but then corrected herself. "I mean, Sister Benedetta." She always forgot that Aunt Ricciarda had taken a new name when she joined the convent.

"Just a minute," the man behind the door said. He slid the wooden slab shut. Zaneta Lucia tapped her foot on the marble, wondering how long it would take. Usually she had to write ahead to visit her aunt.

After she grew bored counting the marble stones lining the edge of the church, the door finally swung open. She saw a very old priest, his white beard trailing into the rosary he wore around his neck. "Follow me," he said, and she stepped into the cool antechamber to the convent.

He led her through a low doorway into the visitors room. It was sparsely furnished, with only a few chairs. Zaneta Lucia hoped that her aunt would be allowed to come to the room this time. Their last visit had taken place through the grates usually reserved for the nuns to take communion and confession from priests.

The elderly priest left, and Zaneta Lucia was once again alone. She listened for the sounds of the convent behind the wall, but the entire building felt silent as a tomb. Finally, she heard footsteps coming from behind the wall of the convent. A moment later another door swung open, and she saw her aunt dressed in the black habit of a Benedictine nun.

Zaneta Lucia leapt up and ran to her aunt, grateful for the woman's embrace.

"What is it, my niece?" Ricciarda asked when Zaneta Lucia pulled back.

"Mother says I have to get married," Zaneta Lucia confessed with a sniffle.

"Ah," Ricciarda responded, leading them to a pair of chairs.

"But I'm too young. And I don't even know the man. And he's so much older." Zaneta Lucia was already a blubbering mess. Ricciarda pulled out a handkerchief and handed it to her. She dabbed her eyes, clutching the scrap of white cloth tightly in her hands.

"I cannot counsel you to disobey your mother," Ricciarda said, and Zaneta Lucia began sobbing again. "Wait, wait, Zaneta Lucia." Her aunt placed a comforting arm on her shoulder. "Please listen. I know all too well that there are not many options for the daughter of a Venetian patrician. I paid a high price for my disobedience, and I would hate to see the same fate befall you."

Zaneta Lucia blinked back her tears. "Is it really so terrible in the convent?" she whispered. "I thought you sometimes put on plays."

Her aunt smiled. "You still remember that story? *Allora*, of course you do, you remember everything. Life here is not terrible. Most of my Benedictine sisters are also from patrician families, and we find ways to entertain ourselves. We spend much of our time reading and praying, but yes, we sometimes put on our own plays or recite poetry together."

Zaneta Lucia's eyebrows rose. "But that sounds wonderful. You read all day and you never have to get married."

Ricciarda shook her head. "You are still so young, my dearest niece, but then, I was about your age when I joined the convent. Right now you can only imagine wanting to escape, but it is not a trade that many women would choose for themselves. I have not wandered the streets of Venice or stopped on a bridge to watch a gondola pass in over twenty years. I barely remember what the façade of the church looks like. We have an interior courtyard for when we yearn for sunlight, but we truly are dead to the outside world."

Zaneta Lucia's heart fell. She chafed at needing an escort for a five minute walk through the city. How would she feel locked up in a convent?

Ricciarda squeezed her shoulder. "You were meant to see the world," she said in a soft voice. "From the moment I met you, I knew you were different. You don't belong in a convent, you belong in the world."

"But . . ." Zaneta Lucia trailed off. She had hoped that Ricciarda would paint a portrait of convent life that was so alluring that Zaneta Lucia would volunteer to join that very day. But her aunt was right. She would whither in the convent, shut off from the city.

Zaneta Lucia buried her face in her hands. Something broke

inside of her, and she could not stop the tears. Ricciarda wrapped her arms around Zaneta Lucia and held her without saying a word.

FIVE

Zaneta Lucia snuck back into the palazzo, her cheeks still stained with tears. She crept up the back staircase, and reached her room without running into anyone. At least here she could wall herself off from the world for a few hours.

But soon the sun began to dip in the west, and it was time for Zaneta Lucia to get ready for the engagement party. She fidgeted as her hair and makeup were applied, unable to sit still. The dressmaker chattered with their housekeepers Maria and Besina, who were busy piling her hair into an artful arrangement atop her head. Thankfully her mother was in another room, applying her own layers of sticky makeup, so Zaneta Lucia could close her eyes and ignore the voices swirling around her.

Instead of thinking about the engagement party, she tried to recreate the lecture from last week in her mind, running over the professor's words. Who was the mysterious Professor Galileo, who seemed to be at the heart of a brewing controversy among natural philosophers? She had re-read her volumes of Aristotle with a newly critical eye, willing herself to find flaws in his theories, but the words on the page made so much sense that it was difficult to find weaknesses.

Of course, thousands of brilliant readers had scrutinized these texts without finding the flaws that Galileo claimed existed. It was foolish to think that she, an uneducated girl, might uncover one in an afternoon of reading.

She let out a frustrated breath of air and Maria scolded her. "Hold still while I apply this rouge, or you'll look like a Carnivale player."

A smile crept across Zaneta Lucia's face at the thought.

After what felt like an eternity of poking and prodding, it was finally time to put on the dress. It felt even heavier tonight.

With a clap of her hands, her mother threw back the doors to inspect her daughter.

Zaneta Lucia stood still under her mother's gaze. Bartolomea gave her a critical look, and ordered her to spin so she could see all sides of the outfit.

As Zaneta Lucia obeyed wordlessly, her mother scowled. She reached up and pulled the fabric tight on the back corner of the dress, signaling to the dressmaker to smooth the area. The woman leapt up to fix the wrinkle.

When she was done, Zaneta Lucia turned back to face her mother.

"You look like you've lost weight. Have you been eating? Did you eat the broth I prepared for you?"

Zaneta Lucia sighed. "Yes, Mother."

"You have to look perfect tonight." Her mother repeated familiar words. Zaneta Lucia had heard them a hundred times that week. "We have to make a good impression."

"Why? They won't call off the wedding if I break social etiquette, right?"

Zaneta Lucia had imagined all sorts of ways to get out of the engagement. She could throw a glass of wine in Mario's father's face. She could slap his mother. She could kick her fiancé in the shins. These fantasies brought a smile to her face. But in truth she could never act so disgracefully. The Barbaros had done nothing to her—other than expecting her to act like a normal Venetian girl.

"You will act appropriately at all times," her mother warned. "The wedding will happen, but it's very important for the family that things go well. We want this union to strengthen our ties with the Barbaros and the other families at the top of Venetian society."

As if the crushing weight of the dress wasn't enough. Now Zaneta Lucia also felt the pressure of her mother's expectations. Was she supposed to single-handedly save the family by reviving their reputation and making them once again part of the elite? It was too much to ask a not-even sixteen year old girl.

Bartolomea had scrutinized every part of Zaneta Lucia's appearance. "Now look in the mirror," her mother ordered.

Zaneta Lucia stepped toward the glass with a sigh. She did not expect to be surprised, since she had already seen the dress once before.

But her reflection took her breath away. The dress, the hair, the makeup. She had been transformed into a young woman. And what's more, she was apparently a very beautiful young woman. The makeup made her green eyes look even larger, and the blush across her cheeks, though unnatural, made her glow with youth. Instead of the untamed locks that usually circled her shoulders, her hair had been curled and pulled back from her face. A few wispy tendrils circled her brow, making her look like one of Titian's muses.

And most astonishingly, the dressmaker's skill made it appear that she had a curving pair of breasts where only hours ago there had been nothing.

Zaneta Lucia did not recognize herself.

"You do look quite lovely," her mother admitted. "The rouge in particular was a nice touch."

Zaneta Lucia lifted a smaller mirror up to her face, looking for the line between the makeup and her own skin. She had never worn makeup before, and though it felt heavy on her face, in the mirror everything blended seamlessly. Had her eyes always been so round? And her cheeks, rosy as a ripe apple, gave her the look of a girl just come in from the snow. The effect made her skin look even more pale in comparison. She was the picture of youth, beauty, and vitality.

"Yes, you do look quite lovely," her mother said again, more quietly.

Zaneta Lucia wondered what her mother was thinking. Was she remembering her own wedding, years ago? Was she impressed that her daughter finally looked like a woman? Or was she calculating the value of Zaneta Lucia's transformation to the Zorzi family?

At that moment her father walked into the room, clasping his hands at his chest. "Oh, Zaneta Lucia, you look magnificent." He turned to her mother. "We really must be leaving. It wouldn't do for us to be the last to arrive."

He stepped forward to take Zaneta Lucia's arm. She reached for him, grateful to have a companion on the long walk down three flights of stairs. Zaneta Lucia nearly tripped twice over the long hem of her dress. She was not used to the slight heel in her shoes. Her father steadied her, and whispered, "I always wondered how women manage to walk in these elaborate gowns." His conspiratorial tone brought a smile to her face, and for a moment she forgot where they were going.

The shock of warm air hit her face as they walked outside. The heat that gripped the city had not faded with the setting sun. Would her elaborate makeup melt off her face?

Her father was on one side of her, her mother on the other. Filippo would meet them at the party with his wife, their young children left at home with a maid. As she stood on the dock, waiting for her turn to step onto the shallow boat for the journey to the Barbaro palazzo, Zaneta Lucia heard neighbors shouting to her, wishing her well on the union. A woman's voice called out that she finally had some birthing hips, and another responded that she would soon fall pregnant. The thought made Zaneta Lucia blush much deeper than the rouge.

She tried to ignore all the commotion and concentrate on putting one foot in front of the other. If she tripped now, she might tumble into the canal wearing a dress that cost more than most Venetians made in a year. On shaking legs, Zaneta Lucia eased herself into the boat while her father steadied her. The voluminous skirt forced her to stand during the journey.

In moments the boat pushed away from the dock and Zaneta Lucia watched her home receding behind her. She felt as though she were in a hazy dream, her mind slipping away from the present into some happier memory.

Zaneta Lucia trained her eyes forward, refusing to look up. If she saw a friendly face, she might burst into tears. Tonight she had to project the perfect air, playing a role in an elaborate play. She imagined herself as a statue, cold like marble and unable to feel anything.

Voices on both sides of the canal continued to call out as their boat passed. Apparently the engagement party was big news in their Castello neighborhood, and it felt like every palazzo had emptied so that people could wave to the Zorzi family and call well-wishes to Zaneta Lucia. A few young boys even ran along the *fondamenta* throwing flowers at the boat. They seemed to see Zaneta Lucia as the target, but thankfully their aim was poor.

Soon they had woven their way through Castello and into the neighboring district of San Marco, the most expensive neighborhood in Venice. Zaneta Lucia knew the Barbaro family owned multiple palazzi. She was not sure which one would host the engagement party, but apparently it was in the very heart of Venice.

They rounded a corner and Zaneta Lucia's breath caught in her throat. Their decorated gondola had turned onto the Grand

Canal, and she gazed up at the beautiful palazzi that lined the waterway, carved balconies competing to outshine each other. Zaneta Lucia had seen views of the Grand Canal from the Rialto bridge, but this was different. She felt dwarfed by the massive stone buildings jutting out of the water.

And the Grand Canal. It was nothing like the narrow strip of water in front of her own house. This was a river, flowing through the city. And it was crowded, with other gondolas and small boats jostling for space. The wake nearly knocked Zaneta Lucia from her feet, and she reached out to steady herself.

In front of them, a mass of gondolas surrounded one palazzo. Rows of tall windows faced the dark canal, with light pouring from each one. Her eyes crept up the front of the palazzo, counting five—no, six—stories of windows.

This must be the Palazzo Barbaro. It cast a warm glow onto the Grand Canal and the surrounding buildings. Zaneta Lucia could hear the sound of violins spilling out from the party, which had already begun.

Her eyes soaked in the scene. It seemed that every gondola on the Grand Canal was heading toward the same place. The boats carried people dressed in finer clothes than she had ever seen before. Pearls twinkled in the candlelight, rubies and emeralds glittered on the surcoats of the men stepping onto the dock and walking toward the party. She searched her memories for anything equivalent to this scene. But she had never attended an engagement party before. Children were rarely invited to attend these events. Instead, they were usually sent off with a nurse.

In fact, as Zaneta Lucia looked around she saw hardly any women at all. It seemed like most of the adult male population of Venice was in attendance—or at least the wealthiest men of Venice—but she could count the number of women on one hand. How strange.

Zaneta Lucia felt a light touch on her arm, and tore her eyes away from the palazzo. It was her father, signaling that it was time to step off the gondola. With a deep breath, she took his arm and followed him onto the dock.

Her legs wobbled on the unstable planks. More than anything she wanted to turn around and run home, but her mother and father were watching her expectantly, along with a growing audience gazing down on her from the rows of balconies. Men cheered and more boys threw flowers, and she had to school her arms not to cover her face protectively.

After all, she could not act as a living embodiment of Zorzi wealth if no one could see her.

So Zaneta Lucia steeled herself to play a part. She painted a smile on her face, and dropped her father's arm. She stepped carefully toward the door. Even though her parents followed in her wake, Zaneta Lucia felt completely alone.

The dock seemed much longer than twenty feet, with the eyes of so many people watching her closely. Any stumble or misstep at this moment would shame the Zorzi family, and she could not bear the thought of causing her family's decline. The crowd opened up a path before her, and soon she reached the narrow stone embankment in front of the water gate. Stepping carefully, still unsteady in the heels and cautious of the long, wide hem of her dress, she made her way toward the palazzo.

When she reached the water gate, she was greeted by some Barbaro who would become a distant in-law after the marriage. He kissed her on both cheeks and guided her into the palazzo, up two flights of stairs until they reached a massive hall inside the building.

Zaneta Lucia's eyes widened at the sight. The ceiling was painted in a fresco of clouds and cherubs, gilt with gold leaf. The walls were hung with paintings, portraits of Barbaro ancestors crowded around a series of landscapes overflowing with majestic animals. And the people. Everyone had donned their finest clothes for the party. Her eyes could not find a single person who was not covered in glittering jewels.

Her mother and father had vanished into the crowd, pulled by social obligations to speak with other guests of the party. Zaneta Lucia felt a rising sense of panic. What was she expected to do now?

But her eyes finally found a group of women, standing in the corner apparently waiting for her arrival. Their large skirts knocked together as a dozen heads turned in her direction. The eyes of so many strangers aimed at her nearly weakened her resolve, but she refused to let it show on her face. She smiled deferentially at the women, who seemed to be mostly Barbaro relatives, though she saw a few Zorzis mixed in the group.

They wore identically elaborate dresses, slightly different shades of blue and green but equally extravagant. Their hair, artfully arranged atop their heads, showed off the white skin of their necks. A few looked nearly as young as Zaneta Lucia, but most were her mother's age. They must all be married women. Unmarried women would probably not attend an engagement ceremony—that is, Zaneta Lucia thought, except for the future bride. With a sinking feeling, she realized that soon she, herself, would be a married woman.

Finally her eyes alighted on a familiar face—Filippo's wife Giulia Maria.

Zaneta Lucia allowed herself to be escorted toward the women and enveloped into their group, surrounded by voices complimenting her complexion (either unaware of the aid she'd received from cosmetics, or simply ignoring it), and oohing and ahhing over her dress. She felt a tug on her gown and realized one of the Barbaro women was weighing the fabric in her hands, assessing its value. The nosy woman gave a nod to her neighbor, and the two began to whisper about the silver threads woven throughout the skirt.

Zaneta Lucia had not realized how literally the Barbaro family would assess her value. She had never wanted to vanish more than she did at that moment. But Giulia Maria, sensing her embarrassment, pulled her aside.

In a quiet voice, her sister-in-law whispered, "I think some of them would eat you alive if it would not reflect badly on their families."

Zaneta Lucia smiled, finally at ease around a friend. "Giulia Maria, I'm so glad you're here," Zaneta Lucia began, her lungs compressed by the tightness of the bodice and the weight of her dress. She pushed down her rising panic.

"I wouldn't miss it," her sister-in-law confided, resting an arm on Zaneta Lucia's. "Did you see that the Doge's son is in attendance?" She pointed off in the crowd and Zaneta Lucia tried to follow the line of sight, but she did not recognize anyone in the sea of people packed into the palazzo.

"The Doge's son?" she repeated breathlessly.

"Filippo told me that your father invited him to impress the guests."

"It really is quite a show." Zaneta Lucia had not pictured anything on this scale when she imagined the party. But, of course, this was the first engagement party that she had ever attended.

"And you are the center of attention."

The blood rushed out of Zaneta Lucia's face. She only wanted to blend into the crowd. She never wanted to be the center of attention.

Giulia Maria turned to face her, temporarily blocking Zaneta Lucia's view of the guests. Zaneta Lucia instantly felt the weight lift as she focused only on Giulia Maria, ignoring the enormous party.

"Filippo and I were thrilled to hear of this union. You will be so happy with Mario Barbaro." She gave Zaneta Lucia's arm a squeeze as she spoke.

Was her sister-in-law truly only a few years older than Zaneta Lucia? Giulia Maria had been married for years, and already had two young children.

"Giulia Maria, what did you think when your parents announced that you would marry Filippo?" Zaneta Lucia whispered, quietly so that no one could overhear.

A tinkling laugh erupted from Giulia Maria's mouth. "To tell you the truth, I was terrified. I didn't want to get married, and Filippo seemed too old."

"Really? But he's still younger than Mario Barbaro."

"Yes, he did marry sooner than most Venetian men," Giulia Maria acknowledged. "But when you're sixteen, anyone over twenty seems old."

Zaneta Lucia relaxed her grip on her skirts. For the first time, she wondered if the marriage might not be a disaster. After all, Giulia Maria and Filippo seemed happy, and they had wed under nearly identical circumstances.

But now Giulia Maria had two young children, and Zaneta Lucia could not even imagine caring for children, or birthing them, or making them.

Another wave of panic washed over her. Giulia Maria reached out and put her hands on Zaneta Lucia's shoulders. "It's normal and natural to be nervous, Zaneta Lucia. All girls feel that way at first. But I'm sure you'll learn to love Mario, just as I came to love Filippo."

Zaneta Lucia mentally listed all the reasons the marriage would be a catastrophe. How could she convey that to Giulia Maria? She could barely put it into words herself.

"But . . . he's so *old*." Zaneta Lucia pulled at her skirt. "I never imagined this happening so soon."

Giulia Maria leaned in to whisper to Zaneta Lucia. "But you

knew it would happen eventually, right? Your family has been planning this day for years, trying to make a good union for you."

Everything Giulia Maria said was true. It was almost unbearable. How had Zaneta Lucia deluded herself into thinking this day wouldn't arrive soon? What did she imagine would happen, that she'd grow up and become some kind of scholar? It was ridiculous. The daughters of Venetian patricians were born to wed.

Her crushing thoughts were interrupted by a male voice. "May I have your attention! May I have your attention!"

The room fell silent and all eyes turned toward the voice. What would happen next? Every possibility that came to her mind seemed terrifying.

"Now, it's the moment you've been waiting for. It's time for the groom and bride to meet for the first time."

SIX

The hall erupted into uproarious applause. Zaneta Lucia was pulled away from Giulia Maria and pushed toward the front of the room. Her heart was beating so fast that she thought everyone must hear it pounding through her chest. But she could only see what was directly in front of her: a path leading to the front of the ballroom. Richly dressed men stepped aside, as others shoved her forward.

At the end of the path she saw a man standing on a dais in front of a broad marble staircase. It was Matteo Barbaro, the father of Mario, and the man who had arranged the union with her father. Zaneta Lucia recognized him—she had seen him at her house a few weeks ago. Of course, back then she was blissfully absorbed in her books and had not wondered why the head of the Barbaro family would visit their home.

Matteo reached out his arms, and clasped each of her shaking, pale hands in his.

He pulled her up to join him on the dais. Feeling faint, Zaneta Lucia's eyes swept over the crowded room. The wealth of Venice truly was on display this evening. Silver and gold, sapphires and pearls, and yard upon yard of expensive cloth floated in front of her eyes. If Neptune rose up and swallowed the palazzo, he would drag hundreds of family fortunes down into the depths of the seas.

For a moment Zaneta Lucia could only see the opulence rather than the people. And then, with a start, she realized that all of their eyes were on her.

"Welcome to the engagement party for my son, Mario Barbaro," Matteo called out to the assembled party. "Marietta and I are grateful for your presence to celebrate this blessed union." He leaned over to kiss Zaneta Lucia on each cheek. He stepped back and held out an arm as if showing off a prize horse. "My future daughter-in-law, doesn't she look beautiful? Introducing Zaneta Lucia Margherita Zorzi, soon to be Zaneta Lucia Barbaro."

The cheers were deafening.

Zaneta Lucia's knees wobbled. She tried to smile, itching under the weight of hundreds of eyes on her, but she felt frozen. In some part of her mind, she was aware that she looked stricken, as though plagued by some natural disaster.

But she knew what came next. She would meet Mario Barbaro face to face.

"She's shaking like a leaf," she heard a man nearby say in a loud whisper, followed by deep chuckles from his friends.

Shame flashed through Zaneta Lucia's body. Had her resolve not to embarrass her family really vanished so quickly? All she had to do was stand still—it was certainly much easier than disguising herself as a boy and sneaking into a lecture. She could not afford to act like a fool tonight, not when her entire family was counting on her and all the most prominent citizens of Venice were staring at her.

She took a breath and threw back her shoulders, trying to imitate the ease and authority of the professor she had seen only a week earlier. Surprisingly, the act touched her mind as well as her body. She felt a sense of calm envelop her, and her hands were finally steady.

Then the cheering started up again, and she saw ripples in

the back of the room. Someone was walking through the crowd, trailing a wake like a boat cutting through the lagoon.

It had to be Mario.

She took another deep breath, counting down from a hundred in her mind.

"Look at her, isn't it precious?" she heard a voice whisper behind her. It had to be Mario's mother, Marietta. Zaneta Lucia had hoped that all eyes were on Mario. But apparently she was still the center of attention, in spite of her panicked prayers to blend into the background.

The waves drew closer, and finally the last row of guests parted. Mario was standing in front of her.

He was well dressed, in a matching shade of blue to her own gown. Her family must have planned this, for the two of them to meet wearing coordinated outfits. How had she missed the complicated arrangements that must have been going on for months?

Mario bowed, with an exaggerated flourish of his arm, and said, "My lady." He reached out for her hand.

She was supposed to take his hand, but instead she studied his face. Mario looked about Filippo's age, maybe a few years older, with dark hair and steely gray eyes. Unlike most men at the party he was clean shaven. He looked nice enough, but she felt no sparks or instant feelings for him.

The room was silent. Everyone was waiting for Zaneta Lucia's response. Mario was frozen with his hand outstretched.

She reached out her hand and tried to curtsey without falling over. It was nearly impossible in such a tight bodice. If only she had practiced in the privacy of her own home. But thankfully she stayed on both feet.

With another flourish, Mario raised her hand to his lips but stopped just before they touched. A fresh wave of cheers broke out in the hall.

Mario released her hand and turned to give the crowd a bow. Following his lead, Zaneta Lucia curtsied again, this time more steady on her feet. At that moment the musicians in the corner began to play again, and couples paired off to dance.

Zaneta Lucia stood stiff as a statue, every inch of her aware that Mario was standing right at her side.

Mario leaned in toward her and asked, "Would you like to dance?"

She knew that she was supposed to say yes, but somehow the words didn't come out of her mouth. The dancing lessons she had taken at her mother's insistence had vanished from her mind. And would she even be able to dance in the wide dress without looking clumsy?

But those fears paled in comparison to the thought at the front of her mind. She did not want to hold Mario's hands and gaze into his face. Every second would remind her of the uncertain future laid out before her as a Barbaro wife.

Mario pulled her aside. "Would you prefer to step out of the room for a glass of wine?"

She nodded gratefully, relief flooding her body. He took her arm, and led her up the stairs at the back of the dais. For the first time that evening, she was not the center of attention, and she relished the return to anonymity, however temporary it might be.

At the same time, she was very conscious of Mario's broad shoulders, bobbing next to her at eye level. Where was he taking her? The stairs must lead, as they did in most Venetian palazzi, to the more private spaces of the house. Her mother never would have allowed such impropriety, but now Zaneta Lucia was his fiancée. What would Mario expect during their first private encounter?

At the top of the stairs, she saw a hallway, but instead of taking her toward the rooms which broke off from the hall, Mario led her to a small balcony overlooking the canal on the east side of the building. Zaneta Lucia let out a breath. The familiar sounds of the small canal splashing against its embankment soothed her. She could still hear the music below, but it was faint enough to block out. She could almost imagine that she was back home.

The fresh air felt good on her skin. The heat of the ballroom had been stifling. Zaneta Lucia rested a hand on the stone rail of the balcony, savoring the quiet.

"It's probably a bit overwhelming from your point of view, I imagine," Mario said.

Zaneta Lucia took another deep breath. "Yes, I must admit it has . . . caught me off guard," she said cautiously. She was not sure what kind of person Mario was, but no man wanted to hear that his fiancée did not want to marry. She might admit her fears to Giulia Maria, but Mario was still a stranger.

But to her surprise, Mario laughed. "I know how you feel. I will confess that when my father first told me about this arrangement, I wasn't sure what to think."

Zaneta Lucia's eyes widened in shock. The engagement had been a surprise to Mario as well? She had assumed that he was involved in the negotiations with her father. After all, he was an adult and a man. But perhaps he had been blindsided as well.

"I honestly think that I'm a little young to marry," he continued, running his hands through his silky hair. He turned to look at her. "I apologize—I forgot that you're so much younger."

He was so calm that Zaneta Lucia felt her anxiety fading into the background. Had she been thinking about the marriage the wrong way? If Mario had not pushed for the engagement, perhaps he would allow her a degree of freedom once they had wed.

"I will admit that I do not feel old enough to be a wife," she ventured carefully. She hoped that Mario would not think her a fool for confessing her fears.

"Hmm," Mario murmured. "I can remember being your age, you know. With all the lessons and rules, I could not wait to grow up."

"What kinds of things did you study?" she asked, leaning on the stone rail. She tried to picture Mario as a teenager.

"Oh, history, and poetry, that sort of thing. I never found it very interesting. I wanted to spend my time learning about my father's business."

Her eyes dropped to the canal several stories below. For a minute she had wished for Mario to share her devotion to science. In her mind, she was already imagining attending lectures together, even though she had never heard of a woman, let alone a married woman, at a natural philosophy lecture. But her hopes were dashed almost as soon as they had been lifted.

She did not want Mario to see the sadness in her face.

"And what kind of business do you do now?" she asked, trying to keep her voice polite.

Mario leaned back from the balcony rail at the question. His voice grew animated. "The Barbaro are very involved in trade," he explained. "But not the little local trades like some of the lesser families. We specialize in trade with Crete, the Greek isles, the Ottomans, Cyprus, those sorts of places."

"Then, do you travel a lot?"

"No, I mostly work from Venice. I let the sailors take the risks, while I take the rewards. I decide what to buy and what to sell, and how much to mark up the prices. And I negotiate our insurance, so that if a ship is lost we don't lose the investment."

He spoke so casually about shipwrecks and dead sailors that a shiver went up her spine. She knew that most patricians in Venice had a hand in trade, but she had never quite connected their opulence with the backbreaking work which funded it. And soon, she supposed, she would be living off the lives of those poor sailors.

She glanced back at the canal, watching a boat tied to a mooring bob up and down with the gentle swell of the water. The city seemed so peaceful from this balcony, lit only by the candlelight of the surrounding buildings. And yet underneath the city's beautiful face was a beating heart powered by the impoverished workers who toiled to make the patrician families wealthy.

Mario cleared his throat, and she jumped. She had been lost in her own thoughts. Zaneta Lucia looked up at Mario's face, and saw a frown.

"I fear that I've been too informal with you." He stood straighter and his voice became more authoritative. "After all, you are to be my wife, and I do expect your obedience."

She froze, uncertain about this change in his personality. It seemed to come out of nowhere. Had she said something wrong? Should she have shown more interest in his business? And what should she do now—did he want her to apologize? She had no idea how engaged women were expected to behave, and suddenly she wished she had thought to ask her mother before the party.

His frown deepened. "You will acknowledge my words when I speak to you," he said, his tone halfway between command and request.

"I understand," she managed to squeak out. "I apologize."

"Good," he said gruffly.

And to imagine, only a few minutes before she had thought that they weren't in such different positions. But Mario could demand her obedience, and she had no equivalent power. They might both have been surprised by the engagement, but in their relationship Mario would always be in control.

They stood awkwardly at the balcony. Zaneta Lucia's mind raced. Did Mario expect her to speak, or did he prefer for her to remain silent?

Finally, he spoke. "I expect you to return to the party shortly. It would be unseemly for us not to share a dance."

And with that he turned and walked back toward the staircase leading to the ballroom. She watched him leave, his footsteps echoing on the cold marble walls.

Zaneta Lucia's knees buckled and she grabbed the rail for stability. Was this what their union would be like? Him commanding, her fearfully obeying?

She screwed her eyes closed, drawing in ragged breaths of air. Everyone expected her to act a certain way: her parents wanted her to raise the family's status, Mario wanted her to act like the perfect wife, when she had no desire to marry in the first place, and even the attendants in the ballroom expected her to bow and dance and laugh, and pretend like this wasn't the worst day of her life.

A tear rolled down Zaneta Lucia's cheek and landed on the rail before her. What could she do now? In her mind, she imagined running from the palazzo, or dramatically tossing her body over the rail and into the canal.

But she knew that her only true option was to return to the ballroom, where she would dance with Mario, a false smile painted on her face. She would be the puppet that everyone expected her to be, because she did not have the courage to make any other decision.

The thought brought fresh tears to her eyes. She fanned her face before they could fall and swallowed her sorrow.

Zaneta Lucia was so consumed with her thoughts that she did not hear the sound of footsteps drawing closer down the hall, until they stopped right behind her.

Was Mario back? Zaneta Lucia turned, hoping it wasn't obvious that she had been crying. A woman stood before her dressed in green, the cut of her gown emphasizing the roundness of her belly. Zaneta Lucia exhaled, scolding herself for jumping in fright at a pregnant woman. The stranger must be another guest at the engagement party, perhaps a Barbaro relative sent to check on the bride.

"I thought we should be properly introduced," the woman said coolly, reaching out for Zaneta Lucia's hand.

Who was this woman? Zaneta Lucia frowned, but took the proffered hand in her own. "Of course," she stammered. "I am Zaneta Lucia Zorzi."

"I know who you are," the woman said as she pulled back her hand. Zaneta Lucia blushed with embarrassment. Had she insulted the woman? After all, Zaneta Lucia was the reason for the party, and Matteo Barbaro had just loudly introduced her to all the guests only moments before.

How could she repair her social faux pas? Her mind raced as the silence drew out. "May I ask your name?" She tried to imitate her mother's most polite tone, using the formal tense.

But her words did not seem to soothe the stranger. Instead, the woman's face contorted into a grimace and her voice dropped to a hiss. She spat out, "I am Anzola Secco, the only woman Mario will ever love."

Zaneta Lucia's eyes grew wide. This woman was Mario's mistress. Her surprise must have shown on her face, because Anzola began to laugh. Zaneta Lucia flushed. She knew that most men had mistresses before they wed, but she had never wondered if Mario Barbaro, her future husband, had one.

And a pregnant one, at that.

Her mother's etiquette lessons had not addressed this situation.

"I am here to warn you," Anzola said, stepping closer to Zaneta Lucia. "I'm not going anywhere, and you will soon learn your place. You might be Mario's wife in public, but he will always love me. His home is my home."

Zaneta Lucia was speechless. Did Anzola really live with Mario? And would Zaneta Lucia be expected to move into the same house with Anzola?

Anzola's eyes narrowed. "I run Mario's house," she said, placing a hand on her swelling belly. "And no woman will change that. Mario is wrapped around my fingers, and he will do whatever I say. He never wanted to marry you. He promised to name me as his wife in a few months when I bear him a son."

Mario didn't want to marry *her*?

Zaneta Lucia did not want to steal Mario from this woman. So why was Anzola acting like Zaneta Lucia was her rival? All of Zaneta Lucia's frustration and anger boiled over. She pointed a finger at Anzola. "You think Matteo Barbaro would ever accept *you* as his daughter-in-law?"

Anzola reacted as though she had been struck. But in an instant her face twisted with fury. "You're no better," she hissed. "Your father pushed for the marriage, not Matteo. He was running around town begging someone to take you off his hands. Your father practically had to bribe the Barbaros with your dowry." Her lips curled up. "They're only taking you for the money."

These words stung Zaneta Lucia to the core. Could it be true? Or was Anzola lying? She pushed those questions down. Her anger surged faster than her shame. She rose up to her full height, enjoying the extra inches gained from her heels. "How dare you speak to me that way? You're a common whore, pregnant with a man's child who isn't your husband, and you think you can speak to me like that?"

In a flash, Anzola's hand darted out and she grabbed Zaneta Lucia by the hair. Zaneta Lucia tried to cry out, but Anzola's other hand was clawing at her face. The force of Anzola's attack pushed her backward, and she let out a gasp of air as her back hit the rail of the balcony. Was the woman trying to push her over the balcony into the canal, three stories below?

After a terrifying moment pressed against the rail, Zaneta Lucia shoved Anzola away and regained her balance.

Anzola's grasp on her was broken. The pregnant woman stood a few feet away, her chest heaving. Zaneta Lucia eyed Anzola warily. The rage that had bewitched Anzola had vanished, and the woman stood calmly, smoothing down her dress as though nothing had happened. Zaneta Lucia reached up to her face, where the fiery tracks of Anzola's nails still burned. Hopefully they weren't visible.

Anzola put her hands on her hips, her swelling belly thrust forward. "Know your place when you marry Mario. He will always favor me, and I have the loyalty of all the servants. If you take one step out of line, I will do worse than throw you off a ledge. I promise you that."

Before Zaneta Lucia could respond, Anzola spun around and stormed off in the direction of the party.

Zaneta Lucia blinked. The sounds of the canal filled the silence. She raised her hands to her hair, tucking in the curls that had fallen loose during the attack.

Had Mario's pregnant mistress really just assaulted her?

Had Anzola actually threatened her life?

Zaneta Lucia's heart was beating out of her chest. This was madness. She was supposed to live with that woman?

Zaneta Lucia tried to slow her rapid breathing. Maybe she could convince the Barbaros to send Anzola away. But Mario had already spoken harshly to Zaneta Lucia. And he did not want to marry her. If he really did love Anzola, he would not send his mistress away because his unwanted wife objected.

Could Zaneta Lucia avoid Anzola, or try to be very deferential and kind to her? Zaneta Lucia snorted. Based on the woman's personality, it was impossible to imagine Anzola suddenly wanting to befriend her. She could never have a peaceful relationship with that woman.

Maybe Anzola would die in childbirth.

Zaneta Lucia felt horrible for even thinking such things, but she could not picture a future where she inhabited the same house as Anzola.

She sighed, chewing on her lower lip. Zaneta Lucia had resisted the idea of marriage from the start. Ever since her parents told her of the engagement, only a week before, she had been single-mindedly focused on how to continue her studies as a married woman. She had even wondered if the marriage might become a happy union with time.

But now she saw it could be much, much worse than she had ever imagined. Her earlier fears seemed small in the face of Anzola's rage.

Zaneta Lucia shivered in spite of the warm air on the balcony, and drew her arms around her body in a hug.

Again, she heard the echo of footsteps in the hall behind her. She spun around, preparing herself for the next encounter. But when she saw it was Mario, returning to find her, she let out a breath of air. At least he wouldn't try to push her over the balcony.

Mario's eyebrows made a thick line across his face, and his expression was one of irritation. "Did you forget what I said? Come back to the ballroom so we can dance."

She faced him, trying to plaster a pleasant expression on her face.

"Of course," she said. She stepped toward him, ready to face the guests.

SEVEN

Zaneta Lucia sighed in relief later that night when she finally peeled off the dress with the help of several servants.

Walking up the three flights of stairs to her room had been punishing. Her feet ached, and her muscles screamed in discomfort after hefting the weight of the dress for hours. Removing the dress felt like shedding a weight that threatened to drag her to the bottom of the canals. But now she was safe in her room, wrapped in her familiar silk dressing gown.

The engagement party had been a disaster.

Mario had barely spoken a word to her as they whirled around the dance floor. When he decided they were done dancing, he had vanished somewhere in the palazzo. Zaneta Lucia was left to stand awkwardly in the ballroom, speaking to guests, until her father appeared at her side to take her home.

Her parents had no idea how excruciating the party had been for Zaneta Lucia. During the entire gondola ride home, her mother had rattled on about the beautiful tapestries in the Barbaro palazzo, and how all the women from the Barbaro family had treated her as an honored guest. Zaneta Lucia's father had been mostly silent, nodding in agreement with Bartolomea's observations.

Her parents only seemed to care about the wealth and status attached to the Barbaro family. Neither asked Zaneta Lucia how she had enjoyed the party. They didn't even ask what she thought of Mario.

The servants carried the dress from the room, which eerily held its form as if worn by a ghost. Zaneta Lucia was finally alone. She collapsed onto her bed, grateful for the moment of peace.

Zaneta Lucia lifted her weary arms to pull the hairpins out of her hair. She slipped the high heels off her feet, letting them fall to the floor, and let out a sigh.

She was born the daughter of a Venetian patrician, but Zaneta Lucia had never felt that her life was particularly easy. She lived in a palazzo, but some days it felt more like a prison than a palace. Her mother heaped expectations on her only daughter, pushing Zaneta Lucia to memorize every etiquette lesson and study dancing rather than natural philosophy. Her father largely ignored her. Her brother was too busy running a business and leading his own small family to bother much with his sister.

Yet in spite of all the rules, Zaneta Lucia had felt in control of her own life. She was able to read as much as she wanted. Sometimes she had to practice sewing, or attend mass, but most of her hours were her own. And it wasn't very difficult to sneak out of the house.

She had struggled against her mother's stifling attention, and yet Zaneta Lucia saw that she had been granted more freedom than most women of her class.

But now it seemed everything would change.

Mario would not allow her to read and continue her studies once she was his wife. She would not be sneaking out to attend lectures. He would expect her to obey his every command. And Anzola would take every opportunity to make Zaneta Lucia miserable.

Mario did not want a wife and Anzola certainly did not want Mario to marry. Where would Zaneta Lucia fit in the Barbaro household? Somehow, she did not imagine they would let her read books all day.

Mario might expect her to manage the household and take a public role as his wife. And he would need someone to bear him legitimate children, even if he continued his relationship with Anzola.

Children. The thought sent a chill up her spine. Would she find herself, five years in the future, raising Mario's children in the same house with his sons from Anzola? Once they married, she could not refuse to sleep with him.

Zaneta Lucia rolled over, her stomach in knots, and faced the wall. She doubted that she would be able to sleep at all, even though it was well after midnight.

She closed her eyes and concentrated on her breathing, trying to quiet her mind.

Zaneta Lucia forced her thoughts back to the lecture, the last time she had been happy. She remembered what Professor Cornaro had said about a professor named Galileo examining the world to learn new things about it. She pictured herself studying with Galileo, the secrets of the world laid out in front of her.

Zaneta Lucia sat straight up in bed. Why should she marry a stranger, a man who didn't respect her or even like her? Why did she have to move into a home with his mistress who was carrying his child?

It was not her decision, and she could not refuse. She had a duty to her family.

Zaneta Lucia could never tell her parents that she refused to marry Mario. That would never work. After the cost of the engagement party, and the nobility of Venice approving of their union, it would be a terrible blow to the Zorzi family if they broke the engagement. Vendettas had started over less.

It was too public. There was no way to back out without her family losing face.

But she could not endure it. She could not marry Mario, have his children, navigate the rivalry with Anzola, and be miserable for the rest of her life.

A voice whispered in the back of her mind. *Did* she have a choice?

Zaneta Lucia leaned off the edge of her mattress to open the wooden chest at the foot of her bed. Rifling through the clothes, her hands hit the book she knew was hidden at the bottom of the chest.

She pulled it out and set it on the bed, throwing back the cover to look for the page she remembered reading a few months earlier.

Finally she found the passage. It was Aristotle's discourse on the purpose of natural and manmade objects.

In it, Aristotle explained that everything had a purpose. The purpose of a tree was to create more trees, the purpose of a chair was to provide a seat. Zaneta Lucia remembered with a smile how she had reacted the first time she read this passage. She had wandered around her house, pretending to be Aristotle, and investigating the purpose of everything she found: the walls, the art, the cat that wandered in the back alley, the canals.

Aristotle also wrote that the purpose of man was happiness. This had puzzled Zaneta Lucia at first, because what made one person happy might be repulsive to another. But after thinking on Aristotle's words and reading the passage over and over again, she had seen the deeper truth. Aristotle believed that happiness came from investigating and learning about the world. Happiness meant gaining knowledge.

Zaneta Lucia had often thought back to that passage to justify her secret studies. She had been taking risks nearly every day. When she asked her neighbor for books, or hid in her bedroom reading natural philosophy, she might be caught. And sneaking out of her house was even more dangerous. But it was necessary if she wanted to gain knowledge.

A life without learning would never make her happy. It would turn her against her purpose.

Her limbs were heavy with sleep but her mind raced. In the dim light of a single candle, Zaneta Lucia studied the words. She ran a finger over the letters. They grew blurry as tears clouded her vision. She closed the book gently and set it on the bed, wiping the tears from her eyes.

Had Aristotle just been writing for men? Did he not consider that women, too, might share the same desire to learn? Or was the happiness produced by knowledge reserved for the male sex?

Even if Aristotle had only thought about men, what if Professor Cornaro was right? Maybe Aristotle had made mistakes.

Zaneta Lucia deserved happiness. She deserved the opportunity to keep learning. And nothing about the marriage made her happy. No one else was going to stand up for her happiness. Her mother, her father, Mario, Anzola . . . none of them cared what she wanted, and she could not count on any of them to make her happy.

The only person who could give her life purpose was herself.

Zaneta Lucia looked out the window. She only saw black night. Her head spun, and she wondered if she was thinking in circles. She couldn't break off the marriage, because her parents would be furious. It would shame her entire family. She couldn't go through with it because she would be completely miserable.

That left a single option. She had to leave Venice.

It was the only way she could avoid the marriage without destroying her family's reputation. She alone would bear the blame. Everyone would gossip, but they would assume she was a frightened girl, and surely that would not tarnish the Zorzi name.

If she ran, her parents would avoid the humiliation, and she could pursue her dreams and her own happiness.

And, after all, she had passed as a boy once before. Maybe she could do it again.

She leaped off of the bed and grabbed the candlestick, carrying it to the small mirror on the wall across from her bed. Her reflection gazed back at her, dim in the flickering light.

Zaneta Lucia looked past the red around her eyes and the pale hue of her skin. Pulling back her hair, she tied it at the nape of her neck in a style she'd seen men wear. It was not much of a disguise, but it had fooled everyone at the lecture.

People saw what they wanted to see.

In a flash she threw open her wardrobe, looking for any clothes that might suit. She had a few loose shirts, and another pair of the casual pants that her mother didn't know she had stolen out of a pile of Filippo's old clothes, in addition to the outfit she had worn to the lecture. She began to pile the clothes on her bed, her heart racing.

Zaneta Lucia froze in place, a shirt drooping in one hand.

What would it mean to actually run away?

She would have to leave everything behind, forever. She could never come back to Venice. She might never see her family again, her mother, or father, or Filippo. She might never step foot in Venice, the only city she knew, the place where she grew up.

It would be a self-imposed exile.

Exile was a fate worse than death, according to the poets. It had driven Dante nearly to madness, igniting visions of the next world. Why would she *choose* exile?

Zaneta Lucia dropped the shirt and sunk onto the bed, suddenly too exhausted to stand. What a fool she had been. She had no food, no money, and no plan, just a vague sense that she wanted to escape her life. Where would she even go?

She undid the tie around her hair and shook it loose. Her eyes threatened to well up once again.

But the tears vanished in a flash, and she tightened her hands into fists. It was not right that she had to give up her happiness because of what other people wanted. She should not have to abandon her dreams just because she was born a girl.

Suddenly her body felt lighter, an echo of the moment when she had pulled off the engagement party dress. A burst of energy coursed through her veins.

She had decided.

Zaneta Lucia wrapped up the clothes and shoved them in a sack, then gently added her copy of Aristotle. Then she resolutely went through her drawers, looking for anything she might be able to sell. She packed a few items of jewelry in the bag. She grabbed the pearl necklace that she had worn to the engagement party and put it around her neck, concealing it beneath her shirt.

She would leave the palazzo dressed as a girl, but once she abandoned Venice, she would change clothes and become Luca Manetti.

And she would go to Padua. To the university. To find Galileo.

EIGHT

The sun rose high in the sky, baking the parched dirt path. A young man walked down the deserted road, leading a donkey who kicked up a plume of dust.

"Go to the fair in Isola di Torre, he said. It's not that far, he said. You'll be able to make some sales." He kicked the dirt. "I walked all day to get there with this mangy beast, and I only managed to make five *soldi*. FIVE *soldi*! I could have spent an hour in the Piazza del Erbe in Padua and made double that amount, with a lot less walking!"

The donkey snorted, and he looked back at it. "Don't say anything. I know, I know, you don't like wheat, you only want barley. You're spoiled."

He continued his walk, sore from a night spent sleeping outside to save money.

"What a terrible day," he said to no one in particular. "I can't believe I have to walk all the way back to Padua. Me, the son of Giovanni di Rinaldo Serravalle. Me, Paolo di Giovanni di Rinaldo Serravalle!"

He glanced back at the donkey, and tipped back his hat, which provided meager protection from the midday sun.

"I can see you're not impressed."

The donkey would never understand the weight Paolo carried on his shoulders. Sure, the donkey carried heavy loads, but he knew nothing of the emotional weight of a father's expectations. Paolo plodded along for a few more steps, until he stopped to look back at the donkey again.

"Do you see that?"

The donkey twitched an ear, swatting away an invisible fly.

"I think someone's on the path, back there." Paolo strained his eyes, trying to see if the tiny moving shape was a person, or a figment of his imagination.

"He's in for a big surprise, is all I can say," he told the donkey with a shrug. "If he's some kind of highway robber." Paolo continued plodding along, giving the donkey's lead a light tug. "All he'll find is five *soldi*."

Paolo laughed. "Along with some worthless merchandise, that even the people of Isola di Torre wouldn't pay for." He slapped the bag on the donkey's back for emphasis.

"You know what, donkey? I'm tired of working for that man. He thinks he always knows best, but in this case, I was right. Did he listen when I said no one in Isola di Torre would want his ridiculous gadgets? No, of course not. Should I say 'I told you so,' when I hand over the five *soldi*? I suppose that would be pointless. But it sure would feel good."

He scratched at an itch. "I think you're right, donkey. I think there might be some invisible flies around here." The donkey plodded along, ignoring him.

"You know what? I think that really is a person back there. And he's getting closer. Well, he looks worse off than us, if you ask me, because he doesn't even have a donkey or a horse or anything." He patted the donkey affectionately. "Even the highway robbers ignore this little back road. And robbers probably don't walk, anyway." He paused. "It looks like that poor fool doesn't even have a sword. Probably just a peasant."

The person was gaining at a fast clip, though. Paolo had to decide if he would stop and wait for the person to pass, or continue and ignore the only excitement of the entire morning. After all, the mysterious stranger might make a good traveling companion for the walk to Padua.

Paolo decided to wait.

He guided the donkey to the side of the road, and adjusted his left boot, which was rubbing his foot raw. The donkey dipped his head to munch on some grass at the edge of the dirt path. "Ah, too good for wheat but you'll eat these weeds, eh? You're a donkey of discriminating tastes, I can tell."

While Paolo waited, he quickly tightened the straps on the donkey's pack, checking that everything was in order for the rest of the journey to Padua. By his reckoning, they were about halfway. He wanted to get an earlier start, but somehow the late night had hindered his plans.

"You know, donkey, I don't really think this is worth it. I mean, I could be taking lessons right now with the most illustrious professors in the world. And instead I'm running errands for my landlord. It's a waste of my time. The rent is cheap, but it comes at a pretty steep price." He plucked one of the weeds and began to chew on the fat, green end.

"Is this sorghum?" he asked the donkey. "It's pretty good. I apologize for slandering your honor."

The person on the path was now close enough that if Paolo called out, the stranger might have heard. Paolo squinted into the sun, hoping for a better look at the approaching figure.

On closer inspection, it looked like a boy. Maybe someone only a year or two younger than his own eighteen years. And was he carrying some kind of sack, maybe grains? Could he also be coming from the fair? It certainly didn't look like it. While his clothes looked well made, they appeared to be hand-me-downs that the boy had not quite grown into. And his hair was rather shaggy.

"Ho," Paolo called out. "You there." He doffed his hat, and

waved it in a friendly manner.

He heard the stranger clear his throat, and call back, "Hello."

"It sounds like a young guy," Paolo said *sotto voce* to the donkey. "His voice hasn't even dropped yet. I wonder what he's doing out here?"

The stranger had drawn near enough that Paolo could finally see his face. The boy's skin was smooth, not even close to the point where he could grow a beard. In spite of the ill-fitting clothes, he looked like he came from money. Paolo couldn't put his finger on why. The boy just looked soft. He had green eyes and hair somewhere between blonde and brown. Sand colored, Paolo figured, although he'd only ever read about sand. There was mainly mud in the waterways he frequented.

"What's your business in these parts," Paolo asked, trying to sound polite.

A cloud seemed to pass over the stranger's face. "Trying to find Padua," the boy said brusquely.

"What a coincidence, that's where I'm headed on this fine day. Care to walk with us?"

The stranger hesitated for a moment, but then gave a nod.

Paolo lowered an eyebrow. The boy's hat didn't seem suited for the hot weather, and it looked like his nose was already pink from the sun.

"You from around here? Isola di Torre, maybe?" Paolo asked. He tugged the donkey's lead, pulling him out of the sorghum and back on the path. The stranger fell in next to Paolo, keeping an arms length between them. He was cautious, Paolo thought, to stand outside the reach of Paolo's sword. Not that his rusty old blade was very useful.

"Uh, no, I'm coming in from Venice," the boy replied. "I caught a ride with a merchant train heading to Isola di Torre for the fair, and they swore it was an easy half-day walk to Padua, but here I am and I can't seem to find it."

"You're on the right path. But whoever told you it was a half-day walk didn't realize how windy this damn road gets. The dust today is terrible." They fell into silence for a few steps. "I'm Paolo, by the way. Paolo Serravalle."

"Luca Manetti," the stranger said, shoving out a hand in greeting. Paolo gripped it briefly, and noticed that Luca had no callouses on his hands. Not a worker, then. Could he be the son of some merchant? It would still be a few hours until they arrived in Padua, and Paolo was curious. In any case, the boy was already better conversation than the donkey.

"Nice to meet you Luca. Now what are you doing out here?"

Luca was silent. Did the boy always pause before every answer? It was odd, as though he was trying to figure out what to say. Or was he worried he might say the wrong thing?

It was perfect. The mystery might entertain Paolo all the way back to Padua.

Paolo's grandmother had called him nosy, but even as a youth Paolo had known that it pays to be inquisitive.

"I'm heading to the University of Padua," Luca finally said. "I want to enroll as a student."

Paolo let out a brief laugh. "Oh, is that all? Well that's easy enough, assuming you have the money and can pass the exam."

"There's an exam?" Luca asked, his face drained of color. "What kind of exam?"

Paolo pulled off his hat and ran his fingers through his hair. "Well, they have to have an exam, or anyone could become a student." Out of the corner of his eye, he studied Luca. He appeared nauseous. Would the boy vomit?

"Luca, is this one of those 'running away from home' things?"

"What?" Luca yelped. The donkey, startled by the noise, jerked up, nearly pulling the lead from Paolo's hand.

"You know, like you got in trouble with your parents so now

you're running off to Padua. Although if you were running away, I don't know why you'd choose Padua. You could go to Rome, or Paris!"

"But Padua has the university," Luca said quietly.

"Universities are boring," Paolo confided. "Trust me, I go to the University of Padua so I should know."

"You do?" squeaked Luca.

The boy—because, really, he was a boy, even if he was only a few years younger that Paolo—was so tightly wound that everything made him jump. Clearly Luca was not a mastermind, or a charlatan. His emotions played out right across his face. He must be in over his head.

Poor guy. He'd probably get eaten alive in Rome.

"So, are you running away?"

"I guess you could say that," Luca admitted. The boy raised his hand to his hair, but then awkwardly dropped his arm.

"We have a few more hours until we reach Padua. Why don't you tell me what happened?" Paolo prodded gently. "Anyway, it's probably a good idea for you to rehearse your story in advance."

Luca froze in place. "What's that supposed to mean?"

Paolo sighed, turning back to face Luca. The donkey took advantage of the break to grab more weeds from the side of the road.

"Look, I'm going to be frank. You aren't a very good liar. So if you're going to lie, you might as well practice a few times so that once we get to Padua, people might believe you."

"I'm not lying. I had to leave Venice. For a good reason."

"Oh, yes, I'm sure that's the case," Paolo said, the corners of his mouth rising. "Very specific."

Luca's eyebrows fell. The boy couldn't take a ribbing. Paolo made himself ease up. After all, Luca wasn't going to say anything if he was afraid. And then what would he do for the rest of the walk?

Paolo pulled the donkey's lead and began walking, and Luca followed.

"Anyway, I'd wager it has something to do with a girl. Am I right?"

Luca made a noise that sounded like choking. "A girl?" he sputtered. "Yeah. I guess you could say that."

"You fell for her, the family says back off. Your father threatens you, but you just can't ignore her. Somehow you cause her to lose honor, and now you have to get out of town fast."

"Something like that." Luca fell silent for several steps, and then continued in a quieter voice. "My parents wanted me to act one way, but I wasn't interested in following orders." Luca shrugged, putting on an air of nonchalance.

Paolo raised an eyebrow. Luca really couldn't pull off the disinterested attitude that Paolo had been cultivating since he could walk. He must not be from a noble family, or he'd be better at hiding his emotions.

"And so you decided to run off to Padua?" It wasn't much of a plan at all. But Paolo didn't want to crush the boy's spirits. There was something endearing about Luca, like an enthusiastic puppy who had not grown into his paws. He was trying so hard that Paolo actually wanted to help him.

"Yes," Luca said firmly. "I'm going to attend the university." He scratched his elbow. "But, could you tell me more about the entrance exam?"

The boy could not hide the nerves in his voice. Luca apparently thought he could waltz into Padua and just enroll at the university. How could he not know about the exam? Maybe his tutor had not been very good. Or maybe he had received a shoddy education.

"Well, it's a pretty typical examination, you've probably taken a hundred just like it."

Luca shrugged. "I'm not sure."

"You know. Faculty members will ask you questions about all sorts of things. You have to schedule it in advance, because the university has to put together a panel of professors to sit and hear the exam."

"It's an oral exam?" Luca asked, his voice cracking.

Paolo's eyebrow shot up. So the boy really hadn't had any exams before. "Yes, of course. And it takes, oh, let's see. I guess it takes a few hours? They ask you all kinds of questions. Usually they have a professor of rhetoric, and one for music, and sometimes one for natural philosophy. It's pretty standard, but it covers a lot of material."

"And, what if you don't know the answer?"

"Well, sometimes it's okay, sometimes it's not. The examination is to figure out how much you know, to see if you're ready for the university. I guess they don't expect you to know everything, otherwise you won't be attending the university in the first place, right? But they do have to test you in the basics, to make sure you know what you're doing. Otherwise anyone could take classes and that would make the university look bad. The best things are always exclusive, don't you think?"

Luca nodded again. They walked into the shade of a copse of trees, and Paolo wiped the sweat from his brow. Luca's face was contorted with worry.

Paolo wondered if the boy might simply turn around and walk back to Venice.

"You took the examination, right?"

"Yes, of course, and I passed, too." Paolo tried not to make it sound like a boast, but he was proud that he'd passed. His father had told him that over half of the examinations ended with a rejection.

"Do you think—I mean, would you be willing to tutor me for the exam? I could pay you of course."

Paolo scratched his head. It would be a nice way to pick up some extra money, and maybe he could avoid these pointless trips to local fairs if he had another job in Padua. And would it really be that hard? He'd make Luca read some lesson books, give him a few tips, and cash in.

"It sounds like a good idea, but . . . do I get paid even if you don't pass? Because it's not fair if you only pay me if you pass. I can't make you into a genius if you're dim, you know."

"Of course," Luca responded quickly. "I would want to offer you a fair amount. I could give half now and the rest after the exam? Maybe a bonus if I pass?"

It was clear that Luca hadn't negotiated many deals. Paolo's palms itched as he imagined how much money he could squeeze out of the boy. But something restrained him. Luca was clearly in over his head.

So Paolo wouldn't count on any bonus for Luca passing the exam.

"That sounds fine. We can agree on the amount later. But tell me, do you have a place to stay in Padua?"

"No, not yet. I've never been to Padua, and I don't know anyone there."

"Well, you might be able to take a room in my boarding house. That would definitely make it easier for me to tutor you." And his landlord would give him a discount for bringing in a new tenant.

Luca nodded enthusiastically.

"There's only one problem," Paolo continued. "The owner usually only rents to current university students." He saw Luca's face fall. "But he's made exceptions in the past, and if I tell him that you're studying for the exam, he might let you take a room."

"I can promise him that if I don't pass the exam I'll move out," Luca added hastily.

"That might work. It's not too expensive, since it's for

students. The only catch is that sometimes you have to do stupid errands for the owner. Like he'll make you do work for him in the house, or send you to fairs. That's why I'm out here wandering in the wilderness. He sent me to the fair at Isola di Torre because he thought they'd want some of his goods. Which, as you can see, they did not." He pointed to the full bags hanging at the donkey's waist. "But it's a good deal, in any case."

"It sounds perfect," Luca said. "What's the owner's name?"

"Oh, him? He's a professor at the University of Padua. His name is Galileo."

NINE

Zaneta Lucia's breath caught in her throat when Paolo spoke.

Had she misheard? Did he really just say Galileo?

It was almost too perfect to believe. How was it possible that fortune had brought her here?

Zaneta Lucia had been plagued with doubts since she had left Venice. But this felt like a sign that she was on the right path.

It had not been an easy journey. After deciding to leave, Zaneta Lucia had written a quick note to her parents, apologizing for running away. She didn't linger long, worried that her resolve would evaporate. She left before the sun had even begun to turn the sky pink.

Zaneta Lucia stopped for one last look at the house where she had grown up. Her eyes soaked up the perfect harmony of the five Byzantine-style arches above the balcony, the twisted pillars beneath the windows, the golden glow of the bricks on the building's façade. But before she could change her mind, Zaneta Lucia turned her back on the palazzo and forced her feet to move.

She walked north, through the streets of Venice that she knew best. The first rays of morning light were just barely turning the sky a paler shade of blue, but between the tall buildings, darkness reigned. The city felt empty. Then Zaneta

Lucia saw a dark shape scurry across her path. She choked back a scream. It was a rat. Swallowing her fear, she quickened her pace, her eyes avoiding the moving shapes at the edges of the canals.

Finally, she reached an unfamiliar place—the Jewish ghetto, where Venice's Jews were forced to live. Zaneta Lucia had to sell her jewelry, and she hoped no one would track her to the ghetto. If she was going to leave the island, she needed money.

The tight ring of tall buildings was surrounded by a circle of water, the only bridge raised for the night so that the Jews could not leave the small enclave. Zaneta Lucia shifted from one foot to the other as she waited near the bridge. She bought a hot roll with some change, and as she ate, she eyed the ghetto.

Sunlight filtered through the sky. Hopefully the bridge would come down soon. She felt exposed, standing on the street wasting time.

A guard finally approached. Zaneta Lucia was struck with a new worry. Would the men inside even talk to a girl without a male escort? Should she find some place to change into pants and tie back her hair?

Before she had time to decide, the bridge was down and a Jewish man walked across it, heading toward San Marco. "Excuse me?" she called out to him. "Excuse me!" He turned and caught her eye. "Sorry, do you know where I might go to sell some jewelry?"

"Go in there and talk to Manfredo," the man said, pointing back over the bridge. She frowned, and he stepped closer. "Don't worry, women are allowed in the ghetto, even young Catholic girls like yourself. It's all legal."

"Oh, thank you," she said, relief washing over her. The man tipped his cap toward her and walked off.

Zaneta Lucia blushed. She had complained about needing an escort. But the entire ghetto was barricaded off from the rest of society. The Jews might be allowed to travel the city during the day, but they were guarded at night. She had to walk past armed guards just to cross the narrow bridge into the ghetto.

Once inside the narrow ring of houses, Zaneta Lucia looked around, trying to sort out the man's directions. These houses were much taller than others she'd seen in Venice. It seemed like there were at least six or seven stories on all of them. A woman stopped to ask if she needed help, and Zaneta Lucia repeated her request. The woman kindly walked her to Manfredo's shop, on the fourth floor of one of the buildings.

Zaneta Lucia took a deep breath before walking through the door. A man sat behind a low counter. He was older, maybe in his fifties, and he seemed friendly, at least judging by the wide smile on his face.

"Welcome, welcome," he said, his accent calling to mind the Low Countries, or maybe Germany. "I am Manfredo. You have jewelry to sell, I presume?"

"Yes. Do many women come here to sell jewelry?"

"More than you might guess. Women from Venice's most prominent families come right here to sell to me. Maybe they have debts they don't want to share with their husbands, maybe they need the money for their lovers, who knows? It's none of my business. But just the other day, I saw a woman in this very shop who claimed she was here to sell some of the Dogaressa's jewelry. The Dogaressa! Can you imagine, the most powerful woman in Venice selling here in Manfredo's shop? Well, I probably shouldn't spread that story around, so let's keep it between us."

Zaneta Lucia smiled, her nerves allayed by the man's friendliness. She wondered if Manfredo told this story to everyone who visited his shop. It did sound impressive, she had to admit.

She reached into her bag and pulled out a few items, setting them on the counter.

"Ah, a gold bracelet, very nice. The inlaid jewels on this one are very fine quality, I think." He pulled out a device that looked like a small circle of glass and studied the jewels near the window. "And the ring is lovely as well. This ruby, it's real?"

"Yes. It was a gift." A gift from the future husband she was rejecting. But she didn't add that.

"This is all very high quality. I can offer you . . . let's see . . . thirty ducats for all three pieces."

"Thirty ducats?" she said, her voice rising in shock. "I was expecting more like a hundred. The jewels are real, as you said, and the gold is high quality."

Manfredo shook his head. "You might be able to get more if you went to the jewelers down by the Rialto in San Polo. But here? I can give you thirty ducats."

"Can you at least make it seventy-five?" Zaneta Lucia shifted nervously on her feet. She didn't want to sell the necklace draped around her neck. It was her last insurance policy in case she needed more money later.

"Look, I can do you a favor and give you forty," he said. "But that is the best deal you can get from anyone in the ghetto."

She sighed. "I need at least sixty. Look again at this gold bracelet, did you see the etchings on the flat side? It's really quite fine. And this other one has sapphires and opals, very nice stones and popular in Venice. I'm sure you could sell them for double that price, at least."

Manfredo looked again at the three pieces. "They are quite nice. You've convinced me. I will make a special deal just for you. I can give you fifty ducats, if you promise to tell your friends that my shop is the best in Venice and that the Dogaressa herself comes here."

Zaneta Lucia grinned. "It's a deal."

He counted out the coins and weighed them in front of her. She would never have remembered to ask for him to weigh the coins.

Zaneta Lucia had never seen so much gold, but she would need it to escape Mario Barbaro. In just a minute, Manfredo pushed the pile of gold toward her and swept her jewelry off the table. She reached out for the coins and divided them. She put half in one purse, and split the remainder between a pouch sewn into the lining of her sack and one under her skirts.

"Thank you, Manfredo. I promise to tell everyone that you are the best jeweler in Venice."

He clapped his hands together, and gave her a friendly wave as she walked out the door.

The heavy coins clinked in her purse as Zaneta Lucia climbed down the steep stairs. It was less than she'd hoped for, but it was enough money to support herself for at least a few months, by her calculations.

Now she just had to figure out how to get to Padua.

Zaneta Lucia walked through the Canareggio neighborhood, and tried to remember everything she knew about boats to the mainland. It wasn't a topic that came up very often, at least not in her presence. She knew ships came to Venice all the time; it was the best port in Europe, or at least that's what her father had said. But did some ships carry passengers? And if so, where did you catch them?

Zaneta Lucia couldn't exactly ask someone. She was in a neighborhood filled with workers, dressed like a patrician girl. And it would be strange for a young girl traveling alone to ask about ships to the mainland. Her chest tightened. From now on, she would always have to avoid drawing attention to herself. The city was now awash with light. Her family might have already found her note and started searching for her. They might even be checking places where she could sell jewelry, or monitoring the boats leaving the city.

She had to leave Venice right away.

Zaneta Lucia finally turned toward San Marco. There were always boats bobbing in the lagoon, and docking in front of the two pillars. Most ships must leave from there, too.

But she couldn't board a boat dressed as Zaneta Lucia Zorzi.

She ducked off the main street and pulled a pair of pants from her sack. Her eyes scanned the alley, and she slipped the pants on under her dress. Then she carefully pulled the dress up over her head, keeping a hand on her undershirt to avoid revealing her skin.

Zaneta Lucia clutched the dress in her hands. She had owned it for two years, and it was still quite fine even though the hem was starting to show wear. She ran her hands over the faded green cloth. She wanted to stuff the dress in her bag. But if her plan worked, it would only weigh her down. And what would happen if Luca Manetti was discovered carrying around a patrician girl's dress?

So she hung the dress on a line of clothes drying in the alley. It would be a nice surprise for the family that found it.

Zaneta Lucia turned her back on the dress, and resolved not to look back.

She put a light coat on over her shirt. There was no mirror in the alley to check her outfit, but it would have to do. Then, she tied back her hair in a loose knot at the nape of her neck. At the last minute, she spun around and pulled the dress off the line, burying it at the bottom of her sack. She had already said too many goodbyes. The dress would come with her.

She stepped out of the alley as Luca Manetti.

Right away the streets of Venice felt different. Zaneta Lucia was used to feeling strangers' eyes following her on the streets. But dressed as a boy she seemed to pass unnoticed, almost as if the pants had transformed her into a spirit.

But that didn't explain all the bumps and shoves. The first time, she nearly yelped in a voice that would have given her away. It must have been an accident. But it kept happening as she wound her way toward San Marco. This must be how men walked through the city, always running into each other. Was it some show of status? She watched, and began to notice a pattern. Only boys her own age would bump her, and there was certainly an implied challenge in the physical contact.

Zaneta Lucia was too terrified to shove back. She had no training in fighting or with a sword, and she didn't want to take any chances.

And then there was the language. The language! She'd never even heard some of the terms. Men would say the foulest things imaginable, and yet if a woman walked by they would instantly cease. Unless the woman was dressed coarsely, in which case she'd be using the same language. Zaneta Lucia figured out those women were working class prostitutes, worlds away from the nobly dressed courtesans that strolled the streets spending their money, rather than looking for work.

The short walk left Zaneta Lucia lightheaded. For the first time, she was seeing a side of Venice that had been hidden from her sight. She had lived her entire life in this city, but she had known nothing about what it looked like through men's eyes.

And right now, it made her palms sweat.

She wandered through the narrow streets, across bridge after bridge, until she reached San Marco. She entered the square from the north, under the massive clock with mechanical men stamping out each hour of the day. Zaneta Lucia wanted one last look at the painted façade of the beautiful Basilica di San Marco, and the bronze horses perched atop it. And she had to visit the exotic ducal palace, which looked almost pink in the new light of the morning.

It might be her last chance to see Venice.

Her skin began to crawl as she stood in front of the massive church. Were people looking for Zaneta Lucia Zorzi? Putting her head down, Zaneta Lucia turned her back on the basilica, and walked through the open Piazza San Marco. She turned left to reach the water on the west side of the square. Here, she followed the water, her eyes trained on the ships moored off the island of San Giorgio, standing alone in the lagoon. These were the large, ocean-bearing ships that might be coming from the eastern Mediterranean and the Black Sea, or even the Atlantic. This sort of ship didn't ferry to the mainland, only two miles away from Venice.

There were also painted gondolas dotting the *riva*, with gondoliers calling out for customers. But those small boats probably didn't go all the way to the mainland either, they were for navigating the maze of islands in the lagoon.

Finally she saw some mid-sized ships, unloading goods at the very end of the marble embankment.

Zaneta Lucia screwed her eyes closed for a moment, and breathed in the sound of waves crashing into the stone. Now she had to truly become Luca Manetti, board a ship, and leave Venice behind. Or she could run home, sneak through the door into Gianna's kitchen, and marry Mario Barbaro.

It was her last chance to change her mind.

"Need a lift?" a voice called out. Her eyes flew open at the interruption. Before her, a man stood on a wooden plank that connected a ship to the embankment. He was looking at her expectantly. "Heading to Mestre in about thirty minutes if you want a ride."

And she knew that she would leave Venice.

"You're going to the mainland?" she asked cautiously, as she studied the man. He was dressed like a sailor, she supposed, having not seen that many sailors in her life. He was in his late twenties or early thirties, with dark hair and tan skin that spoke of more southern origins.

"You look like someone who's planning to get out of town."

"I'm looking for a ride for the right price." She tried to keep the nerves out of her voice.

"And from there?"

"I don't see how that's any of your business."

The man laughed. "I'm not trying to give you a hard time, I swear it on the Virgin Mother. I'm just looking for hands who can help me transport these goods. I've asked every able-bodied boy I've met in Venice if he's looking for a ride, and so far I only have these two," he said, pointing over his shoulder at a pair of young men loitering near the boat.

"So what's the price?" she asked again. He seemed very forward. Of course, he would never speak that way to a girl. But that didn't necessarily mean he was trying to trick her.

"You help me and the others load the goods onto the ship, and unload when we get to Mestre. Pretty simple, and maybe two hours work total. That's all."

Zaneta Lucia chewed on her lower lip. It did sound like a good deal, but she didn't want to make a decision that she would regret. Still, she needed to leave Venice. She nodded. "Fine. I'll help you load and unload, that will pay for my fare. But I want to ride on the deck of the boat, not below deck with the goods."

He thought for a moment and agreed. "I hope you're stronger than you look. Here come the goods we need to load." He pointed at a pallet of wooden crates that four men strained to carry between them. The captain—for he must be the captain, she thought—walked over to it. He spoke some words to the men, who set down the heavy load. "Boys, one of you unloads the wagon and carries the goods to the dock. The other carries them from the dock to the deck of the ship. The last one hauls the boxes down into the hold." He pointed at each, giving them a task.

He gave Zaneta Lucia the first task. "You look like you might trip on the boat," he said with a laugh.

They got to work quickly, and within minutes Zaneta Lucia was winded. The boxes looked light, but after carrying a few they suddenly felt very heavy. She wasn't used to manual labor of any sort. But she had to make a good impression, and she didn't want to be left in Venice.

Maybe she should have paid to get off the island after all. She imagined all the things she could buy with the ducats clinking in her purse, including a sedan chair to carry her to a boat, and a cabin with a private window, or even a private deck. Cold beverages, chilled with ice carried from the Alps. A salve to rub on her sore hands.

"Take off that coat, boy," the captain called out to her. "It's still summer, and you're sweating like a pig in Naples." The other boys laughed, and Zaneta Lucia put her head down to focus on moving the boxes. She did not want the others to see the blush in her cheeks, and she was not going to take off the coat.

It felt like it took hours to load the boat, but slowly the pallet grew empty until there were no more boxes to carry up the plank. Zaneta Lucia wiped her hand across her brow, probably leaving a smear of dirt on her forehead. But she was too tired to care. "Let's load up!" the captain called from the ship. Zaneta Lucia stole one last glance back at San Marco before she walked up the plank. She hopped on the boat.

The crew pulled in the plank and pushed the boat off from the dock.

"I'm Sergio Sargento," the captain said, shaking her hand in a tight grip. He threw her a waterskin, and she gratefully took a gulp. "The ride should take about an hour if the winds are in our favor. And you're free to stay above deck, although it might get wet."

He left Zaneta Lucia alone on the deck. Her throat choked up. Would she ever see Venice again? The strip of dark water separating the boat from the city grew, until it opened up a gap that was too wide to jump. San Marco shrank in their wake. She craned her neck toward her neighborhood, Castello, and prayed for one last glimpse of the church tower near her house. But she could not find it.

Instead, she focused on the Campanile, the red tower growing from the Piazza San Marco. It marked the center of Venice, and stood tall as a symbol of the city's vitality and power. How strange it was to see it from the water. Venice, which had always felt solid beneath her feet, suddenly looked like a floating mirage.

She felt tears welling up behind her eyes and scolded herself. It wouldn't look good to weep in front of the men. But what if she was making a terrible mistake? What if her exile became permanent, and she never saw her family again?

What if she was burning bridges that couldn't be rebuilt?

As the ship pulled farther and farther away from Venice, out into the open water of the lagoon, Zaneta Lucia felt very small. Everything had seemed simpler sitting in her bedroom in the early morning hours. But now, on the deck of a ship watching Venice slip away, she felt completely alone, and knew she was on her own.

TEN

The boat slipped through the Giudecca Canal, picking up speed as they left Dorsoduro behind and entered the open lagoon. The wind whipped around Zaneta Lucia, threatening to pull her hair from its binding. But she couldn't tear her eyes away from the water. It leapt and splashed against the bow, and she wondered how cold it would be, even in August, if she fell overboard.

The boat moved in curious ways under her feet, nothing like the gondolas she'd taken through Venice's narrow canals. Those rolled in the waves of the Grand Canal or the lagoon, as they inched next to the embankments, but this ship was different. The deck felt solid until a wave hit the side and it tipped. Zaneta Lucia almost forgot she was on a boat until those moments when the ground moved beneath her feet.

If she squinted, Zaneta Lucia could see the shore of the mainland. It was almost unrecognizable to a girl who had spent her entire life in Venice. Her hometown was a city of towers, and canals, and magnificent buildings. It was a floating miracle, proof of man's ingenuity, and the perfect marriage between sea and city.

The shore looked like a port, and not a very nice one. Small boats clogged the coastline, and men crawled all over the decks of the ships. She saw fishermen out on the waters checking nets they'd set earlier, and behind them, dozens of broken-down homes doted the shore.

They docked quickly. In minutes, they were in Mestre. Zaneta Lucia sighed as she thought of the boxes in the hold. She looked down at her hands, sore and red from the labor of loading the boat, and wondered if they would be bleeding by the end of the day.

"You, come over here," Sergio called. "We've got other workers on this side, so all you have to do is bring boxes up to the deck."

Zaneta Lucia nodded and made her way down the narrow staircase leading below deck. She raised a hand to her face as the stench struck her, and tried not to retch. She could barely breathe. Had some animal died in the hold, and Sergio didn't want to bother carrying its carcass up the stairs to throw it overboard? She grabbed a box and ran up the narrow stairs.

With the new men helping unload, Zaneta Lucia didn't have to make many trips to the hold, thankfully.

Soon Sergio was shaking her hand. He said she was free to go, unless she wanted to load more goods and take another trip back to Venice. Zaneta Lucia declined. But now she was left alone on the mainland wondering what to do next. It was the first time she had ever left Venice. She had no idea what to expect. In her mind, the rest of Italy looked much like Venice, but Mestre was not what she had imagined at all.

From the docks she wandered through the narrow street that appeared to be the commercial district of town. Mud stuck to her shoes, and she stopped to marvel at it. Venice might flood in the winter, but it was a city free of mud. Everyone she passed wore rough clothes, and their faces were caked with dirt. Most of them seemed to be dock workers, or fisherman. Many of them stank of fish.

No one in Mestre had the wealth that had surrounded her in

Venice.

On her walk, Zaneta Lucia stumbled upon an open field where multiple wagon teams were loading and hitching up. As she watched, one departed, pulled by a team of shaggy horses. She leapt back from the beasts—they were the first living horses she had seen up close. Horses had been illegal in Venice for almost three hundred years.

Once she calmed down, her mind filled with questions. Were some of these wagons heading toward Padua? Could she ask for a ride? She had no idea how people traveled on the mainland.

And just how far was it to Padua? She'd seen a few maps of the Veneto, painted in green, blue, and gold. Her father owed one that made him very proud. It hung in his study. But on those maps Venice was enormous, certainly out of scale. She had traced a finger down the Grand Canal, marveling at the miniature version of the basilica and the Doge's Palace. And when her eyes had drifted to the mainland, the territory was stamped with images of St. Mark, or coats of arms, that made it impossible to judge distances.

Now that she was in Mestre, was it a day's walk to Padua? Two? When night fell, where would she sleep? And, she wondered with an increasing sense of urgency, where could she relieve herself in private? She certainly would not urinate standing on the top of a wagon, as one man nearby was currently doing.

Zaneta Lucia's heart pounded, and she swallowed hard, trying to steady her breath. It was too late to go back now. She remembered the bravado of Tommaso Mocenigo, the brash boy at the lecture, and tried to imitate his confidence.

She studied the wagons. Soon, she noticed men walking through the crowded field calling out the names of cities. Sometimes the wagon train leaders would call out "Yep," and the men would stop, talking.

"Padua," she heard one of the wandering men say.

"We stop near Padua," called out a voice a few rows over. Zaneta Lucia's ears perked up, and she followed the man.

Speaking to strangers still made her hands shake. But Zaneta Lucia stood tall. She was not a young girl running away from home—she was Luca Manetti, on his way to study at the University of Padua. "I'm heading to Padua, too," she said to the men. "Where are you going?"

"Isola di Torre, for a fair. Carting glass from Murano to sell," the wagon train leader said.

Zaneta Lucia had never heard of Isola di Torre. "How far is that from Padua?"

He scratched his head. "It's maybe a few hours away."

The other man shook his head and wandered off. "I'll look for another wagon later today."

"You still interested?" the driver asked Zaneta Lucia. "I'm Umaldo. I charge five *soldi* per day to Isola di Torre; it's a two day journey."

She nodded, ready to negotiate. But she had no idea if that was a good price. Still, she had heard Filippo say you should always reject the first offer. "I'd rather pay for the full distance. Eight *soldi* to ride to Isola di Torre, and I'll eat with your crew." Her stomach growled at the mention of food. She had not eaten since the roll she had devoured outside the Venetian ghetto.

Umaldo whistled. "Fine, it's a deal. Half now though."

She carefully opened her money pouch, making sure not to clink the coins too loudly, and fished out four small coins.

"It looks like you could use this," Umaldo said, tossing her a waterskin. "Keep it for the journey. You're responsible for filling it, and you can return it in Isola di Torre. We should be ready to head out in about a quarter-hour, if you have any business in Mestre."

Zaneta Lucia looked down to hide the red on her cheeks.

She had completely forgotten that she would need water on the journey. Umaldo must think her an idiot, or an easy target. But in her entire life, she had never had to think about where to get water or food, it had always been provided for her.

Zaneta Lucia shook her head. "I have no business here," she said quietly.

"Then just hop on that wagon," he said, pointing at one near the back of the train. "It's not too full so you might even be able to sleep in the back."

Several hours later she was cursing Umaldo. This was her first time in a wagon, and it was so bumpy that sleep was unimaginable. Her entire body was already sore and chafed. She didn't want to imagine how she would feel at the end of the day tomorrow. Or how she was going to walk to Padua after the long ride.

With the wagon jolting up and down, Zaneta Lucia could barely raise the waterskin to her mouth. Finally she decided to stretch her legs and walk next to the wagon for a while. She hoisted herself over the side, steadying herself as she nearly lost her balance. The walking helped, but before long the pace of the wagon train was too fast and she had to try to climb back into the wagon, which was harder than it looked.

Just as the sun was tipping from its zenith, Umaldo rode by on his horse. "Here you go," he said, tossing her a heel of bread and some dried meat. "Lunch."

That night, they stopped in a little town that was halfway to Isola di Torre. Umaldo and his gruff crew were planning to sleep under the wagons, and had already lit a small fire. Umaldo called that she was welcome to join. Zaneta Lucia declined, heading toward the local inn alone.

The inn was relatively empty, although it seemed a natural stopping point between Venice and Padua. Not too much traffic came through this time of year, according to the chatty innkeeper who stationed herself at Zaneta Lucia's table and talked her ear off. Zaneta Lucia was exhausted. She had not slept the previous night, and that day she had left her hometown for the first time, done hours of manual labor, talked with more men than she'd spoken to in her entire life, and ridden in that cursed wagon. All she wanted to do was climb up to her room and sleep, but she didn't want to appear rude.

The innkeeper's monologue stopped, and Zaneta Lucia realized that she had asked a question.

"What?"

"Oh, I was wondering if you wanted a companion in your room," the innkeeper said.

A companion? Did she mean a shared room?

"We have several young women, all very beautiful, and at very reasonable rates. We offer discounts like you won't find anywhere else."

Then Zaneta Lucia understood what the innkeeper was offering. "Oh, no thank you!" she burst out. "I appreciate the offer, but I will have to decline." Was this how men lived? Did they really look for a different woman every night?

Zaneta Lucia quickly excused herself from the conversation and climbed the stairs to her room. When she stepped into the small space, exhaustion hit her like a pile of stones. She collapsed into the bed and fell into a deep sleep, still wearing her dusty clothes, and dreamed about her mother putting a spell on her for ruining the family's reputation.

~ ~ ~

The next day was much like the previous one. Zaneta Lucia rode on the wagon, her muscles clenching at every bump. By the early afternoon, she was starting to get a headache.

"Are we almost to Isola di Torre?" she called out to Umaldo.

"It's just over that ridge," he replied, turning his horse back toward her wagon.

"Could I get to Padua tonight?"

"The fair starts tomorrow, so you probably won't find a wagon heading to Padua for a few days. And the sun would set before you could walk there. Unless you want to buy a horse?"

Zaneta Lucia shook her head. She'd just have to spend the night in Isola di Torre. Staying at inns wasn't too expensive, but she couldn't afford a horse. She needed to save her money.

The next morning, the fair started in Isola di Torre. Zaneta Lucia couldn't leave before she walked through the booths. She had never been to a fair. Her mother had let her go to Carnivale in Venice, but only before dark and only with a male chaperone.

But this was different: there were hundreds of booths, each overflowing with different goods. She saw golden spices, dried apricots, and fat wheels of cheese on one row of booths, across from carved wooden toys, strips of painted leather, and colorful glass marbles.

Zaneta Lucia caught herself touching some blue fabric wistfully, thinking how nice it would look sewn into a dress. She pulled her hand back before anyone noticed. A boy wouldn't look at fabric like that.

She watched the men wandering the fair, and studied their movements. Zaneta Lucia noticed that almost all of them were carrying some kind of weapon. Should she try to buy a knife, or a sword? Shaking her head, she decided against it. Even if she knew how to use a weapon, wearing one might make her more of a target.

Stall after stall, she saw woven fabrics from all over the world, exotic fruits and grains that she didn't recognize, including some type of black rice and dozens of dried herbs. One table even sold coffee. Zaneta Lucia sniffed at the hard beans. She'd heard coffee was coming into fashion across Europe, but she grimaced at the bitter, acrimonious scent. It was hard to imagine anyone drinking it for pleasure.

In other booths she saw all sorts of utensils and cooking pots, as well as clothes already fashioned in the most current styles. Zaneta Lucia touched a pair of pants and wondered if she should buy more men's clothes. But she would not try anything on in the fair, and she couldn't afford to waste her money. For now, her two pairs of pants and two shirts would have to do. She could buy more in Padua.

And then she saw a booth overflowing with books. Zaneta Lucia stopped in her tracks, breathing in the familiar scent of paper, ink, and glue. They were cheap books, bound in already cracked leather. She saw religious texts, and some books of poetry, but nothing on natural philosophy. Still, her eyes devoured the offerings, and she had to stop herself from grabbing them all up.

"You like to read?" the bookseller asked from behind the stack of books.

"Oh, yes, very much," Zaneta Lucia breathed.

"Then you might like this. It's brand new," he said, handing her a volume. Was it just her imagination, or was the book still warm from the press? It couldn't be.

She turned it over and read the title. "Don Quixote? What's it about?"

"Some crazy Spaniard."

She wanted to sit and read the book immediately, but she handed it back reluctantly. "Thank you, but I can't afford it."

It was past time for her to get on the road to Padua.

Walking through the fair felt significant, in some way. These were the goods that had made family fortunes in Venice, these were the items that wealthy patricians coveted. Zaneta Lucia was suddenly immersed in a whole world of goods and experiences that she hadn't even realized existed. Her Venetian life had been so sheltered. She rarely left the house, and spent most of her time speaking with the same small group of people.

And now there was an entire world to explore, a world she'd only read about in books, and it was filled with all sorts of amazing things.

By the time she finally set off to Padua, it was already close to noon. Her legs were sore, and her hands were chapped. Zaneta Lucia's stomach rolled as she thought about arriving in Padua. Where would she live? How would she enroll at the university? She was exhausted and overwhelmed before she even began the walk.

So when Zaneta Lucia overtook the young man walking next to a donkey, she was shocked to learn that he was a student at the University of Padua. Everything was falling into place—Paolo would tutor her, and help her find a place to live.

And when Paolo mentioned the name Galileo, her heart almost stopped. Galileo! The man she'd heard about at the lecture in Venice. The man who was revolutionizing the study of the world and nature. How could she be so lucky?

Her aches and pains faded away, and she grinned as she walked next to Paolo on the road to Padua.

ELEVEN

The porticos surrounding the University of Padua were wide and shaded, even in the depth of summer. In the early morning, they were also deserted. Students were still asleep in bed, and most professors had not yet roused themselves from slumber. The streets outside the portico, which would be bustling with commerce in a few hours, were silent.

But in the shade of the portico, two men walked toward each other.

In spite of the wide, empty space, they were on a collision course. Before they were even within an arm's length, one man flinched and leapt back.

"Watch where you're going," the man scolded, giving his white beard a quick tug of irritation. "You aren't the boss of this place, no matter how much your head has swelled since you began corresponding with kings."

The offender chuckled. "Calm yourself, Fanelli, or you'll cause the vessels of your heart to contract until you begin foaming at the mouth."

"Is that your idea of a joke?" Professor Fanelli responded, his shoulders stooped with age. "That sounds like a threat. I don't know what you're up to, Galileo, but you better stay away from me." Fanelli huffed off down the corridor.

Galileo tried to suppress another chuckle. He raised a hand

to his close-cropped beard, and continued down the portico away from Fanelli.

He knew that many of his colleagues were jealous of his achievements, but what was he supposed to do? Reassure Fanelli that his research into a letter penned by Cicero was going to gain him the same level of fame? It was a ridiculous notion, and even Fanelli must realize that. No wonder the man was prickly.

Fanelli was at the end of a long, though not illustrious, career, while Galileo's star was on the rise. And Fanelli's letter had been studied by dozens of other intellectuals. Galileo's work was original.

Plus, Galileo knew how to work the system, unlike poor old Fanelli.

Fanelli was probably furious that the Holy Roman Emperor himself had written back to Galileo's letter. Maybe Galileo should have reminded Fanelli that he corresponded with both kings and an emperor. And the pope. Of course, that might actually give the old man a heart attack.

The truth was, Fanelli's linguistic analysis merely repeated the work of previous scholars all the way back to Petrarch, nearly three centuries ago. It was no surprise that few people cared. But Galileo's work was shaking the very foundations of knowledge, challenging the great Aristotle and finding the errors in his view of nature. Galileo was rewriting the book of nature in a language that everyone could understand, while Fanelli muddled along in his dusty Latin prose.

Galileo continued his ambling walk down the portico bordering the University of Padua, heading in the general direction of the small lecture room where he held a seminar once a week. The students complained about the early hour, but Galileo's time was valuable. If they wanted a moment with the rising star, they would have to rise early.

Today he was lecturing on mechanics, though he would do it

from memory without any notes. It was a popular topic at the university, or maybe Galileo was just a popular professor. Students flocked to his classes, and he had been forced to turn some away, much to his chagrin. He was paid per student, after all. Still, the small room held only ten students comfortably, and he had stretched his goodwill with the university by somehow fitting fifteen in the room each week.

He had been turning away students more frequently lately. Ever since word had gotten out about his newest experiments, a veritable mob of young men followed him through Padua, begging to learn from him.

Experiments. They were the future of science, Galileo schooled his students. Aristotle had not performed experiments, and his followers even today claimed that experiments distorted nature rather than revealing her secrets. But Galileo knew they were the key to harnessing the potential of nature, which Aristotle had not seen. With the right experiment, you could even unlock the secrets of the universe itself.

One day soon they might all be running experiments.

Of course, many of his own experiments were *thought* experiments. He didn't have time to run each of his experiments on falling bodies a hundred times, so he did them five times and rounded up. But he still built the ramps and put in the effort to understand the material principles behind his tests.

He used his experiences and his reason to understand the world. After all, he didn't actually plan to climb the mast of a fast-traveling ship to drop weighted balls and record the results. As it turned out, he was a little afraid of heights. But he knew, without doing it, what would happen.

Galileo turned the corner and walked into his classroom, carrying nothing with him. He shushed the chatting students with only a look. Galileo stood at an average height, and his hair had not yet shown the grey of men considered experts. Still, he commanded authority when he entered a room. He thought it must be because of his confidence, which came from knowing he was right.

Without an introduction, he began speaking to the group of young men.

"Mechanics. The study of motion. Learning the laws of the universe through observations. That is the topic of our lecture today," he began. And for the next hour he spoke extemporaneously, never interrupted by the students who sat listening. A few appeared to be writing down every last word that came out of his mouth.

After his confrontation with Fanelli, Galileo was feeling more confident than usual. So near the end of his lecture, he took a few swipes at Aristotelians and their logic about mechanical forces.

"You all study the works of the Great Aristotle, yes?" he asked rhetorically. A handful of boys nodded. "From ethics, to politics, to logic, Aristotle has been the textbook of our university curriculum. But in one area, natural philosophy, Aristotle's theories are flawed."

His reward was a gasp from a few of the boys in the room.

"Yes, you heard me, Aristotle's theories about nature are not always correct. And our discussion of mechanics will prove it."

As the students shifted in their seats, Galileo explained his own experiments on mechanics, and compared them with Aristotle's predictions. Without stating it directly, he led his students to the areas where Aristotle fell short.

Galileo knew that most professors at the University of Padua were committed Aristotelians. They would certainly hear about the lowly mathematics professor criticizing the Great Philosopher. Some of his students were already eagerly leaning forward, as if ready to leap from their seats and trumpet Galileo's attack through the streets of Padua.

As a mathematics professor, Galileo was not allowed comment on the nature of the world—he was supposed to restrict himself to equations and figures. But his work was a much more vigorous tool than Aristotle's old books. Mathematics revealed the order of nature. So why shouldn't a mathematics professor discuss the universe?

Galileo already knew how the Aristotelians would answer. Mathematics professors were menial "counters," unqualified for the highest intellectual pursuits, and the university agreed. Professors of natural philosophy, who declared a monopoly on studying nature, were paid three times his salary or more. It was patently unfair, but every time Galileo asked for a raise he was turned down.

At the end of his lecture, the room seemed to deflate. Galileo, too, was drained from the mental exertion. He didn't want to simply read from a book, like most of his colleagues. His lectures pushed students to confront unanswered questions about nature. Galileo wanted to spark their curiosity, drive them to solve those mysteries.

But Galileo knew that he had crossed a line today.

He stood at the front of the room while his students filed out, and then walked out into the corridor. He should head back to the boarding house. Being a professor barely paid the bills. His books brought in a small trickle of money, as did the rent from students at the boarding house. His wife, Marina, had suggested opening the boarding house for students. Well, Marina wasn't technically his wife, but she was in all but name. She thought it was a good way to bring in extra money, especially with three young children. They did not live together, because of the potential damage to Galileo's career, but he always sent money to Marina and visited his daughters and young son whenever he could.

And now, he was working on a new book that could change

everything, not just for him but for all of natural philosophy. But the stack of letters on his desk was piling higher. He could not afford to ignore the missives from Venetian patricians and French noblemen. Plus, he needed to check on his workers, to make sure they were keeping up their numbers.

A mathematics professor's salary was not very much, after all, not compared with the high wages brought in by the Aristotelian philosophers.

Galileo's mind was stuck on the familiar topic. Was he underpaid because mathematics was somehow easy? No, more likely the university thought mathematics was simply running calculations, while the natural philosophers described the world.

How foolish.

After all, nature is written in the language of mathematics.

As he exited the portico into the light of the mid-morning sun, he nodded at the nice turn of phrase. He would have to remember that one.

~ ~ ~

Zaneta Lucia gasped when they reached Padua. In the two days since she had left Venice, she had not been impressed by the mainland. Mestre had been a muddy mess of workers, and Isola di Torre was not much of a town outside of the tents for the fair.

But Padua, perched on the slope of a slight hill topped by a massive brick basilica, was like nothing she had ever seen. The domes on the basilica reminded her of the Basilica di San Marco, but here the façade was so different, with its row of delicate arches cascading down the front. She wanted to run up the hill to inspect the building in more detail, and discover what wonders were hiding inside the massive church.

Zaneta Lucia soaked in the sight of the buildings crawling up the hill toward the basilica. Paolo pointed out the university as they crossed the bridge over the river.

She had never seen a real city on land before, strange as that sounded. On the road into Padua they had passed villas, some of which looked almost Venetian, but others that appeared foreign to her eyes. Zaneta Lucia tried to conceal her reaction from Paolo. She did not want him to think she was ignorant or sheltered. But she could not help but gape at the sights.

Soon the city had folded itself around them and they were walking near the university. The wide main building of the university was layered with porticos on every level, like a fantastical mirage in the middle of the city. The colonnaded structures reminded her of the Piazza San Marco, but this had been built for learning and education. She gawked at the sight of hundreds of students flocking in the square, many carrying books and talking in loud voices.

Was it possible that in a few short weeks she might count herself among their numbers?

"Most students here at the university are from Venice," Paolo said casually. "You know, because Venice doesn't have its own university, and the University of Padua is the best in the world."

Zaneta Lucia nodded, her eyes glued to the students. "What kinds of classes do you take?"

"Well, I plan to be a lawyer. But first I have to finish all my requirements, like rhetoric, and music, and geometry. It's really rather dull most of the time. I just want to graduate so I can start practicing law and make some money."

It didn't sound dull to Zaneta Lucia at all.

"Will you stay in Padua, or are you planning to move somewhere else?"

He swatted the donkey, who was trying to bite the cloak of a man who looked like a professor. "I'm from Rome, and maybe I'll go back there some day. I'd love to travel, though. I want to see Constantinople, and Paris, and London. And Alexandria."

His voice sped up as he listed the cities, and a smile crept across Zaneta Lucia's face at his enthusiasm.

"But first I have to finish my degree," he said, tugging on the donkey's lead. "Which means I have to pass a thousand different exams before I can go anywhere."

She nodded in silence.

"Anyway, that's the university." He led her away from the square. "And just on the next street over here is the boarding house." He pointed toward the block, which looked very similar to the university. If Paolo hadn't told her the university was behind them, she would have thought they had not left it.

"I heard Professor Galileo got a discount on the building because he's a faculty member. Students usually just arrange their own housing, but I guess the university has an incentive to provide inexpensive housing near campus, you know?" Paolo said.

Paolo was constantly steering their conversation back to money, Zaneta Lucia realized. He did not dress like a rich man. His traveling clothes were coated in a layer of dust from the road. But if his family had sent him all the way from Rome, they must be wealthy.

Zaneta Lucia had never given much thought to money. She grew up in a palazzo, but her mother was always complaining about how poor they were compared to other patrician families. When she crossed the Rialto and marveled at the houses on the Grand Canal, she didn't feel rich.

But now Zaneta Lucia was carrying her entire life savings, and she could not stop worrying about money. Would her ducats hold until she could enroll in the university? How could she make more money once she had spent them? It scared her to walk around with so much gold, and yet it was more terrifying to imagine leaving it somewhere where it might vanish.

Paolo stopped in front of a five story narrow building on the edge of the university district. Zaneta Lucia looked up at the structure and wondered if she would sleep there tonight.

"I have to take the donkey around back. You should wait here," Paolo said, and disappeared down the alley.

Zaneta Lucia stood by the door, her eyes tracking the people on the street. Most of them were young men around her own age. They had to be students at the university. They ignored her, not making eye contact, which she appreciated. Her nerves had returned. She forced herself to relax the hand gripping one of her pant legs.

She wanted to sit down somewhere and rest. Her legs ached with exhaustion. But no one else on the street was sitting, and she did not want to draw attention to herself.

Zaneta Lucia realized with a jolt that she had barely seen a woman since they walked past the university. Women were not allowed to attend the university, and of course all of the professors were men. As she waited, Zaneta Lucia saw a small handful of simply-dressed girls scurry by. They must be housemaids. But if Padua had patrician families, their daughters avoided the university.

Her thoughts were interrupted when the door behind her squeaked open. Zaneta Lucia spun around to see a boy walk out. He was tall and thin with dark hair, and his eyes smiled when he spoke to her. "Are you waiting for something?"

"No. I mean, I came here with Paolo. I'm here to see about a room?" she managed to stammer out.

"Ah, okay," the boy said. "I'm Mazzeo. I've been here a few years and it's a great place to live. But I should warn you, Messer Galileo expects all his tenants to work for him."

Before she could ask what he meant, or even give her name,

he waved and ran off down the street toward the university. "Maybe I'll see you around later. I'm late for class!"

A minute later, Paolo came out the front door and beckoned her inside. "Sorry for the wait."

She shrugged off his apology and followed, grateful to be away from the bustling street.

"This is the entry hall, of course," he said, showing her the dark interior behind the door. "Up these stairs are the rooms, mainly on the third and fourth floor. Professor Galileo lives on the fifth floor, and he sometimes runs experiments in his rooms, so don't go up there. The second floor has the workshop, and the ground floor is mainly storage and that sort of thing."

He walked to the staircase, which was dark even in the mid-afternoon, and she trailed behind him "Galileo isn't here right now, so why don't you just come up to the common area on the third floor? He should be back soon."

Her heart pounded at the thought of meeting Galileo. If he was a genius, would he somehow see through her disguise? She shook off the foolish worry.

The common room on the third floor was an open space with a few chairs, and a row of tables in the corner. Thankfully, it was empty. Zaneta Lucia wondered if most of the tenants were in class, like Mazzeo.

"This is the place. It's nothing fancy, but I spend a lot of time in this room." Paolo collapsed onto an upholstered chair, and Zaneta Lucia settled into the chair across from him. Her feet ached. She tried to mimic Paolo's posture, conscious that she had no idea how men did even the simplest things, like sit in a chair.

"How many people live in the boarding house?"

"Oh, we have about eleven or twelve right now, although it's usually a little higher than that," Paolo said. "But last year there was a plague down in Emilia Romagna, and a few students ended up having to drop out to go home for good."

"And what exactly is the workshop?"

"Galileo makes instruments."

"Instruments, like musical instruments?"

Paolo laughed. "No, instruments to investigate nature. Like compasses and astrolabes. We make them in his shop, and sometimes we help sell them, like I did on the trip to Isola di Torre."

Zaneta Lucia had never heard of instruments to study nature. Aristotle had written that you only needed a sharp mind to investigate the natural world. "So you know how to make the tools he uses for natural philosophy?"

Surprise flittered across Paolo's face. "You've heard of Galileo then? I hadn't realized his reputation had spread to Venice."

Zaneta Lucia cursed silently. She could not afford to make mistakes. Paolo was acting like a friend, but she barely knew him.

"Yes, I heard about him in a lecture on Aristotle a few weeks ago."

"Ah, let me guess. The lecturer was a stodgy old man who vowed to defend Aristotle to his dying breath?"

Zaneta Lucia frowned. "No, he spoke highly of Galileo's work."

Paolo chuckled. "Just let Galileo hear you say that, and he'll definitely want you to stay in the boarding house." He leaned forward and lowered his voice. "The way he talks most days, Galileo thinks he only has enemies. He'll be happy to know that he has allies in Venice."

"I'm very interested in natural philosophy."

"If you show an aptitude with the instruments, I'm sure Galileo will talk your ear off about experiments."

Zaneta Lucia silently vowed to be the best instrument maker that Galileo had ever met.

Paolo continued, "Galileo uses this boarding house to bring

in more revenue. We even have a small printing press on the ground floor where we print the manuals that explain how to use his instruments. But he's very secretive about the techniques. He only lets trustworthy people stay in the boarding house. He can trust you, right?"

Zaneta Lucia froze. She was lying about her identity. Every word she spoke was a deception.

"Of course," she replied, holding her voice steady.

TWELVE

Paolo left Zaneta Lucia alone in the common room. When a church bell tolled four o'clock, Paolo had yelped and leapt up from the chair. He was late for a lecture. As he hurried from the room, he yelled that he would be expelled from the university if he kept skipping classes.

Zaneta Lucia was baffled—what could be more important than attending lectures? If she passed the exam, she would never miss a class.

Zaneta Lucia exhaled, finally able to drop her guard. But before she could relax, her eyes darted to the door. Someone might come in at any minute. She was quickly learning that being Luca Manetti was a full-time job.

She stood, and stretched. A stack of books on one of the tables caught her eye, and she walked over for a closer look. Her fingers brushed against the binding of one book, and she picked it up. It was by Galileo.

She hurried back to the chair, the book clutched in her hands. She settled down to read. Within minutes she was deeply immersed into the book. She nodded along as she read, flipping the pages so quickly that she thought of the time Gianna had been caught reading a romance. The maid's face had turned beet red, and her mother had confiscated the book.

Zaneta Lucia turned her eyes back to the slim volume. In it,

Galileo explained mechanics and motion, using all sorts of experiments. The topic was similar to Aristotle's works, but Galileo proved his points so differently. Experiments, the book explained, were a way to investigate nature and understand how it worked, uncovering the mathematical principles behind motion. Zaneta Lucia was delighted to see new ways of explaining nature laid out before her eyes—and unlike Aristotle, Galileo's book included diagrams and drawings to drive home his arguments.

It made so much sense that she wondered how anyone could possibly disagree.

"That's nice to hear," a deep voice responded, and Zaneta Lucia nearly fell out of her seat in shock. She must have spoken her thoughts out loud.

Zaneta Lucia turned to see a man standing in the doorway. He was around forty, with a shortly cropped beard, and he wore professor's robes. Zaneta Lucia's heart pounded, and she had a sinking feeling in her stomach. This man had to be Galileo. And she was a trespasser, reading his book in his boarding house, without his permission. Though there was a slight smile on his face, her shoulders itched as though she had committed a crime.

"I'm so sorry," she sputtered, leaping to her feet. "I didn't realize I was speaking out loud."

"Don't apologize," he said, his smile widening. "My work could always use more supporters. Are you a student of natural philosophy?"

She opened her mouth to answer and closed it. Finally she found her words. "So far I have mostly studied on my own. Mainly Aristotle."

"That's a good place to start," he said with a twinkle in his eye. "In fact, that's where I started, too."

"But here," she said, clutching his book to her chest, "You show that Aristotle fundamentally misunderstands the nature of motion. You prove that Aristotle was wrong!"

He chuckled. "I'm glad you think so." The corners of his mouth dropped and he sighed. "Unfortunately, my detractors disagree. Many are so firmly committed to Aristotle that they would deny what you can see with your own eyes. They would even deny the power of mathematics to understand the world around us."

"But mathematics will define natural philosophy for the next century, at least," Zaneta Lucia said, repeating what she'd heard in the lecture at Venice. Reading Galileo's book had firmly convinced Zaneta Lucia that his mathematical abilities were the key to his breakthroughs. The equations, the geometry, it was all so convincing. He had converted the world into numbers and figures, transforming his observations into equations. She had never imagined that so much could be understood in the language of numbers.

"I'm glad to hear someone say that," Galileo said, his smile returning. "And for what it's worth, I agree with you."

Zaneta Lucia felt her cheeks redden. She had been speaking with the illustrious Galileo as if he were an old acquaintance. Had she crossed a line? Had she even remembered to use the formal *Lei* when addressing him? She thought so. Maybe her mother's etiquette lessons hadn't been such a waste of time.

"Now that we agree on natural philosophy, can I ask who you are and what you're doing in my boarding house? Besides admiring my work, of course."

Her blush deepened. She had not even introduced herself to the man who owned the building and had written the book in her hands. "I met one of your tenants, Paolo Serravalle, on the walk back from the fair at Isola di Torre," she explained.

Galileo interrupted with a raise of his hand. "Ah, Paolo. I know he wasn't looking forward to that fair, and I probably shouldn't have sent him. But it's good to get him out of the city at times. He needs to be reminded that most people work hard with their hands for their living."

"I told him that I'm planning to enroll at the university. Paolo suggested I might be able to find a room here," she trailed off. "But then he had to go to class, and I was waiting here to talk to you, and I started reading your book—"

"Calm down, you've done nothing wrong," Galileo reassured her, raising his hands. "And yes, I do have a few empty rooms. Although I normally reserve them for current students."

"Oh, but I'm going to start studying for the examination today, and I will take it as soon as possible, and I promise, I will move out if I don't pass the exam."

"You can stay here. But first, will you tell me who you are?"

She still hadn't given him a name. "*Scusi.* I'm Luca Manetti, from Venice." The lie sprung to her lips easily this time. "I have been studying for a few years and I came to Padua because the university is the best in the world. And also," she added, her breath tightening in her chest, "because I want to study natural philosophy and I heard you are the best in the world."

Galileo threw back his head and laughed. It was such a reflexive movement, done without thought, that Zaneta Lucia was instantly put at ease. "Flattery will get you everywhere," he said with a grin. "I am happy to hear my reputation precedes me. So. Let's say you pay for one month, and we'll see how the exam goes."

"Thank you," she said, relief flooding her body.

"And do you have a tutor yet?"

"Paolo offered to tutor me."

"Then you might want to get someone else for the mathematics portions of the examination. One of my other tenants, Mazzeo, is quite advanced in that area and I'm sure he would be willing to help. I believe there are also several study groups among the tenants that you might find useful in preparing for the examination."

"That would be amazing." Her body felt light and airy, as though she might float to the top of the room. "I appreciate your generosity."

"Let's be clear, I won't be giving you a room for free. You can have the same arrangement as my other students: it's twenty *soldi* per month, and you also have to spend at least six hours a week working in the shop. I can start you with something easy, like putting together the booklets. If you seem proficient, Paolo can train you in some of the more advanced tasks."

"Of course."

"There is an empty room on this floor," he said, "And two on the fourth floor. You might prefer the fourth because it has more of a view."

She reached for her purse, but he held up a hand. "No, find a room first. You can pay me tomorrow."

"Thank you again."

"Nice to meet you Luca Manetti. I hope you continue to enjoy the book," he said, nodding toward the volume that she still held in one hand.

"I'm sure I will. It's a very good book."

"Yes, you mentioned that," he said with a smile. "If you'd like to chat some time about natural philosophy, I'm often in my office on the fifth floor. But now I must get back to work." With a slight tip of his head, he walked out of the room. Zaneta Lucia heard his steps creaking up the stairs.

She just spoken with Galileo!

Zaneta Lucia shook her head. Was she dreaming? Everything had gone perfectly since she woke up that morning in Isola di Torre.

The first day of her new life had been a challenge. She had managed the practical matters of selling her jewelry and finding a boat to leave the island, though both had left her heart pounding and her nerves on edge. And saying farewell to Venice had been hard. She still wondered if she would ever see the beautiful floating city or her family again. The long journey to Isola di Torre had also been physically grueling, and she had constantly questioned her decision. She even wondered if Mario Barbaro was really so bad after all.

But now she was in Padua, she had rented a room, and she had one, or maybe even two, tutors for the examination. And she had met Galileo and actually spoken with him. Less than two weeks ago, Zaneta Lucia had been listening to a lecture about the brilliant professor at the University of Padua, and now she was renting a room in his house.

Had he really invited her to discuss natural philosophy with him? She was a novice, and he might be the most brilliant scientist alive. How could she possibly impress him? She would have to finish his book, and ask Paolo for all of his other writings, to prepare for their discussion.

But before she returned to the book, she closed her eyes and sealed this moment in her memory. Life wouldn't always be this easy, and she wanted to remember the feeling of floating on a cloud.

~ ~ ~

Paolo walked out of his class after a long and boring lecture on Cicero's rhetoric. Normally he enjoyed rhetoric, since it was all about convincing people to do what you wanted, but this professor could turn even the most fascinating subject into a dull, plodding lecture.

And if that hadn't been bad enough, Paolo had been caught talking during class. As a punishment, he had to write a thousand words on Ciceronian style.

Still, it had been worth it.

"If Cicero is so amazing, why did he get his hands chopped off?" Paolo had whispered to the boy next to him. "I guess he couldn't rhetoric his way out of that one." Everyone in earshot had laughed. And Paolo had been caught.

After the other students filed out of the room, several patting Paolo on the back for his jest, Paolo's mood had darkened. As if he didn't have enough work on his plate, now he had to find time to write a boring treatise.

He walked out of the building and into the sun. An idea struck him. Maybe he could assign writing the treatise to Luca, as part of the boy's preparation for the exam. The examination board always asked about Cicero, so it would be useful for him to start practicing right away. And then Paolo would have an extra hour of free time.

His step lightened and the corner of his mouth rose in a grin.

Paolo had planned to head back to the boarding house after class, since Luca was waiting for him. But now that he had extra time, he decided to run a quick errand.

Paolo waded through the crowds in the square outside the university, waving to a few friends, and walked up the hill south of campus. The winding Via del Santo connected the university at the bottom of the hill with the basilica at the top. It was less crowded with students, but carts carrying goods rolled up and down the road. Paolo had to watch his step.

When he reached the top of the hill, he stood before the enormous basilica, the largest building in Padua. If he could climb on the roof of the basilica, Paolo thought he might be able to see all the way to Isola di Torre—not that there was much to see, he admitted. But the view alone would be worth it.

He filled his lungs with air, breathing in the sight of the magnificent building. From his position in the square, he could just see the domes topping the basilica and the large chapels jutting off the sides of the church. Paolo gazed up at the building, the heat of the afternoon sun on his back. The sunlight struck the basilica's façade, and the dull bricks shone in shades of red and orange. The massive door at the center of the façade was the height of three men. But it looked small compared with the rising arches and the expansive stretch of the tower climbing higher and higher from the church's peak.

Even from a young age, Paolo's father had always called him a "city boy." Back in Rome, Paolo wanted to be where things happened. And he had never found much excitement out in the fields with the workers and farmers. But cities pulsed with energy. No one ever said they wanted to go visit a field in England—they wanted to see London. And no one travelled all the way to distant China just to see the rice—they went to see the Forbidden City and the Emperor's palace. The bigger the building, the better the city.

That's why Paolo loved to visit the basilica. He wasn't very devout. His father had carted their family to church most Sundays back in Rome, but in Padua Paolo rarely attended mass. Instead, he came to admire the buildings and marvel at the work that must have gone into designing them. And to think about the money that flowed through the basilica, gathering up wealth from all around Padua and investing it in the treasures of the church.

Paolo settled onto a low stone wall to watch the sun move across the front of the building. He thought about his childhood in Rome. He had always loved visiting St. Peter's Basilica, where he gawked at the enormous dome designed by Michelangelo. He wanted to go to Florence and see their dome as well, just to compare the two and decide which was more magnificent. Paolo longed to travel the world until he found the largest, most spectacular building that man had ever built. Wherever it was, he would live there, because he would know it was the best city in the world.

He dropped his eyes to watch the people scurrying through the square. Most of them didn't even look at the massive basilica. Paolo let out a sigh. He'd never travel anywhere if he didn't finish his degree. He had already been at the university for nearly two years, and it seemed like he was no closer to completing his required courses.

To be fair, he had dropped out of a few classes in his first year. Now he had to retake several of them. He had been short-sighted last year, and unfocused. In truth, he had been too interested in taking classes with the highest demand, so he could say that he studied under the most brilliant minds at Padua.

That was why he had sought out Galileo's boarding house, not because of an interest in natural philosophy, which he found rather impenetrable. All those rules, but what did they really mean? Everyone could see what happened in the world around them, so what was the purpose of writing all those equations? And how were you supposed to use experiments about balls rolling down ramps to make money?

But Galileo was supposed to be an up-and-comer. Everyone was abuzz with his latest project, which he was apparently hiding from the world. Even Paolo, who worked in Galileo's shop every day, had no clue what the mysterious project might be. And everyone whispered about Galileo's audacity, challenging the nearly two-thousand-year dominance of Aristotle. Galileo might have a number of enemies, but everyone knew his name.

Paolo didn't care about natural philosophy, but he did want to make connections with people who knew Europe's most powerful rulers. Rumor had it that Galileo had received a letter from the Holy Roman Emperor, though Galileo refused to confirm the correspondence when Paolo had asked.

So for Paolo it was not a tough decision. Galileo might not be rich, but he certainly was notorious. Paolo was learning some of the mechanical arts working in Galileo's shop, and as much as he complained about going to the fairs, he did enjoy the contacts he was making with merchants who traveled throughout Italy and the entire Mediterranean.

His father would say such things were beneath his son. Paolo heard the man's voice in his head: Serravalles do not work with their hands or go to fairs and spend time with merchants. But Paolo saw where the money was these days, and many of the wealthiest families in Italy had made their fortunes not from being born into wealth but from their work. Paolo knew if he wanted to travel the world he would need to make money, so he wasn't going to draw artificial lines about what he would and would not do.

Only a few months ago, Paolo had received a letter from his father scolding him for wasting time. Paolo's father, Giovanni Serravalle, had also attended the University of Padua, and now he was a well-established lawyer. Giovanni had raved about Padua, calling it the best university in Europe for legal training, but Paolo had been disappointed by the size of the city. It was nothing like Rome, which was a sprawling mass of buildings, churches, and ancient ruins. Padua, by contrast, seemed small.

Paolo's father had pushed him to earn a degree in the law as well, so he could join the family business. And while Paolo enjoyed arguing, he was less interested in absorbing the minuscule details about the Justinian Code, and ecclesiastical law, and all the minutia that was necessary for the legal practice. He was more interested in the merchants, carrying goods through the city and hawking their wares outside the university. He wanted to see their ships, crossing the Mediterranean to collect spices and silks from far-away places. The powerful merchants of Venice, who ruled that city, seemed to work less than his father, but he had heard that their palazzi were much larger.

Paolo turned away from the basilica and headed back toward

the boarding house, visions of riches dancing in his mind.

THIRTEEN

Over the next few days, Zaneta Lucia worked harder than she'd ever thought possible. After visiting the vacant rooms, she had picked hers. It was on the fourth floor at the end of the corridor. Through the small window, she could just see the university. She hoped it would give her some privacy, since it shared only a single wall with any of the other rooms.

She had met many of the boys who lived at the boarding house, though they all seemed busy with classes and rarely spent much time in the building. The other tenants were only a few years older than she was, but most stood a head taller. She worried that her size could reveal her secret, but no one had given her a second look yet.

Zaneta Lucia had run into Mazzeo on her second day in Padua. Mazzeo remembered their brief meeting in front of the boarding house, and he agreed to tutor her in mathematics and natural philosophy. Mazzeo usually had a smile on his face, but it was rarely visible since his nose was always in a book. He was quiet, but his face lit up when he talked about mathematics.

Paolo had whispered that Mazzeo was brilliant—though, he added with a laugh, Mazzeo should be, after all those hours reading. Zaneta Lucia found nothing puzzling about wanting to read, which she had said to Paolo. He had just grinned in response. Zaneta Lucia was quickly learning that Paolo remembered everything with barely any effort. Because he was such a quick study, he didn't have to work very hard. And he certainly didn't seem to understand the pleasure of sinking into a book, losing yourself in the pages.

Mazzeo wrote down a long list of volumes for Zaneta Lucia to read before their next meeting. When she stared at him blankly, unsure where to buy or borrow the books, he shook his head.

"Come on," he said, leading her down the hall toward his room on the third floor. When he swung open the door, Zaneta Lucia's breath caught in her throat. Inside, Mazzeo had filled the space with books, stacked on every surface and practically covering his bed.

"Where do you sleep?" she stammered.

He grinned. "I just move the books when I want to sleep." He quickly pulled a handful of volumes from different piles, revealing some organization that Zaneta Lucia could not fathom. "Here," he said, handing her six books while he looked for more. "That should be enough to get you started. Just take good care of my books."

Zaneta Lucia thanked him, clutching the books to her chest. She could not imagine how much money Mazzeo had spent on the library in his small room.

But in her first full day in Padua there had already been a slip-up. The room with the bathtub didn't have a lock, but Zaneta Lucia needed to bathe after her travels. Her ankles from the bottom of her pants to the tops of her shoes were caked in sweat and clay, and she had trailed dust all over her face when she had wiped the sweat off her brow on the long journey from Venice. She had avoided bathing at the inns along the way, afraid that her secret might be exposed. But once she had settled into her room, Zaneta Lucia admitted that she could not walk the streets of Padua in her current state.

She had waited until midday, when most of the other tenants were in class, and the building was usually empty. She had carefully filled the tub, using the pump outside the building, and not caring that the water was still cool from its journey down the Alps and through the Po River Valley. The late summer sun baked the city during the day, and she sighed with relief as she dipped her feet into the crisp water.

In minutes the water turned cloudy and brown from the dirt that washed off her body. Zaneta Lucia was about to lift the large wooden ladle to splash water over her hair when she heard a bang at the door. She jumped and threw her hands over her chest, even though there was not much to hide. A voice from outside the door called "sorry!" and she heard steps retreating into the building.

Zaneta Lucia had thanked her patron saint that she had placed a deep bucket full of water in front of the door in case someone tried to enter.

She quickly finished her bath, her heart pounding the entire time.

And every minute of every day, she wondered if someone was suspicious of the new boy, Luca Manetti.

But she barely had time to worry with her new schedule. Her mornings were filled working in Galileo's shop. Paolo had shown her the workshop when he finally returned from class. It was a large open space on the second floor, divided into several different workbenches where tenants labored busily to staple together the sheets of paper for the booklets Galileo sold to his students. The more advanced workers pieced together brass instruments, building compasses and other measuring devices.

The headmaster of the shop, a bulky man named Francesco Burano, had scowled when Paolo had introduced the new tenant, Luca Manetti. Burano grumbled about the difficulty of training new workers. But still, he had sat down right away to show her how to bind together the booklets. He said that she had very nimble fingers for a boy, which almost made her blush, and he promised to teach her how to use some of the tools.

But as much as she enjoyed working in the shop and seeing how things were made, she loved her afternoons even more. She would meet with Mazzeo or Paolo, depending on who had time, and they would quiz her for the exam.

Zaneta Lucia liked the afternoons where she studied with Mazzeo because they focused on natural philosophy and mathematics. Her knowledge of mathematics was embarrassingly scant, especially compared with boys who had grown up in merchant families where they had learned to run figures as young children. Her education in decorum, poetry, and classical literature had not included many equations. But she was motivated after reading Galileo's book, and wanted to learn everything right away. Mazzeo was a kind tutor, not mentioning her poor preparation. He even encouraged her, and said that she was picking up algebra quite naturally.

But she really looked forward to the afternoons with Paolo. He seemed to know something about everything, and if that knowledge could give him a monetary advantage in some way, he'd tell her all about it. He talked about art and literature as fluently as he spoke on economics and politics. It was certainly an education, in everything she'd been sheltered from growing up as a girl.

"You mean the pope declared a crusade against the Holy Roman Emperor?" she asked one afternoon, astonished.

"Yes, back in the thirteenth century. It was a huge scandal," Paolo said. "They each declared the other was the Antichrist. You've really never heard of it?"

She had read history books, of course, but mainly those written for women, which tended to tell stories of valiant rulers and their obedient wives. Paolo gave her a book on politics written by Machiavelli, and she was shocked at what she saw inside. It was so different from the books she'd been allowed to read where the prince was always good and benevolent.

After her afternoon tutoring sessions, she would sit in the common area or her own room reading. She had a growing stack of books to read, and each time she finished one, Paolo or Mazzeo would add two more. It felt like she would never catch up. She burned through the candles she had purchased from a candlemaker down the street, staying up late into the night reading. And yet by the end of the week she had to ask Paolo and Mazzeo for more books.

Zaneta Lucia was finally reading the works she'd always heard about. It was thrilling to learn something new every day. Back in Venice, it had felt like she was studying hard, but one week in Padua showed her the gaps in her knowledge and the vast world of materials that she still had to learn. She ignored her exhaustion and continued to fly through her stack of books. With each passing day, she was more confident in her decision to come to Padua.

On Friday, Paolo promised to help her schedule the entrance examination. He met Zaneta Lucia after his morning class and they walked over to the university together. Paolo told her about the course he'd just come from, on international trade.

"It's probably the one class at this university that can make a student wealthy without needing an advanced degree," Paolo explained.

Paolo was so open and straightforward. He didn't think about each word before he spoke. And he didn't need to have a plan behind every action, like some people she'd known in Venice. Zaneta Lucia was humbled by his quick wit, and his willingness to share his knowledge with her.

It was strange, but she wondered if Paolo was her first true friend. Or was it even possible to build real friendships when she was lying about her identity?

Paolo's words shook Zaneta Lucia from her thoughts. "This is the administration hall," he said, pointing to a tall building on the square next to the porticoed university. "Most of the classrooms are in that building, over there," he said, pointing. "But you need to go up to the second floor and ask for the examination scheduler."

Zaneta Lucia gazed up at the building, her jaw clenched. Even though she had been studying for hours a day, she had not been thinking about the exam.

"I'll wait out here," Paolo said, sitting down on a bench.

Zaneta Lucia hadn't expected to go in alone. Her palms suddenly felt cold even in the heat of midday. She watched students walking confidently into the building, and tried to imitate their stride. Giving a casual wave to Paolo, she entered the administration hall.

Once inside, Zaneta Lucia walked up the stairs slowly, finally reaching the second floor. A large wooden door stood ajar. She took a deep breath, and pushed it open. She asked the man behind the desk for the examination scheduler. As she waited, sitting in a chair, her foot tapped the floor nervously.

Finally, the scheduler appeared. "*Buon pomerriggio*," he said. "You would like to schedule an examination?"

She nodded, leaping to her feet.

"What kind of examination?" he asked, flipping open a large, leather-bound book.

There was more than one kind? Paolo had not prepared her for this question. But of course the university must have multiple types of examinations.

"An entrance exam?" she said quietly, gripping her shirt in both hands.

"Yes," he said, his finger tracing through the calendar inside the book. "The next available slot is October 22nd." He held a quill in his hand expectantly. "Shall I put you down?"

"That's almost two months from now!"

The scheduler arched an eyebrow. "Yes, and if you had come earlier in the year I might have been able to schedule your examination sooner."

She bit her lip. The man was rather brusque. She could see why Paolo had waited outside.

"Then put me down for October 22nd."

He asked her name, penning it in the book. He raised his eyebrow, and told her it cost twenty *soldi* to schedule the exam. She counted out the coins from her dwindling purse. Zaneta Lucia had not expected her money to vanish so quickly, but between rent, the examination fee, paying her tutors, and the books and supplies she had already bought, she was not sure her funds would even last until her examination date. And then, if she passed the exam, she would have to figure out how to pay tuition.

Zaneta Lucia retraced her steps down the wide staircase. There was a silver lining to scheduling her exam for over six weeks in the future. It meant that she would have more time to study. After a week of reading for hours a day, she was even more conscious of the gaps in her knowledge.

But she hoped that Galileo would allow her to stay in the boarding house until the exam. She didn't want to imagine trying to find somewhere else to live, especially considering how much she loved working in the shop.

When she exited the building, Paolo was still sitting on the bench.

"How did it go?" he asked.

"You knew the scheduler is a cranky old toad, didn't you?"

He shrugged. "No one likes him, but you have to visit him every time you complete a course, to arrange the final exam. He's already mad at me because I haven't scheduled exams for three courses I took in the spring. Anyway, if he saw you come in with me, he would have been even crankier."

Zaneta Lucia raised one corner of her mouth. "Well, he wasn't in a good mood either way. He said the earliest I can take the exam is October 22nd." Just speaking the words aloud made her feel like the day would never come. In the heat of the square, it was hard to imagine that fall was just around the corner.

Instead of mirroring her disappointment, Paolo nodded. "It's for the best."

"For the best?" she groaned, "I wanted to start at the university as soon as possible."

"But you aren't ready yet," he said matter-of-factly.

She knew he was right, but she was still disheartened.

"Anyway, if you want, you can attend a few of my classes to see what they're like."

"Really? That would be amazing!"

"Yes, students who have scheduled an entrance exam are allowed to sit in on two classes a week before their exam. Didn't he tell you that upstairs?"

She shook her head.

"Figures. They act like it's a bother for new students to enroll here, which is stupid because it's how they make their revenues," he said. "And now we should get back to the boarding house for your next lesson. I thought we could discuss Aristotle's *Ethics*. If you've finished reading it yet."

"Of course I've read it. I finished it last night. Or maybe it was technically this morning," she admitted.

~ ~ ~

Later that evening Zaneta Lucia sat in the common area, another of Aristotle's books open on her lap, preparing for her session the next afternoon with Mazzeo. She tried to focus on Aristotle's description of the soul, but her eyes were drooping and before she knew it, she had fallen asleep in the corner of the study room.

Zaneta Lucia woke to an empty, dark room. A narrow curve of moonlight streamed through the window. She was nestled into a large, soft blanket, much too warm for daytime but cozy at night. She didn't want to get up and climb the stairs to her room. So she scooted down even further in her chair, until she thought she might be invisible to anyone who walked past the room at this hour.

As if her thought had summoned a presence, she heard a sound in the hallway. At first she assumed it was just someone coming home late. She'd heard them before, the boys in the boarding house who came back at all hours of the night, usually while she was still awake studying. They were usually intoxicated, or at least their loud laughter and occasional singing seemed to imply inebriation.

But this was different. It sounded like someone who didn't belong, for lack of a better phrase. And she realized that the footsteps were coming down the stairs, instead of heading up.

Zaneta Lucia tried to make herself invisible. A nameless and undefinable anxiety rose in her chest. The steps themselves might have brought it on: they were so slow, so deliberate, as if to imply the person was nervous, or waiting for something.

The footsteps stopped on the landing outside the common room. A few seconds later she heard them descending again. She listened for the creaks on the stairs to the second floor landing, the first floor landing, and finally silence returned.

The entire episode must have only lasted for a minute or two, but it felt like hours. The eerie steps almost seemed to echo in the stairwell.

Well, whatever it was, it was gone now, she told herself. And it was past time for her to go to bed.

But she was glued to her seat. Had the strange footsteps left behind a sign in the stairwell? For a moment, she considered sleeping in the study room. Apparently it happened sometimes. One morning she'd come down early to find that one of the third floor boys, Ugolino, hadn't made it all the way to his bedroom and had crashed in the common area.

Zaneta Lucia scolded herself for being foolish. She stood up, grabbed the book she'd been reading, and walked toward the doorway. She reached out and placed a hand on the doorknob. She froze, then scolded herself again. Zaneta Lucia turned the nob.

The stairwell was empty, of course, and there was no tell-tale sign of the cautious footsteps. She was being ridiculous, imagining things. She walked up the stairs, making a conscious effort not to tip-toe, and went to her room.

But as Zaneta Lucia walked down the fourth floor hallway, she did glance under the other doors, just to check if anyone else was awake. The mysterious trespasser might have come from her floor. She couldn't shake the uncanny feeling that had descended with the footsteps.

The hallway was dark, though, and by the time she was in her sleeping clothes and under the covers, she had forgotten everything except for the last words she'd read from Aristotle. "The soul is the first actuality of a natural body that is potentially alive."

"Potentially alive," she whispered. "What does that mean?"

And before she could get out another thought, she was asleep. But the feeling that came with the footsteps didn't leave her as easily.

FOURTEEN

Galileo leaned back in his chair. He sat in his room on the fifth floor of the boarding house, a pen in his hand. Admittedly, it was more to give the impression of productivity than because he was actually working.

Instead he was looking out the window.

From this vantage point, if he craned his neck to the left he could see past the university and down toward the river. The little chapel stood there, hidden by a copse of trees. Giotto had painted its interior so many centuries before, and it had put Padua on the map, much like the basilica on the hill.

The two buildings were so different: the enormous basilica perched on the hilltop, unashamed of its stony weight or the fact that it monopolized the high ground. People from Padua claimed that the hill had been the site of some Roman structures, long before the basilica had been built.

In many ways it reminded Galileo of Pisa, the city of his birth, and where he had attended university. Another river town, although in spite of Pisa's silted port it was still on the sea. Another town where the high ground was dominated by churches. And, like Padua, Pisa was constantly in the shadow of its more powerful neighboring city.

The other building, the tiny chapel, had originally been built for a single family. But on rare days it was open to the public.

Galileo had gone in once, during one of his first years in Padua, to see the frescoes for himself.

The blues, golds, and reds had been faded by the centuries, but he could still picture what it must have looked like fresh from Giotto's brush. The figures, in agony but also in ecstasy, had moved Galileo in an unexpected way.

Galileo had always thought of himself as a religious man. He attended church regularly and firmly believed in the scriptures of Catholicism. He was, however, aware that certain positions held by scientists did not fit with the church's interpretation of nature.

It's foolish, that's what it is, he thought to himself. God created nature, so how could anything in nature contradict God? It made sense to him, even if others disagreed.

Well, they wouldn't be able to disagree with his findings. He picked up the hollow tube. It didn't work yet. He was still figuring out the perfect ratio between the lenses of ground glass. But soon he would perfect the tool, and he would be the first man to look into the heavens.

He would see what no one had seen before! If Giotto could imagine elaborate scenes on earth, then Galileo's mind could picture the planets and stars, drawn before his eyes. But to see it, to prove it—that was a different matter.

What an amazing tool. Galileo firmly believed that God had granted mankind the skills to understand the universe, if only people would look.

Galileo placed the tube back on his desk. Its surface was covered in papers, stacks of half-written manuscripts, and even some of the booklets he produced and sold from this very boarding house. But a worry tugged at the back of his mind. Something was out of place.

No one else might notice, because he was the only person who understood the order behind the seemingly disorderly stacks. But he felt strongly that something was missing.

He began to shuffle the papers, lifting each stack, looking under and behind the desk, but he couldn't find the sheet he remembered seeing somewhere.

Or had he imagined writing it in the first place? He recalled scrawling down some notes, unsure if he would ever use the material but wanting to record it nonetheless. It was something about the nature of the universe, and what he expected to find when he looked through the new spyglass he was making.

"An imperfect universe," he muttered. "Something like that. Marred by imperfections."

It didn't seem so important, but he did wonder if he'd never written it down in the first place. Or maybe it was simply hiding under stacks of paper.

A knock jolted the professor out of his thoughts. "Come in," he called, his back still turned to the door. He heard it creak open quietly, but his guest was silent.

Galileo turned and saw young Luca Manetti, standing in the doorframe with a worried look on his face.

"Excuse me, Professor Galileo, I don't want to disturb you . . ." Luca trailed off.

Galileo waved the boy over. "It's no problem, Luca," he spoke warmly, trying to put the boy at ease. He had seen Luca working hard in the workshop, and Paolo reported that he spent more time with his books than most university students. But in Galileo's eyes, the boy looked far too young for university. Was he thirteen? Fourteen? His clothes were too big and he carried an anxious air with him.

Then again, Galileo might be the first professor that young Luca had ever met. That might explain his timidity.

Galileo signaled for the boy to join him, and moved a pile of papers from the second chair in the room. "Please, sit," he gestured.

"Thank you, Professor," Luca said, "If you're busy I can

come back, it's just that you said we might talk about natural philosophy." The boy trailed off.

Ah yes. Galileo remembered making the offer, and the boy looked terrified at having to remind him. "Now would be a good time, Luca. Did you have a topic in mind?"

The boy looked down, a blush growing on his cheeks. He really was young. Years from growing a beard. "I wanted to ask you about— I mean, what are your thoughts on Copernicus?"

Galileo suppressed a laugh. Of course the boy would be interested in that controversial theory. And what timing—Galileo had just been ruminating on religion and science. "Have you read his book?"

"I read it. I didn't understand some of it, but I got the general idea. The earth revolves around the sun, he says, not the other way around. It goes against Aristotle and Ptolemy and all the classical astronomers. But I have recently learned that Aristotle was wrong about a few things."

"It does not contradict all of the classical astronomers. Aristarchus of Samos proposed a heliocentric universe in the third century before Christ. Still, I am glad to hear you are willing to question received wisdom."

"Then you agree with Copernicus?"

"I didn't say that." Galileo leaned back in his chair, choosing his words carefully. "There are problems with Copernicus' theory."

"You mean like the issue of wind?"

Galileo nodded and signaled to the boy to continue.

Luca took a deep breath. "If the earth is traveling around the sun, the planet would be moving very quickly to make a rotation in one year. And if we were also turning on our axis, making another rotation every day, you'd expect lots of wind."

"Winds of nearly a thousand kilometers an hour, by my calculation," Galileo added. "You're right, Luca, that our senses tell a different story."

"Then doesn't that disprove Copernicus? Our senses are our most valuable tool for understanding nature."

"Not so fast," Galileo warned. "Our senses do not always tell the whole story. Let me give you an example." He stood and walked to one side of the room, gesturing to Luca to follow him. The boy jumped up and joined him next to a large wooden ramp. "See the ramp? I used this in my tests on motion."

"I read your book, Professor," Luca responded.

"Then you should have no trouble answering a question. Let's say I have two metal balls." Galileo reached into a basket and pulled out two shiny balls. "One is twice the size of the other. Now, using only your senses, what do you think will happen when I roll the balls down the ramp?" He laid the balls next to each other on twin grooves in the wooden ramp.

"My senses would say the larger ball would travel faster. It has more mass, and thus it would be pulled back to the earth faster than the smaller ball." Luca reached out to point to the other ball. "That is what Aristotle would predict, too. But I know that is not true. You have shown the balls travel at the same speed, regardless of size."

"Bravo," Galileo said. "Now you know that what we *think* will happen is not always what *will* happen."

"But, Professor, you can run experiments with ramps and balls. How do you run experiments on the entire universe?"

Galileo nodded. The boy was sharp. "For that, let's take another example from Copernicus. He predicts that in a heliocentric universe, all of the planets would have phases, just like the moon." He led Luca back to the seats. "If we could observe Venus, for example, it would appear full at certain times, and vanish at others."

"So that would be an experiment on the universe," Luca reasoned. "But it's impossible. We can't see Venus that closely.

No one has good enough eyesight."

"That's true. No one can see if Venus waxes and wanes with the naked eye. But perhaps in time we will develop a tool that will allow us to test Copernicus' hypothesis."

Luca furrowed his brow. "Are you saying there's no way to prove whether Copernicus was right or wrong?"

"Not yet," Galileo admitted. "For now, we can only discuss the theory as a hypothesis."

"But then what does the universe look like?"

Galileo held his tongue. They were on dangerous ground, and he always watched his words when discussing such ideas. "It might appear one way from our vantage point. But it might look very different from another perspective."

Luca gave a little nod, chewing on his lower lip. "We see one thing, but the reality is something else?"

"Exactly. And a lesson worth keeping in mind when you read natural philosophy."

"Thank you, Professor," Luca said, standing. "I won't take up any more of your time."

"Please, Luca, it was a pleasure." Galileo found speaking with the boy much more rewarding than debating with his students, who seemed more interested in grades and exams than learning.

Luca gave Galileo another nod, and left.

Galileo turned back to the window. He suddenly reached out for the tube resting on his desk. If everything went as planned, he would be running experiments on the universe before the month was up.

FIFTEEN

The weeks flew by, and it was late September. Summer's hold had not yet broken on the city, and the heat made it hard to believe October was around the corner.

One night, as she sat reading Aristotle by candlelight, Zaneta Lucia realized it was her sixteenth birthday. She hadn't even remembered until the sun had already set. Sixteen didn't feel any different from fifteen. But now, according to her parents, she was old enough to marry. Zaneta Lucia leaned back in her chair, her gaze drifting out the window. The empty night sky made her feel more alone.

Would today have been her wedding day, if she had stayed in Venice? If not today, it would have been soon.

She fell back into her book, and pushed aside the unpleasant thoughts.

Zaneta Lucia loved her new life. She worked in the shop every morning, studied with Paolo or Mazzeo in the early afternoon, and read long into each night. Some evenings, Paolo would force her out of the boarding house to visit a local tavern popular with students. Zaneta Lucia protested that she was already behind in her studies, but secretly she was grateful for Paolo's attention. He wasn't just friendly to her because she paid him as a tutor, he actually enjoyed their time together.

And she had never laughed so hard as she had on the

evening when Paolo, in the middle of a story, had thrown up his hands and upended a tray of wine all over his head. He had looked so shocked, his mouth a perfect 'O' as wine dripped from his nose, and then he quickly dissolved into laughter with her.

The days blended together. Zaneta Lucia was so busy that she almost completely forgot about the late night footsteps. She convinced herself that it was just her imagination. Staying up late, alone in the dark, your mind could play tricks on you. At least, that's what she told herself. But she never fell asleep in the common area again.

Zaneta Lucia was trying to absorb all the most important works written in the last two thousand years. Or at least that's how it felt. Even as she tinkered with the instruments in the workshop, her mind was consumed with history, and poetry, two of her weaker areas. Paolo joked that she couldn't possibly fail since she spent half the hours of every day reading. But Zaneta Lucia worried that she was too far behind to catch up. Mazzeo, on the other hand, thought she was doing quite well and said he was impressed with her improvements.

And yet, even though she knew she was struggling when it came to literature, and rhetoric, and musical theory, and all of the material she reviewed with Paolo, Zaneta Lucia still wanted to spend her time reading Aristotle, and yes, Galileo.

It came easily to her. Geometry felt like a language that she had spoken from birth; her mind only needed a reminder to awake and speak it fluently. She found herself measuring angles in her head, and running equations as she walked the streets of Padua. The world around her was a blank canvas, waiting for someone to transform it into numbers and figures. Even reading Aristotle was different than it had been back in Venice. She had somehow unlocked a new perspective on the text after her conversations with Galileo. Now she saw the holes in his reasoning, which she imagined herself filling with mathematics.

The fact that she was actually good gave her hope. Maybe she really could study natural philosophy at the university.

Of course, that fantasy never got too far. Zaneta Lucia would stop in the middle of a sentence, her chest tight, and realize that she couldn't pretend to be Luca Manetti forever. At some point she was going to slip up. Or she'd finally grow some hips and breasts, and her secret would be revealed.

But Zaneta Lucia wanted to put off that moment as long as possible. She could not even imagine what would happen if she failed the exam. So she focused all her energy on her studies, and tried to ignore everything else. One night, she even shoved Paolo away when he wanted to drag her off to the tavern. "My exam is in three weeks," she cried.

"That's why you have to enjoy yourself *now*," he explained. "Once you're a student, you'll be so busy studying that I'll never see you!"

The next day, she sat in the common room with a stack of books to read before her meeting with Mazzeo. Some boys were talking loudly in the corner. Zaneta Lucia tried to ignore them, and trained her eyes on the book lying open in front of her. It was a selection from Ptolemy on the shape of the world. But then she heard something that pulled her from her book.

" . . . the scandal of the century, I heard him say. She ran off, that's what he said."

Zaneta Lucia's eyes glanced up. It was Ugolino, talking with two friends.

Her eyes went back to the book. The world contained three continents: Europe, Asia, and Africa. No, that wasn't right. Oh, wait. Ptolemy left out the Americas, because they had not yet been discovered. So why did she have to read a book that had been proven wrong?

Another voice jolted her out of the book.

"And what did Mario Barbaro do?" Ugolino's friend Timeo

asked.

Mario Barbaro? Could it possibly be the same one?

Her head jerked up and locked onto the three boys. They shared the same sandy hair, and she knew two of them were brothers, but she couldn't remember which two.

Zaneta Lucia searched back through her memory, trying to recreate their conversation. All she could remember was something about a scandal, some affair. Why had she paid so much attention to Ptolemy?

And she couldn't exactly ask what they were talking about. That would be strange.

Or would it? She was Luca Manetti to them. They would never connect her with some runaway girl from Venice. Right?

Her thoughts were scrambled.

The third boy, Nonni, interrupted her thoughts. "I heard he went back to the mistress. He was probably relieved."

Ugolino and Timeo laughed. The sound made Zaneta Lucia jerk in her seat.

"Yeah, who wants to get married?" Ugolino put in.

"I never want to marry," Nonni said. "I'll just have a dozen mistresses, one for each of my castles."

"Where are you going to find a castle?" Ugolino said, rolling his eyes.

"Marriage is a bunch of rubbish if you ask me," Timeo added. "Women only cause problems and spend your money."

Zaneta Lucia was rooted to her chair, paralyzed with fear. But she could not remain silent. She had to know more.

"What happened to the girl?"

Three sets of brown eyes turned toward her. "Probably fell into a canal and drowned," Nonni said. "Everyone knows women are as dumb as a clump of twigs."

Ugolino swatted Nonni with a book, a grin on his face. "What would our dear mother say if she heard you now?"

Nonni chucked a booklet back at Ugolino's head, which the boy managed to dodge. "Nothing, because she'll never hear of it," Nonni said. "Right, Ugolino?"

"Oh, yes, on my honor. I won't tell," Ugolino said, crossing himself.

"I heard she ran off with the gypsies," Timeo said to Zaneta Lucia. "Women have insatiable urges. If she turned down this Barbaro fellow, she was probably getting it from somewhere else, if you know what I mean."

Zaneta Lucia plastered a false smile on her face. Inside, she fumed. "And who told you about this scandal?"

Ugolino answered. "I heard about it two days ago at Umberto's, you know, the tavern by the river. Some merchant was telling tales, and he said the story is on the lips of everyone in Venice. They're calling it the Zorzi Affair."

The blood rushed from Zaneta Lucia's face, and she gripped the arms of her chair until her knuckles turned white. The boys took no notice, and continued speaking.

"That spoiled girl, can you imagine? She had everything in life handed to her, but she ran off because she didn't want to marry." Timeo shook his head. "I can't understand it."

"Are you saying *you* want to get married?" Ugolino shot back.

"No," Timeo sounded wounded. "Of course not. But she's a girl. What else is she going to do?"

"And did you hear?" Nonni cut in. "A man rode into town this morning. He says he was hired by the family to find the runaway girl."

"He's looking in the wrong place if you ask me," Timeo said. "Check the gypsy camps, I'd wager she's there."

"No one asked you, *stronzo*," Nonni said. "But if you're so confident, go look for her yourself. I heard there's a reward for information about the girl. Her family is so angry they want to roast her alive."

The boys' laughter drowned out the sound of Zaneta Lucia's low moan. Her stomach flipped, and for a second she thought she might vomit on the desk.

"Can you imagine?" Ugolino said. "She must be one selfish witch, to spurn her family like that and ruin their reputation."

"You had *one job*," Timeo said, pitching his voice low as if he were a patrician father. "And you couldn't even do that!" The boys dissolved into laughter.

Zaneta Lucia wanted to bury her face in her book and destroy it with tears. Or run out of the room sobbing. But she couldn't.

Her emotions roiled through her body, pitching from terror to fury to confusion. What if she was caught, and sent back to Venice? Would her family hate her forever? And if she was caught, she would never get to study natural philosophy. And did strangers really think she was a slut or a witch?

The boys took no notice of her, and moved on to talk about the next scandal. Zaneta Lucia vaguely heard them mention a married woman in Padua who was sleeping with one of her husband's students.

Zaneta Lucia stared at her book, the words blurring together. Finally, enough time had passed that she could leave without drawing attention. She stood, watching the boys smile and joke, and left the room. Once she reached the stairs, she ran up to the fourth floor. She had no energy to worry about who might see her. She barricaded herself into her room.

The silence pounded in her ears. She didn't know whether to cry or yell.

But she kept coming back to one simple fact: someone was in Padua, and that someone was looking for her.

~ ~ ~

The next morning, Zaneta Lucia was still a nervous mess. She kept thinking in circles. She had to learn more about the investigation into her disappearance while also keeping distance from whoever was in Padua looking for her.

And would her family really hire someone to chase her down, like a criminal? Or had they sent one of her relatives to find her? Her disguise would never hold if she ran into her brother Filippo on the street.

She had missed her family dearly in the last month. Well, to be honest, she had not missed her mother every day. It was a relief not to hear her voice constantly correcting Zaneta Lucia for every minor breech of etiquette. But she often thought about her father. She wondered how he felt about her abandoning the family. Her heart ached at the thought of his disappointment.

And some days she couldn't think about Filippo or Giulia Maria without tearing up. She even missed Gianna the scullery maid, and the smelly alley behind their palazzo.

Zaneta Lucia had sat down to write a letter to her family multiple times in the weeks she had been in Padua. But each time she stopped. What could she possibly say? Any letter would be a one-way communication. She could not ask questions and expect to ever hear the answers.

And she could not put to paper what she truly wanted to know: if she returned to Venice, would she still have to marry Mario Barbaro?

Zaneta Lucia needed a plan. But every time she ran through her options, she tied herself in knots. She was like the cemetery island in Venice—alone, isolated, silent. Removed from the living world.

Her worries were interrupted by the sound of a knock at the

door.

"Luca, are you in there?" a voice asked quietly.

It was Paolo.

"Yes," she said, quickly checking her face in the reflection of her glass window. Did it look like she had been crying? She opened the door.

"Are you feeling okay?" Paolo asked. "We were supposed to meet in the common room ten minutes ago. You said you wanted to come to my class today."

"Oh, I completely forgot," Zaneta Lucia said. How could she have forgotten? Her life as Luca Manetti had crumbled under the smallest hint of scrutiny. "I'm sorry. Are we too late?"

"Not at all. Anyway, I don't show up to class on time very often myself," Paolo said with an easy grin.

Paolo's tone calmed her. Zaneta Lucia took a deep breath and let it out slowly. She would not ruin her chance to attend the University of Padua. She'd just have to be more careful, that's all. She grabbed a notebook and a cap for their walk through town, and followed Paolo out of the building.

They stepped out onto a crowded street. Zaneta Lucia's eyes darted around, looking for anyone who might be watching her. She pulled the hat firmly on her head, as though it were a magic talisman that made her invisible. They headed toward the university.

"How's the studying going?" Paolo asked.

Zaneta Lucia was so deep in thought about her own problems that she jumped at the question, and it took a moment to regain her bearings. "Good. Thank you again for your tutoring. I'm learning so much."

"It's no trouble," Paolo said. "It's good for me, too. I'd forgotten most of this stuff myself."

Zaneta Lucia searched his face for any hint of sarcasm, and found only his usual cheery smile. "You, forget something?" she joked. Paolo remembered everything. He could switch from discussing Petrarchan verse to papal monetary policy with complete ease. Zaneta Lucia was certain he would make a name for himself once he graduated.

"I've probably forgotten more than you've ever learned."

"Oh please."

"Well, maybe not. I am starting to worry that your hands have fused to the books you're always reading."

She looked down and realized that she had brought a book. She didn't even remember picking it up in her room.

Paolo laughed at her expression. "Anyway, I hope that working in the shop doesn't distract too much from your studies."

"No, it doesn't. I love learning about all the instruments."

Paolo grabbed her arm, just above the elbow, and pulled her to the side of the street, out of the flow of traffic. "There's something you need to know about the shop," he said, his voice low.

Her problems flew away, and she felt a jolt of energy pass through her body. "What?" Her heart was beating faster. Was she curious about what Paolo might say, or was it because he was leaning close to her? She looked up at Paolo's face, framed by dark hair. The glimmer of a smile still touched his eyes. Zaneta Lucia quickly dropped her gaze to the ground.

"It's about Burano," Paolo continued. "The master of the shop. I think he's been skimming off the profits."

"Really? Why would he do that?" Zaneta Lucia whispered.

Paolo raised an eyebrow at her. "For the money, I'm sure."

"But do you have any proof?"

He shook his head. "I know how Galileo's workshop runs, and he should be making more money. See, he makes booklets, and the compass. The materials aren't very expensive, at least not after he bought the press a few years back. And he sells the compasses for a very large profit."

"I don't know how much he charges."

"You don't? That's the first thing I asked!"

Zaneta Lucia suppressed a smile. Of course Paolo was thinking about the profits. "But how do you know he's not making enough money?"

"I ran the figures. I know how many compasses we make, and how many booklets. I probably know better than Burano, even though he's supposed to be running the operation. I also know that the discount Galileo gives us on rent for working in the shop is a great deal for the professor, but not so good for us."

"But he's also giving us an opportunity to learn about the compass and the other instruments," she pointed out. "That's useful for anyone planning to study natural philosophy."

"Okay, I'll grant you that. Galileo is smart. He's got his salary from the university, and he just got a raise last year. And then there's the rent from the boarding house, plus the money from the workshop, and he tutors on the side. He's probably one of the highest paid professors in town, and the majority of his income isn't from the university itself."

Zaneta Lucia glanced around. No one seemed to notice their conversation. Still, her neck tingled at discussing finances in the middle of the street. "How do you know all this?"

"I pay attention."

Paolo's brain must work differently from hers. He picked up financial information without even thinking about it, as though it was second-nature. But still, wasn't it prying?

"So you know a lot about Professor Galileo's finances," she admitted. "But that doesn't mean someone is stealing from him. And it certainly doesn't make Burano guilty."

"Wait, listen. His shop should be more profitable, I would guess at least twenty-five ducats a month above what he's actually earning. It has to be someone stealing the money. And Burano is the only one who makes sense." Paolo's voice rose. "Who else has access to the shop and all the instruments?"

Zaneta Lucia shrugged her shoulders. She didn't want to concede defeat. "What if there's something you overlooked? Like Burano's salary, or rent on the building, or raw material costs?"

"No, I thought of those things already. Burano doesn't make enough to buy that new house on the edge of town. Where did he get the money for such a nice house?"

"Maybe he inherited the money, or maybe his wife's family has money. Maybe he knew the owner of the house and got a good deal—"

Paolo cut her off with a glance. "I'm not confiding in you so we can make a case before the magistrates. I'm just telling you to watch your back. If he gets caught, Burano will blame someone else." Paolo locked eyes with her. "I wouldn't want you to get caught up in that."

Zaneta Lucia's heart start to race again. Paolo was worried about her?

No, wait, she thought. He's worried about Luca. Not *me*.

Still, he was acting like a true friend. And she had done nothing to earn his trust. "Thanks for the warning. I'll remember."

Paolo touched her arm again. "If you notice anything outside of the ordinary, let me know."

"I will," she vowed.

Paolo nodded. "Fine, let's go to this class."

They entered the building and snuck in the back door of the classroom. The professor was in the middle of his lecture. Paolo led her to the last row of desks.

Zaneta Lucia had a hard time concentrating. The topic was logic, and the professor was rather dull and old-fashioned, droning on about the logical conclusions of the scholastic authors. But Zaneta Lucia's mind kept returning to Paolo's suspicions.

Paolo thought something was going on at the boarding house. What if he started investigating the other tenants? Would he wonder if Luca Manetti had any secrets?

Paolo could look at a building and know its value. How could her disguise fool him for long?

The knot of anxiety in her belly seemed to have taken up permanent residence. She shivered in spite of the heat.

SIXTEEN

The next day, Paolo sat in his room flipping through a book. It was late in the afternoon, and the fourth floor felt empty. There were probably a few boys in the workshop, or downstairs in the common area, but here, it was silent.

Paolo dropped the tome, and it made a loud bang on his desk. It was time to be honest—he wasn't really going to read the book.

He leaned back in his chair and thought about his conversation with Luca. That boy was something of a surprise. Paolo had not expected much when they met on the dusty road to Padua, but he had underestimated Luca. The boy seemed so young, but he was so eager to learn. Had Paolo been like that before he enrolled at the university? He shook his head. He had never been that naive. And, in truth, he had never been that devoted to studying.

Luca absorbed books as though they were water. He could listen to a lecture or read a passage, and somehow boil it down to the central point. Paolo was jealous of that skill. His mind jumped around like a flea, never settling long on one surface.

His young friend always asked the right questions. Paolo had been thrown off by Luca's resistance when he explained his suspicions about Burano. How did Luca drill down to the core of the matter so quickly?

Paolo stood, and wondered if Luca was in his room. In a few weeks, Luca had become his closest friend in Padua. Something about his earnestness was charming. Maybe it was like having a younger brother. Paolo had been the baby in his family, so no one had tagged after him on the streets of Rome, or looked up to him like Luca did.

And he wanted to protect the boy. Paolo had heard Timeo making a joke about Luca, something about his clothes, and without thinking, Paolo had punched him in the arm. Already, everyone in the boarding house knew to leave Luca alone.

He stepped out into the hallway, and made the short walk to Luca's door. He knocked, but heard only silence. The fourth floor really was empty. And Galileo was off teaching, so the fifth floor was empty, too.

Paolo wanted to prove himself to Luca. He wanted to convince his friend that Burano was up to something. And now would be the perfect time to look around the place.

If he found proof of the stealing in Galileo's financial records, Burano would be fired. And Luca would see that he had been right all along.

Paolo headed to the stairs in a flash. He opened the door to the staircase and slid through. He stopped, listening for noise from the lower floors, and heard nothing. He didn't like sneaking around, but sometimes it was justified. He was only doing it to help people. And Galileo would thank him, if Paolo saved him twenty-five ducats a month in wasted money.

Paolo took a creaking step up to the fifth floor. When a voice broke the silence, he nearly jumped off the stairs. But it was just someone talking in the third floor common room. Paolo shook his head, and quietly crept up to the fifth floor.

He knew that no one was allowed in Galileo's private rooms. But the reward was worth the risk. If his suspicions were right, he would be a hero. He reached for the doorknob and pulled open the door. The hinge squeaked, and he winced at the sound. To him, it sounded like an avalanche reverberating down the stairwell.

But no one came out to check on the noise.

Paolo slowly stepped into the room and surveyed the floor. He had only been in these rooms on a few occasions, months ago. But the room directly in front of him, with the door ajar, was Galileo's office. Paolo crossed the large, empty space and slipped inside the room.

Afternoon light filtered in the window, giving everything a golden halo. Paolo gawked at the mess of books, scrawls of writing on sheets of paper, and random piles filling nearly every surface of the room.

Where should he begin? He took a step toward the desk, and looked at the paper on the top of each stack. Most seemed to have nothing to do with business. A few were lecture notes or maybe notes for future books Galileo was planning to write. Some were private correspondence, letters to and from a list of names Paolo did not recognize.

Paolo had expected to find a ledger or some type of financial record, but instead the office was filled with works on natural philosophy. It was not going to be easy to prove Burano guilty.

Before he could take another step, he heard a noise.

Paolo froze in place, straining to hear it again. Was someone climbing the stairs? There was only one staircase, and he was trapped on the fifth floor. He searched the room for a place to hide, but found nothing. He could not duck behind the wooden ramps in the corner, or slip under a pile of papers.

But he didn't hear the noise again.

Paolo's earlier conviction had evaporated. Why was he trying to play detective? It was a foolish whim. He shook his head. He needed to leave the fifth floor right away.

He was halfway turned away from the desk when a paper caught his eye. It appeared to be a diagram, for some sort of instrument.

Paolo didn't care too much about instruments, but he knew Galileo was making a lot of money selling the ones he'd designed.

Without much thought, Paolo grabbed the single sheet and stuffed it into his sleeve. He hurried back to the doorway. He listened for sounds before he eased the door open, waiting for the squeak. The stairs were empty, so he flew down to the fourth floor.

When he threw open the door to the fourth floor, Luca was standing in the hallway.

"Oh, there you are," Luca said. "I knocked on your door and looked for you downstairs, but I couldn't find you."

Paolo's heart pounded. "Well I'm here now." He tried to sound relaxed. The rolled sheet of paper stuffed up his sleeve shifted, and he threw up a hand to keep it from falling out. He pretended to scratch his arm.

Luca frowned. "It's just, I came from downstairs, so how did you . . ." Luca trailed off. "Never mind. I wanted to ask if I could borrow that astronomy book from you? The one by the monk? Mazzeo refuses to lend me his copy. He says it's too valuable."

"Of course!" Paolo said. "Mazzeo is so crazy about his books. Let me see where it is." He stepped past Luca and walked to his door. Luca followed. "Just give me a second." He stepped inside, keeping his back to the door, and grabbed the roll of paper from his sleeve. He shoved it under his desk, and pretended to check for the book. Then he grabbed the slim volume off a shelf and carried it back to the door. "Here it is. We can talk about it, if you want. I heard a lecture on the book, not at the university but a private lecture, you know, because it's so controversial."

"I was planning to review it with Mazzeo, but I'd like to hear your thoughts, too."

"I'll give you the outsider's perspective," Paolo said with a grin.

Luca shook his head. "You know more about natural philosophy than most people," he reminded Paolo.

"I only read that stuff so I can sell more of Galileo's instruments."

"That's what you say."

"So how about tomorrow?"

"That would be perfect. After your classes?" Luca asked.

"Great," Paolo said.

Luca still stood in the doorway. "Are you sure you're okay?"

"I'm fine," Paolo lied. "Now aren't you late for something?"

Luca stepped back. "Tomorrow, then?"

"See you then," Paolo promised.

Luca headed off to his room. Paolo collapsed on the bed with a sigh. That had been too close.

~ ~ ~

Paolo had been acting very strange in the hallway. Had he skipped another class? Zaneta Lucia didn't have time to wonder. She was supposed to meet Mazzeo in the common area for a tutoring session. She ran back to her room long enough to drop off the new book and grab the volume for her meeting with Mazzeo.

Zaneta Lucia took a deep breath before she walked down to the third floor. She had been avoiding the room since overhearing the conversation between Ugolino, Timeo, and Nonni. But her tutoring sessions were too important. When she walked in, she saw Timeo and Nonni sitting at their usual table, laughing about some shared joke. Zaneta Lucia's pulse raced. It was nothing, it didn't mean anything. They were just using the common area, like they always did.

Timeo gave her a quick nod as she walked by.

She settled down at one of the tables and flipped through her book. But her thoughts kept coming back to the Zorzi Affair. Timeo and Nonni might act friendly with Luca Manetti, but they would turn her in if they found out she was the runaway girl. She didn't doubt that for a second.

Thankfully, Mazzeo walked in a minute later. He folded his lanky body into the seat across from hers, and dropped a stack of books on the table.

"I hope those aren't all for me," Zaneta Lucia said with a grin.

"I wish. My rhetoric professor wants me to read all of these books by next week. As if I didn't have enough on my plate already." Mazzeo rolled his eyes.

Zaneta Lucia shrugged. It didn't sound so bad.

Mazzeo slapped the top book on the stack. "And can you believe it? Half of these were written by *women*."

Zaneta Lucia's head jerked up. "What?"

"Some female humanist is visiting the university, and I'm supposed to go to her speech."

A *female* author? In all her reading, Zaneta Lucia could not recall any books written by women. And now a female humanist was coming to the university. Zaneta Lucia wanted to ask Mazzeo if she could attend the speech, too.

But Mazzeo was still ranting. "Can you imagine? A speech by a woman?"

From across the room, Timeo jumped in. "Next thing you know, women will want to run for Doge of Venice, and boss all the men around."

Nonni laughed, shaking his head. "And then we'll have a

woman as the pope! Signora Pope will throw all the men in prison!"

Mazzeo scowled. "Ignore them," he said to Zaneta Lucia.

She lowered her voice to match his. "So you don't agree?"

"Well, first, they'll never let a woman run Venice. Can you picture it? She would spend the city's entire treasury on jewels and baubles, and the Ottoman Turks would simply sail up and seize the Armada. It's too foolish to take seriously."

A flash of embarrassment slapped Zaneta Lucia, and she practically shook in her seat. Is that what her friend thought about women? That they were ignorant, empty vessels, incapable of intelligent thought?

She should drop it. She didn't want to draw attention to herself. But she couldn't.

"What about the female humanists?"

Mazzeo raised an eyebrow at her. "I've read some of their writings. They aren't all bad. But I don't see why they want to publish books. They pretend to have manly virtues, but at their core, they're still women."

Zaneta Lucia set her mouth in a thin line. She wanted to rip off the leather band holding her hair back and tell Mazzeo that he had been tutoring a woman for weeks. But that would accomplish nothing.

After she passed the entrance exam, she would prove them wrong.

She pushed down her anger. "I'm sure they publish for the same reason that men write books."

"And what's that?"

"To be remembered." Zaneta Lucia leaned forward and reached out an arm to pull one of the books to her side of the table. She flipped it open. The title page read *The Worth of Women*.

Mazzeo was watching her with an unreadable expression on his face.

She tried to keep her voice light. "What do female authors write about?"

"Oh, all sorts of things. Religion, education." He waved off her question. "We really should get back to Aristotle. He's much more important than these distractions." He gestured to the stack of books on his side of the table. "After all, they ask about Aristotle in every entrance exam. I don't think they ever ask about female humanists."

Zaneta Lucia closed the book. "Well, I'd like to read *The Worth of Women*," she said. "What if I read it, and tell you what it says so you don't have to read it yourself? It could be payback for all the tutoring."

"Fine, one less book for me to read," Mazzeo said with a shrug.

Zaneta Lucia slid the book off the table and into her bag. She could not wait to learn what the author had to say about the worth of women.

SEVENTEEN

Not long after the sun rose, Zaneta Lucia was in the workshop, packing up stacks of booklets to send off to students at other universities. A yawn split her face, and she threw up a hand to hide it.

She had stayed up late into the night reading *The Worth of Women*.

The book had been written by a Venetian woman, Moderata Fonte. A Venetian! Had she walked the same streets as Moderata Fonte? In her mind, Zaneta Lucia saw the city transformed into a map marking the location of female intellectuals. What other female writers had crossed the city? Zaneta Lucia had to know more.

She had devoured the text, immersing herself in the dialogue between seven noble women who debated the virtues of women. Zaneta Lucia had never imagined anything like it—a gathering of intelligent women, advocating for women's value. At one line, she had dropped the book into her lap, as though struck by a bolt of lightening.

She had re-read the line, her eyes lingering on the words. "Do you really believe that everything historians tell us about men—or about women—is actually true? You ought to consider the fact that these histories have been written by men, who never tell the truth except by accident."

Zaneta Lucia had glanced up at the stack of histories on her desk. She had been reading those very books in preparation for her examination, so she knew exactly what they said: the great deeds of history had been carried out by men, driven by valiant, noble motives. Women only appeared in history books as a distraction or a disaster, like Helen causing the Trojan Wars or Cleopatra bewitching Mark Anthony. In the history books, women were seductresses and witches, ignorant and foolish. They were the forgotten mothers and wives of heroes, who never seemed to receive any credit. Or women did not appear at all, erased from the past as though they had never existed.

And now, sitting in the workshop, Zaneta Lucia could not stop thinking about the book. It had upended the way she saw her world, and made her question everything. She wanted to go back through every history text and scrutinize each line. Just as Galileo's work had shattered her belief in Aristotle's world view, Fonte had shaken her view of history.

What would Paolo would say about Fonte's claim that history was written for men? Zaneta Lucia tried to imagine how he would respond. Would he laugh, like Timeo and Nonni, at the idea of a female writer? Or would he roll his eyes at her like Mazzeo?

Zaneta Lucia had learned a great deal in her short time as Luca Manetti, but the most disturbing truth was that men's opinions of women were even worse than she had imagined.

As her mind wandered, Zaneta Lucia's eyes scanned over the order list, noting where different packages should be sent. She cross-checked the inventory lists, checking how many booklets they had on hand, and how many still needed to be printed.

It was easy work, and she quickly fell into a familiar rhythm. It felt good to set her mind to a task that she could finish, and cast aside.

Out of the corner of her eye, Zaneta Lucia saw Burano walk

into the room. He had been away for the last three days, so it was their first encounter since Paolo had shared his concerns about the man. Zaneta Lucia watched Burano walk around the room, stopping at different desks to speak with people. Was that unusual? It did not seem suspicious, at least not from her point of view.

Then again, would anyone watching Luca Manetti find his actions suspicious? There was a reward for information about Zaneta Lucia Zorzi, but she was still walking the streets of Padua in disguise. If she had raised suspicions, someone surely would have turned her in.

But it had not happened yet. She tried to find assurance in that thought.

Zaneta Lucia turned her eyes back to the inventory. She had been paying closer attention to how many items were leaving the shop and how many were being produced. She didn't have the same mind for numbers as Paolo, but even to her, something seemed off. There should be a surplus, but she saw no boxes of booklets waiting to be sold.

Were the extras going out as gifts, maybe to Galileo's patrons? Or did Galileo take them to class, to sell directly to students?

"How is everything, Luca?" a voice asked next to her shoulder.

She jumped. She had been so deep in thought that she had lost track of the workshop. Instead of stacking booklets she had been staring into space thinking.

The voice was Burano, of course.

"Everything is going well, thank you," she answered, clearing her throat. "I apologize, I was doing figures in my head."

"Make sure you count those correctly. We've had some problems balancing the books lately and I don't want to send out extra booklets. We lose money if we do that."

Zaneta Lucia nodded, and went back to her work. Burano walked away. Why would he mention problems balancing the books if he was guilty? Or was he trying to point the finger at her, so he could claim she hadn't been doing her job?

Zaneta Lucia hated how tense and on-edge she felt. She was constantly worried that someone would unmask her secret. And the strange footsteps in the stairwell, and Burano's possible stealing didn't help. On top of everything, she was falling behind in her studying.

The last month had been more exhausting than the rest of her life combined. Had fleeing from Venice been the right choice? The soothsayer had predicted one path would lead to happiness, but what if she had chosen incorrectly?

Then again, at least she was in charge of her own destiny. At least she wasn't married to Mario Barbaro.

When her shift at the workshop was over, Zaneta Lucia decided to go for a walk. She had barely spent any time enjoying Padua. Since her arrival, she had been so busy working in the boarding house and studying for the exam. And once she learned that someone was looking for her, she started avoiding the streets.

But Padua was so different from Venice—it had contours, and topography that was unimaginable on the lagoon. The self-imposed home arrest was grating on her nerves. She wanted to walk through town unchaperoned. That was why she had left Venice in the first place. She wanted freedom, and she didn't want to stay in her room all day.

So Zaneta Lucia stepped outside the boarding house. Instead of turning toward the university, she walked the other direction. She wanted to see something new.

She strolled by small buildings with shops on the ground floor and homes on the upper levels, until she reached a large square near a church. She stopped for a moment to watch the people hurrying by. Then she walked on until she reached the edge of the city, ringed by a tall stone wall. She traced a finger along the wall and felt the heat of the afternoon sun in the boulders. Galileo would call it transferred energy. The world looked different when she imagined it through his eyes.

Zaneta Lucia turned right and walked along the wall until she reached a bridge heading out of the city.

A handful of wagons were crossing the bridge, along with some people, and she decided to follow the road out of town. As she walked across the bridge, she lingered for a moment to listen to the water rushing under the stones. It reminded her of Venice. Early in the morning she would hear the water slapping the stones edging the canal. She sighed, picturing those days when she would lie in bed listening to the soothing sound of the waves.

On the other side of the bridge the city dissolved into the endless fields of the countryside. Zaneta Lucia had not spent much time in the country, aside from the wagon ride and the walk from Isola di Torre. She marveled at the vast, empty expanses of land. It was like nothing she had ever seen in Venice.

Zaneta Lucia filled her lungs with air and sensed the first hint of fall. Her face broke out into a wide grin, and she left Padua behind her.

She saw people working in the fields. It must be the end of harvest season. Were these foods destined for Venice, which had to import everything since nothing could be grown on the island? Zaneta Lucia paused to watch a woman carrying a basket of fennel. Another few minutes down the road and she was surrounded by vineyards, overflowing with ripe purple grapes. Men and women walked the rows, filling woven baskets with the fruit.

Her anxiety evaporated in the fresh air. After hours of reading, it felt good to use her legs.

But then she heard the sound of footsteps close behind her.

At first she thought it was just someone else on the road, maybe a merchant leaving town or a farmer heading back to his fields. But the footsteps didn't fade away, and they matched her own when she sped up.

Zaneta Lucia rounded a bend in the road, where it cut through a forest of trees between fields. The sun was blotted out, and it took her eyes a minute to adjust to the shade of the small woods. Should she turn around? Or run? She pulled in deep, steady breaths, but her heart was pounding. What if someone had recognized her?

She quickened her pace, her eyes trained on the narrow slit of sunlight at the end of the dense patch of forest. But before she could reach it, a hand grabbed her shoulder.

She spun around to face the person.

It was a man, in his thirties perhaps. His shaggy brown hair was chopped off at the shoulders, and he was wearing an expensive-looking cloak the color of freshly spilled blood.

Zaneta Lucia searched his face for familiar features, and found none. He must have been following her. Why else would he track her nearly twenty minutes outside of the city, on her slow and wandering tour of the Paduan countryside?

The man frowned at her, still holding her arm. "Luca Manetti?"

Zaneta Lucia froze, fighting against her instincts to break free from his grip and run. She forced out a quick nod.

"You live in the boarding house of Professor Galileo, is that correct?"

She nodded again, swallowing hard. Who was this man, and what did he want from her?

"Ser Galileo is in serious trouble," the man said. "We want to know if you are willing to help him."

Her fear faded into confusion—so this man didn't think she was the runaway Zorzi girl. But what could he want with Galileo?

"We?" she managed to whisper.

"I can't say more than that."

"What kind of trouble is he in?"

"I can only tell you if you promise to help."

She racked her brain. How could Galileo be in trouble? He was one of the most respected professors at the university, and he was known across Europe. Could it have something to do with Burano or someone else stealing from him?

The man was watching her. She needed to give him an answer. "Yes, I'll help you," she told him. "I want to help Professor Galileo."

The stranger nodded, and released her arm. She wondered for a moment what he would have done if she had said no. A shiver snaked through her body. Was it a coincidence that he had stopped her in the forest, right around a bend in the road? She could hear the distant sound of wagons, but she was invisible to them from this spot.

Instead of explaining himself, the mysterious man stepped away. "Wait for our instructions," he said, and walked past her on the road out of town.

Zaneta Lucia watched until she could no longer see him. She collapsed on a stump next to the side of the road. Terror had struck her when she imagined the stranger dragging her back to Venice, back to her family and her former life. But now, as her fears receded, she was left with questions. If the stranger had nothing to do with the Zorzi matter, why had he approached her, out of all the tenants at the boarding house? And was Galileo in some kind of danger?

Who did the man work for, and what was he hiding?

Zaneta Lucia had only agreed to help to get answers, but she was still in the dark.

She had wanted a relaxing walk in the countryside, but her problems only multiplied. She turned back to town, her steps heavy.

Her eyes darted around, waiting for the next disaster to strike. Then, a thought entered her mind. Paolo had acted very strangely yesterday when she ran into him on the fourth floor. How had he appeared in the staircase, only a minute after she climbed the stairs?

Was Paolo on the forbidden fifth floor?

Paolo had told her that someone was stealing. But what if it wasn't Burano at all?

A cold sweat covered Zaneta Lucia's body. She didn't know who to trust or what to believe. And now, she wondered if her only friend was lying to her.

EIGHTEEN

Paolo lay on his bed, studying the sheet he'd taken from Galileo's study. It looked like a schematic drawing for some new instrument. But no matter which way he turned the paper, Paolo could not figure out what the strange cylinder was supposed to do.

He dropped the sheet, and sighed. He never should have taken the paper. What had he been thinking? Paolo slapped his forehead. He hadn't been thinking at all. That was the problem.

Galileo's office was a mess, but the professor would eventually notice that something was missing. He had to return it. But he couldn't afford another disaster like when he had run into Luca. He would have to be more careful this time.

Paolo tucked the paper into his sleeve and lingered outside the fourth floor stairwell. The building was quiet, and Galileo was off with his children. Paolo scurried up the stairs, raced into the studio, and stuck the sheet under a thick book. Hopefully Galileo would assume he had misplaced it.

He ran back down the stairs, out of breath. Instead of stopping at the fourth floor, he kept going until he was out the building to the street. His heart was still pounding.

How could he have been so stupid? He was trying to prove that there was a thief in the boarding house, and so he stole something. Paolo silently promised not to rush into anything so foolish again.

He walked aimlessly through Padua, circling around the university and the town hall.

Paolo's mind wandered. He needed to write back to his father's latest letter. And finally schedule his rhetoric exam. His thoughts landed on Luca Manetti. How could he convince Luca to trust him again? It was easy to confide in Luca, who seemed incapable of lying, or manipulation. When Paolo began to suspect Burano, Luca was the first and only person he told.

Paolo sighed. He had given Luca reason to be suspicious. Paolo *was* sneaking around the boarding house, after all, and he'd stolen one of Galileo's plans. Yes, he had returned it the next day, but he was still a thief. Luca was right to doubt him.

Paolo stopped outside a small church and thought about going in. He hadn't attended church in a while. Most of his fellow students only visited the university's chapel infrequently. Maybe confession would help him clear his mind.

But there were some things he couldn't even trust with a priest.

Paolo wandered away from the church, and instead walked into a store.

"Paolo Serravalle!" the shopkeeper called from behind the counter. "Do you have anything for me this week?"

Paolo always supplemented his monthly stipend from his father with extra money he would pick up in Padua. He had even considered selling the plan he'd taken from Galileo's office, but quickly discarded that idea. He didn't even know what it was, so how could he know a fair price?

"I have a rumor that might turn a profit for you," Paolo said. "But let's just exchange information today, not money."

"Fine, I don't mind saving some money. And I heard something that might interest you."

Paolo leaned on the counter, which was covered in colorful

packets of sweets. "Do you sell a lot of these things?" he asked the shopkeeper, pointing to the candies.

"More than you can imagine. And mostly to university boys like you. They love them." The shopkeeper tossed a packet to Paolo, who caught it with one hand. "On the house."

Paolo grinned, ripping off the paper wrapper and popping the candy in his mouth. It tasted of licorice. "I heard that the bishop is planning to make another visit up the mountain to the parish in Feltre."

"That's not news," the shopkeeper said, straightening up a stack of broadsheets. "He's supposed to do that every year, although I wager he doesn't make it quite that often."

Paolo swallowed the last of the candy. "That's not the best part. He's planning to censure one of the priests for inappropriate relations with a woman in the town. The bishopric is hoping to keep things quiet, but I happen to know the woman is pregnant, and she isn't likely to go away."

The shopkeeper laughed. "Sounds like a bad day for the bishop. But how does that benefit me?"

"I'm sure the bishopric might be willing to pay a good shopkeeper to keep the story quiet," Paolo said with a grin. "After all, they don't want it to become public knowledge."

"Ah, I see your point. And who told you this secret?"

Paolo shook his head. The man was always trying to ferret out his sources. "I'll never tell, and you know it. Now, what do you have for me?"

The man turned away from the stack of papers. "Have you heard about the man from Venice who's looking for that runaway girl?"

"Of course. Who hasn't?" Paolo snatched another candy when the shopkeeper turned his back. Maybe the red ones tasted better. "I hope you have something more than that, considering I probably just made you fifty ducats. Or if you're smart, you'll ask the bishop to buy his goods from your store, which could make you hundreds of extra ducats a year."

The shopkeeper raised an eyebrow. "You're too clever for your own good. Of course there's more. This Venetian has been visiting nearly every shop asking questions. He even hired a printer to copy a likeness of the girl on a broadsheet to post around town. But the man thinks he's very crafty and that he's doing a good job keeping the matter quiet."

Paolo rolled his eyes. Gossip had a way of getting around even when people tried to keep it quiet—especially in Padua. "So, what's the news?"

"He wants to offer a reward for her return to Venice. Five hundred ducats."

Paolo nearly choked on the stolen candy. "Five hundred ducats?" he repeated. "That must be the girl's entire dowry!"

"Just about, from what I heard. And that's why the Venetian is keeping things quiet. He thinks too many people will falsify stories to get the money."

"I'd make up a story for that kind of money," Paolo said, thinking of all the things five hundred ducats could buy. "But why offer a reward if you don't tell anyone about it?"

"That's a good question. I think he's trying to spread it around quietly to see if anyone will come forward before the whole town knows about it."

Paolo turned his thoughts back to the mysterious girl. "Why do they think she's in Padua?"

"It's the closest city to Venice. And from what I heard, the girl has a thing for reading. Aristotle and all that business, what you boys are always talking about at the university."

Paolo laughed. "A girl who wants to study Aristotle? And I thought the priest impregnating the mayor of Feltre's daughter was funny."

"I heard the family sent people to other towns as well.

Verona, Vicenza, even Bologna. No one thinks she went that far, though."

"How far could she go without help? She's, what, sixteen? Seventeen? She wouldn't know the first thing about living on her own." Paolo pictured the sad life of the runaway girl. "And they don't think she might be dead, or worse?"

The shopkeeper shook his head. "They know she sold some jewelry in Venice on the morning she disappeared, but no one is sure how she left the island. I can't imagine she's hiding out in Venice, not without an accomplice, and where would a girl of that age find someone to help her?"

"So how do I find this girl?" He was already spending the five hundred ducats in his mind. A boat. He would sail around the world. How much did boats cost, anyway?

"I don't know. I only wanted to tell you about the reward. And the rumor about her selling jewelry, so she must have some money."

Paolo threw up his hands. "That's not enough. How am I supposed to find her with that?"

The shopkeeper opened his account books and began to study the rows of figures. "That's not my job, Paolo," he said with a smirk. "I just pass along what I know."

Paolo balled his hands into fists. The man was no help. But he didn't want to sour their relationship. "Then at least tell me where I can find this Venetian man."

The shopkeeper looked up. "I can see this has caught your attention. I could give you the man's name. But what's it worth to you?"

Paolo cursed the shopkeeper silently under his breath, but apparently he wasn't quiet enough, judging by the grin on the shopkeeper's face. "I just told you about the bishop."

"But that's not worth five hundred ducats, is it, Serravalle?" The man leaned forward. "Look, I'm having trouble with some of my less desirable sweets. I'll sell them to you, and you see if you can turn a profit. Both of us win."

"Unless no one wants your disgusting candies," Paolo said, but he agreed anyway. Hopefully it would be the red ones, not the licorice ones. He fished some coins out of his pocket and took the proffered sack of brown candies. "Now, what's the name?"

"Leonardo Sorto. He's staying at the inn next to the public gardens, down past the university. Do you know the one?"

Paolo nodded, and tipped his hat to the shopkeeper. He wasn't sure which of them had come out on the better end of their exchange. But at least he had a lead on a big payoff.

~ ~ ~

Galileo squinted, and lifted the lens to his eye. He was trying to fit two ground glass pieces into a tube of thick paper wrapped in leather. The building was silent, and he could finally set aside a few hours to work on his latest project. He had been fiddling with the tube for months, looking for the right balance between the two lenses, the length of the tube, and the material to hold them in place.

This was only the latest in a series of tests. He wasn't sure if the lenses were right. The tube had been the easiest part to manufacture. Galileo had calculated that the tube should be two feet long, and the leather kept it both sturdy and dark.

With a sigh, he eased the first lens into the slot at the end of the tube. He tapped it to make sure it was in place. Once he was confident that it would hold, he flipped the tube and picked up the second lens, sliding it into the slot. He rotated the glass. When it was secure he took a deep breath.

This was the moment he had been waiting for. Now he

would learn if his efforts had been in vain. For months he had been quietly grinding lenses, not trusting the delicate work with anyone else. He would not even whisper about this project outside of his fifth floor rooms.

If he succeeded, it would revolutionize the world. Not just natural philosophy, but the whole world.

But the previous tests had failed to yield results. All those hours of work, all the energy and money spent on materials. And every time, he failed.

This time, he might have solved the problem. He had sunk hour after hour into analyzing his previous shortcomings. He didn't know what he was doing, after all.

"Isn't that the point of invention?" he muttered to himself. "Doing something for the first time?"

Galileo stopped for a moment, the tube clutched in one hand. His eyes scanned the room, taking in the barely ordered chaos. He had been on this earth for forty-five years, and he'd come so far in that time. He had used his education wisely, building a name for himself.

But that would pale in comparison to the prestige and wealth he would gain if this one invention worked.

Galileo raised the tube to his eye, aiming it out the window. He froze, his eye screwed shut. What if it failed again?

He said a prayer and opened his eye.

In an instant, the university building two blocks away was directly in front of him. He could see through the window on the building, directly into a classroom. It was a little fuzzy, but he could just make out the hair color of the students in the row nearest the window.

Galileo adjusted the tube, turning it to the west. His gaze jumped over the rooftops to the church several blocks away. The frescoes painted on the upper wall of the building looked close enough for him to touch. The glass barely distorted his view.

Distant objects leapt right before his eyes.

Galileo began to laugh, quietly at first and then louder. "It works!" he cried out. He clapped his hands over his mouth, laughing too hard to stop, and called out again, "It works!"

NINETEEN

Paolo left the shop with a new sense of purpose. He would find Leonardo Sorto, and then figure out some way to get the five hundred ducat reward. But first, he had to attend a lecture. If he skipped any more, he might get kicked out of the university. And if he survived the expulsion, his father would kill him.

Then it was time for another tutoring session. Paolo couldn't abandon Luca. He pictured Luca's crestfallen face, and practically ran back to the boarding house. Luca peppered him with questions about church doctrine, as if Paolo was a priest.

The sun set, and Paolo finally admitted that it was too late in the day to find Sorto.

He vowed to go the next morning, but then he ran into Luca in the common area. Luca was shifting from foot to foot. His eyes kept darting to the door whenever there was a sound in the hallway.

"What's going on?" Paolo pressed.

"Nothing. I've been meaning to ask you something." Luca gripped a book so tightly in his hands that Paolo could see the white in his knuckles.

"Is it about the book you're strangling?"

Luca nearly dropped the book on the floor. The boy's face was red as a beet.

"Luca, out with it."

His friend swallowed. "Did you hear about the female humanist?"

"That sounds like the set-up to an odd joke, 'did you hear about the female humanist.'" He laughed, but Luca's face went ashen. "I'm sorry, I didn't mean to tease."

Luca looked like he was going to pass out if he didn't slow down and breathe. "Mazzeo said a woman is coming to the university to give a speech."

"Yes, I heard about that. Lucrezia Marinella, I think?"

"What do you know about her?"

"Not much. She wrote a book on the Virgin Mary. And something about women's nobility? I haven't read it myself."

"When's her speech? Do you think— I mean, would I be allowed to attend?"

"I don't see why not."

The color rushed back into Luca's face, and he finally smiled. The boy was obviously intrigued by this woman. Paolo shook his head. Young men had the strangest tastes.

"Luca, I'll find out more about the speech. We can go together, alright?"

"Oh, thank you, Paolo!" Luca burst out. He reached out to grab Paolo's hand. In a second, Luca dropped it as though he had been burned.

Instead he shoved the book at Paolo. "I just read this, and it really made me question things."

Paolo promised to look at the book—something about the worth of women, was it about dowries?—and patted Luca on the shoulder. The boy walked off with a smile. Luca reminded Paulo of a fawn just finding its footing. His floundering was one of his most endearing qualities, though he seemed completely unaware of it.

It wasn't until the next day that Paolo finally set off to look for Sorto. The chance of five hundred ducats, however slim, was worth his time.

At midday, Paolo left the boarding house for the short walk down toward the public gardens. He would start by visiting the inn where Sorto was staying.

Paolo found the building easily, but the door was locked. He stood in front of the narrow doorway and scratched his head. What kind of inn locked their door in the middle of the day? Paolo nearly turned back to the boarding house, but since he was right outside the gardens he decided to continue his walk. He could always check back at the inn on his way home.

As Paolo strolled along the dirt paths of the garden, he imagined his life with an extra five hundred ducats in his pocket. He could travel for months with that much money. He could go all the way to China.

But for some reason, the thought of leaving everything behind didn't bring a smile to his face. Maybe he'd stay in Padua long enough to finish his degree. Money didn't spoil, after all.

He reached a small church nestled amongst the trees, and stood for a moment looking up at the red brick edifice. Its narrow façade just reached the tops of the oak trees that ringed it. It was a private chapel owned by Padua's leading family.

And the door of the chapel was ajar.

Paolo looked over his shoulder. He had never seen the church door open. It was a private chapel for a rich family, after all. Why would they invite Paduans to peek in? Such chapels were usually draped in gold and silver, the wealth of the family thrown on the altar of the church. Paolo took a step forward, suddenly craving a look inside.

But before he could take another step, two men walked out of the door. Paolo quickly ducked into a grove of trees, only a dozen yards from the men. Had they seen him?

His curiosity got the best of him, and he cautiously peeked around a thick tree trunk. Yes, his first suspicion had been correct: one of the men was Enrico Scrovegni. His family had built the small church generations earlier. Even though the family's fortunes had dwindled in the intervening centuries, they were still one of the wealthiest families of Padua, and their name would always be attached to the opulent chapel.

The other man was tall, with wispy, greying hair. Paolo did not recognize him, but an itching between his shoulders told Paolo the conversation might be important. And to his relief, neither paid attention to the grove of trees where he hid. They must not have seen him.

Paolo inched closer to the men. He stayed in the shade of the trees, and strained his ears.

"And how do you expect me to help you?" Scrovegni said.

The response was muffled. Paolo let out a silent curse.

"Are you accusing me of something? I don't know why you would think I was involved," Scrovegni said, his voice rising.

If Scrovegni was caught up in a scandal, Paolo had to know. It could be worth a lot of money. But he had reached the edge of the grove, and could go no closer without exposing himself.

The stranger turned away from Scrovegni, his voice carrying. "You've heard my offer. Think about it and get back to me." The man walked right toward Paolo's hiding place, and he retreated into the oak trees. Paolo waited a moment, until he was sure the stranger was gone, and dared another look at Scrovegni. The patrician was shaking his head, and worry lines creased his face. Paolo watched him walk away in the opposite direction.

He let out a low whistle. Scrovegni was in some kind of trouble, that much was clear. Paolo would pay more attention to the man. It never hurt to have a backup if the reward money didn't pan out.

Paolo took one last look at the door to the chapel. It was firmly closed. He had missed his chance to sneak inside.

He waited a few more minutes among the oak trees, and

then emerged. Once he was back on the path, he retraced his steps to the inn.

This time, the door was unlocked.

Paolo pulled the door open and stepped inside. He came face to face with the inn's proprietor, a short, cheerful woman named Anna, sweeping the floor in the empty common room.

"Signora Anna," Paolo began in his most respectful voice.

She cut him off. "Paolo Serravalle, as I live and breathe. I thought I told you not to show your face around here ever again." But she said it with a smile in her eyes, so he brushed it off.

"You're not still sour because the tip I gave you about that horse race turned out to be wrong, are you?"

"'Wrong,' is that really how you would describe it? The horse I bet on died before he even got halfway down the track! I've never seen such a thing."

Paolo shook his head. "I was shocked, too, but who are we to question God's will? Clearly it was that poor horse's time, and no one could have predicted such a thing."

Anna lowered her eyebrow at him. "And yet, somehow, I heard that you made quite a bit of money betting on the winning horse."

Paolo shrugged. "You know I'm not one to brag."

At this, Anna laughed out loud.

Paolo changed the subject. "Is Leonardo Sorto one of your guests?"

Anna narrowed her eyes. "What is this about? You want to harass my customers? Maybe give them some bad tips on horse races?"

"No, I simply had some business with the man and heard he was staying here."

"Business, you say?" Anna tapped the broom in her hand against the floor. She glanced toward the stairs at the back of the common room. "This doesn't have anything to do with a certain missing Venetian girl, does it?"

Paolo's ears perked up. "It might." He was on the right track. If the girl had come through Padua, what if she had sought out a female innkeeper? Anna might hold the key to a five hundred ducat payout.

"I wish you men would leave that poor girl alone," Anna said bitterly.

Paolo felt his pulse quicken. Was she confirming his suspicions? She was more likely to open up if she didn't know the information was valuable. Even if she felt sorry for the girl, Paolo figured Anna wouldn't give up a five hundred ducat prize. But he could keep her in the dark. "Why is that, Anna?"

Anna halfheartedly swept a small patch of the wood floor. "Think about it from the girl's perspective," she said quietly. "Her family is only worried about their reputation. But this poor girl must have had her reasons for running away. What sane person would leave everything behind without a good reason?"

Paolo frowned. Anna was right. If he hoped to find the girl, he needed to understand her motivations. Why had she left Venice in the first place? She was a patrician—she lived in a palazzo, she had everything provided for her, a house filled with servants and whatever she might desire. Fancy dresses, jewels, all those sorts of things. So why would she leave?

Anna interrupted his thoughts. "Don't you see? She's still a child, younger than you, and her family wants to marry her off to some stranger, some man she doesn't even know. How does she know if he's a good person? They might barely have a conversation before she was expected to sleep next to him and spend her life with him."

Paolo saw, to his discomfort, that Anna's passionate speech had brought tears to her eyes. He needed to steer the conversation back to more productive questions. "What about the rumors that she ran off with a man?"

Anna shook her head, grimacing at Paolo. "A man that *she* chose, instead of one chosen by her parents, you mean? Good for her."

"Are you saying you've met this girl?"

Anna emitted a noise tinged with disgust. "I don't know her. But I know thousands of girls just like her. Daughters who are treated more like property than people by their families. I'm sure *you've* never given girls like that a second thought."

Paolo's chest tightened. Anna was right. He'd always assumed young patrician women were lucky. They didn't have to scramble for money, or fight to make a name for themselves. Their fathers didn't force them to take a degree and enter a profession. From his point of view, they lived a life of leisure. And yet, Paolo had always known from a young age that he would be able to attend a university, run his own business, or travel the world. He could do as he pleased. Anna's words struck a guilty chord in his heart—he had no sisters, only three older brothers, and his mother had died before his first communion. He lived in a world of men, where women were rarely a consideration. And when he did think of women, it was just a pleasant diversion.

Paolo locked eyes with Anna. "Is it really that terrible?"

Anna set down the broom and sank onto a wooden bench. Her face drooped as she spoke. "It's not all bad. But I can understand the girl's troubles."

Paolo had never seen Anna so unsettled. He wondered if his words had hurt her. He knew Anna had been married once, years earlier, but her husband had died, and she had no children of her own. And in all those years she had never remarried. Paolo had never asked whether Anna's marriage had been happy. And why had she not remarried? Did she have more freedom as a widow? Certainly she must, because she ran her own inn and managed her business without a husband. Only a handful of women in Padua ran businesses, and, it dawned on Paolo, most of them were widows.

The innkeeper stood, picking up the broom. "Now get out of here, Paolo Serravalle. You've wasted enough of my time."

He tipped his head to Anna. "My apologies, Signora." He did feel guilty for drudging up Anna's bad memories. Paolo ducked out the door and let himself be swept up by the people walking purposefully toward the university.

As he walked through the streets of Padua back to the boarding house, he replayed the conversation in his mind. Anna had distracted him from his task—she had never admitted whether Sorto was staying at her inn. He'd have to return to look for the man later.

But she had given him a new perspective on the runaway. The girl was probably afraid. She was alone, and she was likely quite ignorant. If, as Anna hinted, she had led a sheltered life, treated as a pawn by her family, was it possible she would seek out the comforts of her home? Maybe she had approached a female innkeeper or businesswoman, or perhaps a convent or other religious organization. Or the girl might have run in the opposite direction, eloping with a boyfriend to escape the strict rules of her family.

Paolo suddenly remembered the book that Luca had given him the day before, about women. Maybe reading the book would help him figure out what motivated the runaway girl. He vowed to pick it up as soon as he got back to the boarding house.

His visit with Anna had taught him one thing: if he wanted the five hundred ducat reward, he needed to learn more about this girl.

~ ~ ~

Zaneta Lucia paced back and forth in her room at the boarding house. The room was too small to make the route satisfying. It held a bed in the corner next to the window, a basin for water to wash her face (though it seemed most boys at the boarding house didn't use it), and a small cabinet for her possessions, meager as they were.

Her money was running out. The rent, plus food and a handful of books, had placed a sizable dent in her purse. On top of that, her few items of clothing were also becoming noticeably threadbare. She needed to buy clothes, but that required money. And she couldn't visit a tailor and try on clothes. She couldn't even get her measurements taken.

She put herself at risk whenever she left her room. Someone could recognize her at any time.

Zaneta Lucia had taken extra steps to strengthen her disguise in the last few days. She had visited a barber on the opposite side of town. He didn't ask questions, and chopped her long locks into a shoulder-length bob that many young men were wearing. It was just long enough to tie back, but now she didn't have to braid it every day to hide the length. And she almost always wore her new cap. The shadows it cast on her face made her appear more masculine. Plus, she could tilt her face down to hide under the brim if anyone tried to look at her too closely.

Zaneta Lucia had also spent hours practicing the mannerisms of men. It went against all her instincts, and required constant thought. She walked differently, holding her hips steady. At first it had felt so odd, but it was quickly becoming second nature. Men were more physical, too. She was still nervous when anyone smacked her on the shoulder, but she no longer flinched. And her hands were rougher, from working in the workshop and making instruments.

In spite of the flatness of her chest, she also bound her breasts every day. One wrong glance could destroy her disguise, and she wasn't going to take any chances.

She gazed in a small mirror, searching for Zaneta Lucia in her features. Would her own family recognize her now? She looked very different without the long hair and a dress. Had she ever even seen a woman in pants before? There was one time, during Carnivale, when her brother had pointed out a woman wearing men's clothes, but her mother had quickly grabbed her hand and dragged her away.

It was illegal for a woman to wear man's clothes. Or at least that was the rumor whispered in Zaneta Lucia's ear. Was it true? Was she breaking the law simply by dressing as Luca Manetti every morning?

Zaneta Lucia turned away from the mirror and picked up the book on her bed. It was October, and her entrance examination was only two weeks away. She could not afford to get distracted. She had to throw herself into her studies.

Some days, it felt like she'd learned more in the past month than in the rest of her life combined. She knew how to compose a Petrarchan verse, which volume of the Justinian Code explained civil crimes, and she could discourse eloquently on the history of the Roman Republic.

Other days, she was struck with panic at everything she still didn't know, all the books she had not read, and the dwindling time before her exam. There was so much more to learn.

When Zaneta Lucia left the boarding house, which was rare, she visited the university's library. Paolo had reassured her that students studying for the exam were allowed to use the collections. On her first visit, she had been struck dumb by the rows and rows of books, more than she had ever imagined in one place. The library held printed books as well as manuscripts.

She could ask the man behind the counter for any book and he would find her a copy. Zaneta Lucia loved the days that she spent in a dusty corner of the library, pouring through stacks of books.

And she had found more books written by women. First she had looked up Lucrezia Marinella, who would soon be in Padua to give a lecture. Then she had found volumes by Laura Cereta, Isotta Nogarola, and Christine de Pizan. She had never imagined that so many women had written books. The stack at her table grew and grew, and she devoured the words that had been conceived in the minds of other women.

Zaneta Lucia knew the books would probably not help on her entrance exam. Mazzeo had dismissed female authors as largely pointless, while Paolo had never mentioned them, at least not until Zaneta Lucia had raised the subject. The faculty who ran the examinations had probably never asked about female authors, but that was not going to stop her. Zaneta Lucia had finally found female role models, women she could admire for their intellects. She would stay up every night reading if that's what it took.

Money and time, money and time. She kept coming back to the conflict between the two. Zaneta Lucia had asked Burano for a temporary reprieve from some of her workshop duties so that she could increase her study time, but then she had to pay more in rent. But she needed the time if she was ever going to pass the examination.

And how would she pay for classes, if she did pass? That was one question she refused to consider. She would find a way. Somehow.

She flopped over on the bed. Suddenly her room felt claustrophobic. She needed fresh air. Grabbing her book, Zaneta Lucia set out toward the university. She walked quickly, peeking up from the brim of her hat to see if anyone was watching her.

No one seemed to notice. The students and professors wandering around the university were caught up in their own thoughts and problems.

In minutes, she was in front of the library. She entered the building and walked to the third floor, waving to the man behind the desk. He handed her a stack of books she was keeping on reserve, and she looked for a table as far away from the door as possible. She spotted one behind a shelf and headed for it.

Placing her books on the table, she settled down to pick up reading where she had left off. She was looking through medieval commentaries on Aristotle, so that she could compare them with the more recent works of Galileo and Kepler. Mazzeo had claimed that the examiners wanted students to have a good overview of Aristotle but they also wanted to hear more recent opinions on his works. The faculty was very committed to Aristotle's viewpoint, but there was always the possibility that someone might ask about problems in Aristotle's worldview.

Mazzeo told her to completely avoid the controversy brought about by Copernicus' book, which claimed that the earth revolved around the sun. Mazzeo thought it would just cause more problems for her examination. In his view, most of the faculty was firmly opposed to the theory, and others might be offended or think she was not well-versed in Aristotle if she kept contradicting the Great Philosopher.

"They want to know that you understand Aristotle," Mazzeo had explained, his patience wearing thin.

"Isn't questioning Aristotle the best way to demonstrate you understand him?"

"No," Mazzeo had said, shaking his head. "They mostly care if you can repeat his words. If you start questioning him, you'll make enemies."

"But what about Galileo's work?" she had asked. "Aren't they proud to have the best mathematician in the world here at the University of Padua?"

"No. Most of them think he's overreaching. To them, he's just a number cruncher and an instrument maker. He's an artisan pretending to be a philosopher. Bringing up Galileo will only anger the examiners."

Sitting in the library, Zaneta Lucia shook her head. It was silly. She wanted to study Galileo's works. She wasn't going to plead ignorance or pretend she didn't know about his new findings. If the older faculty members weren't willing to break with Aristotle, that was their problem.

She was so deep in thought that she didn't notice someone sitting at the table behind her. When he tapped her arm, she turned with a jump.

Her heart pounded in her chest. It was the same man who had approached her in the forest.

"Have you thought about my offer?" he asked quietly.

Zaneta Lucia glanced around to see if anyone could overhear their conversation. "What do you want me to do?" She had been wondering when the man would appear again. Zaneta Lucia had lain awake at night trying to puzzle out their encounter in the woods. Finally, she had decided to play along with his requests until she knew what was going on. Then she'd decide whether or not to tell Galileo. He had done so much for her. She didn't want to abandon or betray him.

The man slid a folded sheet of paper onto her desk. It was sealed with red wax. "Read this. Then meet me back here in one week at this same time."

Zaneta Lucia snatched up the paper, and turned back to her desk. Before she broke the seal, she looked over her shoulder to ask the man a question, but he had already vanished.

Her gaze returned to the folded sheet of paper. She didn't want to open it. What if Galileo was sick? Or what if his family was in trouble?

But she had to know. With trembling fingers, she broke the red seal.

Inside, she saw words scrawled in a nearly illegible hand. At the bottom of the sheet, a heavy wax insignia caught her eye. The hardened disc held the imprint of the Catholic Church.

She looked at the signature above the wax. It was signed by an Inquisitor.

What could the Inquisition possibly want with a mathematics professor?

She quickly scanned the rest of the note, deciphering the scrawl. It ordered her to report any "irreligious" activities or meetings that occurred at Galileo's home. The letter was vague about what that meant. How was she supposed to know what looked suspicious to the Inquisition? Did they care, for example, that she had spoken with Galileo about the phases of Venus?

Then she read the last line. The failure to report information would put her under penalty of the Church.

Her stomach dropped.

She didn't want to report on Galileo. The man had asked her to help the professor, not spy on him. She would never have agreed to this.

She reread the last line. Did that mean she would be in trouble for simply telling Galileo about her contact with the Inquisitor?

Zaneta Lucia folded the letter and stuffed it into her pocket. She stared blankly at the books in front of her, but her eyes refused to focus on the text. Suddenly her readings on Aristotle didn't seem so important.

TWENTY

Paolo dropped everything to chase after the five hundred ducat payday. His classes could wait, and so could his chores for Galileo.

He criss-crossed the streets of Padua, searching for rumors, gossip, or any tiny morsel about the runaway girl. A shop owner near the basilica claimed that he saw the girl only the previous day, walking arm-in-arm with her lover. A tavern owner by the university said she was dancing on his table the previous week. And a baker from near the west wall of town confided that she came in every morning for a piece of his world-famous *focaccia veneta*.

Paolo wasn't desperate enough to believe any of the stories. The girl had hidden herself for weeks. She wasn't stupid. She wouldn't visit the same bakery every morning, or dance on a table. But everyone in Padua wanted to claim a connection to the richest prize in town.

Paolo leaned against the city wall one day, chewing one of the disgusting brown candies. No one wanted to buy them, so he had to eat them himself. A thought struck him. If the girl was in Padua, she must have heard the rumors of people looking for her. She would be frightened and probably alone. As a sheltered patrician, she would have no idea how to look after herself. Still, if she had an ounce of sense, she would change her routines. She would move to a new inn, or even leave town.

Paolo cursed every time he heard the rumor on a new pair of lips. The more people talked about the girl, the more they risked scaring her off before he could find her.

The next day, Paolo collapsed on a bench near the university. Should he give up on the search? He had spent hours looking for the mysterious girl, with nothing to show for it.

And what if the rumors were just rumors? What if she was dead, or in Rome, or already back in Venice? Shaking his head, Paolo decided it was time to finally attend a class.

But as he stood, ready to plod to a boring lecture, something caught his eye. It was the grey-haired man that had been walking with Enrico Scrovegni by the chapel a week earlier. Paolo replayed their mysterious conversation about a possible scandal in his mind, and his mood brightened. There might be more than one payday in Padua. He was on his feet before he gave it a second thought, winding through the crowds of boys heading to class. He followed the stranger from a safe distance.

The man walked with a purpose, but after five minutes Paolo still had no idea who he was or where he was headed. They passed the university without stopping. Fortunately, the stranger stood stiff and tall, and it was easy for Paolo to keep an eye on him. He let the distance between them grown as they left the university behind and the streets grew empty.

The man walked without pausing to look at anything or talk to anyone. In fact, he didn't even nod to anyone—which was odd, because in a town like Padua you always ran into acquaintances on the street. Paolo had nodded to at least five while following the stranger.

He must be from out of town. Or maybe he worked for the Scrovegni, and people were afraid of him.

The man might be heading back toward the chapel, where Paolo had first seen him talking with Scrovegni. Paolo slowed his pace in anticipation of entering the public garden around the chapel. But then the stranger veered off.

And he walked right into the inn run by Anna.

Paolo stared at the closed door of Anna's inn, his mouth agape.

He screwed his mouth shut and stepped forward. At just that moment, Anna opened the door and caught his eye. "Paolo, you're back! The man you asked after is here."

Paolo blinked twice. Then Anna's words sunk in. All around him, the air crackled with static. He had been following Leonardo Sorto. Sorto, who was looking for a runaway and offering a five hundred ducat reward. But what business would Sorto have with Scrovegni? What were they discussing that evening near the little chapel?

Paolo mentally replayed the conversation. Sorto had been asking Scrovegni for help, and Scrovegni had resisted. Could it have to do with the girl?

He slowly returned to his surroundings, and realized that Anna was staring at him. She shook her head, almost audibly tsking.

"What?" he asked, his cheeks reddening.

She rolled her eyes at him. "I've never seen you at a loss for words before. Are you drunk?"

Paolo could see why Anna might wonder. But it was money, not alcohol, that had intoxicated him.

Still, his mind felt cloudy as he tried to make the pieces fall into place. He would never get the reward money if he couldn't shake this haze off his brain.

Paolo smiled at Anna. "I apologize. Perhaps I just need a cup of your fine red wine."

She gestured at him to follow her, and turned back into the inn. "You're in some mood today," she muttered. "I've never seen you like this."

But Paolo ignored her. He only had eyes for Sorto, who was sitting at a table in the corner of the inn's common room. Thankfully, the man was alone.

"I'll take my wine with him," Paolo said, nodding at Sorto.

Anna gave a quick nod, her eyes darting between Paolo and Sorto. Then she vanished back to the kitchen.

Paolo took a step toward Sorto's table, sizing up the man. Sorto's gaze was steady, but Paolo got the impression that the man was on high alert. Several of the other tables were occupied, and Sorto was keeping an eye on all of them.

And, Paolo saw, Sorto was wearing a sword. That was unusual, sitting in the common room of his own inn. Had the man been carrying the sword on the street? Paolo wouldn't have missed a detail like that. So the man felt more threatened at his inn than on the streets of Padua. Curious.

When Paolo was within three steps of the table, Sorto locked eyes on him.

"Hello," Paolo said. "May I sit with you?"

Sorto lowered one eyebrow, but he silently pushed back a chair with one foot. Paolo took that as an invitation and sat.

"My name is Paolo Serravalle."

Sorto continued to watch Paolo with a blank face, his expression equal parts boredom and irritation. It was an effective combination, unnerving Paolo to his core. He filed away the look for future use.

Paolo waited for Sorto to speak, but the man held his tongue. Sorto's indifference made no sense. Wasn't Sorto desperate to find the girl by now? Why wasn't he curious about what Paolo had to offer?

There was no point in beating around the bush. It was time to see if Sorto would take the bait. "I have information on the runaway from Venice."

The man's expression changed in a flash, his eyebrows rising infinitesimally and his lips parting. Sorto tried to cover his interest, dropping back into the blank expression, but Paolo had seen the change and knew that he had the man.

"What information might that be?" Sorto asked, brushing an imperceptibly small piece of dust from the table.

Paolo would string Sorto along, dolling out hints and rumors to keep the man interested, until he actually found the girl. Or, if he never found her, Paolo could still get a few ducats out of Sorto in the process. The man was hungry for information, and Paolo knew just how to feed that kind of appetite.

"First, I hear there's a reward." In his imagination, he pictured Sorto offering even more money, double or triple the original amount. If the family was desperate, they might be willing to pay. Never mind the fact that he had no idea where to find the girl. Yet.

Sorto leaned back in his seat. "Fifty ducats if you can tell me where she is."

Paolo raised an eyebrow. If he hadn't heard the higher figure, he might have believed the man. Sorto was calm, his voice even. The shopkeeper had said that Sorto wanted to keep the affair quiet. Maybe that explained his nonchalance.

"That's not the figure I heard."

"And yet that is the amount."

The serving girl approached the table with Paolo's wine. He grimaced at the interruption. But he could turn it to his advantage. Paolo grabbed the cup in his left hand and stood. He stepped back, as if planning to move to a different table.

"Wait!" Sorto said, his voice finally losing its smoothness. "Tell me what you know and maybe we can come to a mutually agreeable number."

Paolo lowered himself into the chair with a grin. He loved this sort of negotiation.

~ ~ ~

Zaneta Lucia tapped her heel against her chair in the common area of the boarding house. She could not stop thinking about the letter from the Inquisition. Yesterday, after coming home from the library, she had stuffed it down to the bottom of the cabinet in her room, under the cloth bag she had carried from Venice.

The letter might be out of sight, but its message consumed her. She wanted to tell Galileo he was being investigated, but then the Inquisition might punish her. She thought about telling Paolo, but would he even help her? Or would she be forced to go against all of her instincts and follow the letter's orders?

There were no good options.

Zaneta Lucia tried to ignore the letter, and bury herself in reading. But no matter how long she stared at a single page, the words could not break through her anxiety.

Still, Zaneta Lucia read and read, moving between her room and the common area on a daily rotation. She visited the library when she couldn't stand to sit in the boarding house for another minute. She read by daylight, and when the sun went down she would light candles until their wicks were drowned in melted wax. She talked to Paolo and Mazzeo during their tutoring sessions, but she barely spoke two words to anyone else.

Mazzeo had noticed—he asked her what was wrong when they met to discuss Euclidian equations. She had lied and said that she had a cold.

"You look terrible," Mazzeo had said. "Get more rest."

And Paolo was acting strangely. At their last session, he had canceled their tutoring meetings for the rest of the week. He claimed to be too busy with his own work. But she knew he was skipping most of his classes. She had heard Ugolino and his friends gossiping about Paolo being on academic probation.

Zaneta Lucia's stomach tied in knots whenever she thought about Paolo.

And she had been intentionally avoiding Galileo. She wanted badly to tell him about the Inquisition's investigation—but it was too risky. Still, what if he saw the truth in her eyes? What if she broke down in front of him?

Then it was the day before she was supposed to meet with the Inquisitor. Zaneta Lucia still didn't have a plan.

She was up late in her room, reading by the flickering light of a candle, when she heard a noise.

Everyone else in the boarding house was asleep, as far as she knew. But her heart pounded in her chest. She eased off the bed and stood next to the door. Could it be another tenant returning home, drunk and loud, laughing at some jest? She pressed her ear against the cool wood of the door. No, it was quieter than that. Was someone sneaking back to his room?

Zaneta Lucia was so tightly wound that she would jump at her own shadow. It was probably nothing.

But her breath caught as she recognized the noise. It sounded exactly like the footsteps she'd heard in the hall weeks ago, the ones that she had nearly forgotten.

Zaneta Lucia swallowed her fear and eased the door open, wincing at the squeaking sound of the metal hinge. She stepped into the hallway, then stopped to listen. Yes, the footsteps were coming from the stairs, and they were clearly heading up to the fifth floor.

Galileo never worked this late. And anyway, the steps were too cautious and slow to be Galileo walking into his own rooms.

Zaneta Lucia padded silently toward the stairwell door. Suddenly she heard a creak above her. She froze, her bare feet stuck on tiptoe. The person must have opened Galileo's door.

She tried to remember if Galileo had come home that

evening. When she had left the common area, he was not back from class. Then, later, she had gone down to the third floor for a bite of bread and cheese. Timeo, Ugolino, and Nonni had been laughing in the corner. But thinking back, she hadn't seen Galileo all day.

And Zaneta Lucia did not remember hearing any footsteps on the fifth floor while she was studying.

Which could only mean one thing: someone was snooping in Galileo's possessions.

Her hands clenched so hard that her fingernails dug into her palms. In so many parts of her life, she felt trapped. She had to wait for the examination, which would judge her fitness for study, and wait for the Inquisition to demand answers about Galileo, or throw her in prison if she refused. And every day she had to hide, and worry, and wait.

She was tired of feeling helpless.

Without a second thought, Zaneta Lucia threw open the door to the stairs. She raced silently up the steps, fueled by anger. At the top, she saw a dim light shining through the door, which was ajar.

She stopped, nearly tripping over her own feet. Was she really going to confront an intruder? She looked like a wispy young boy, and she certainly would not be able to put up much of a fight. What if the person was dangerous, or had a weapon?

Or what if it was an Inquisitor, coming to investigate the professor?

She had almost talked herself out of going any farther when a rush of wind blew past her.

Someone inside the room had pulled the door open.

Zaneta Lucia bit back a scream at the shadowy figure standing in the doorframe. The shadow lifted a candle, and she recognized him.

"Burano?" she sputtered. "What are you doing?"

He scowled, holding the flickering flame near his face. "I could ask the same thing of you, Luca Manetti. Why are you trying to enter Ser Galileo's room at this late hour?"

She gasped. How dare he accuse her of trespassing when he was the one sneaking around. "I have done nothing wrong. You were in Professor Galileo's rooms, not me."

Burano narrowed his eyes. "You have no right to question me. I was merely dropping off some records from the workshop." He frowned and leaned closer. "You should not mention this to anyone. Your involvement could easily be misconstrued."

Was that a threat? It felt like one. But if she backed down now, he would know he had bested her.

"I don't know what kind of records you would need to drop off in the middle of the night, but it looks like you forgot to leave some." She pointed at the folded papers sticking out of Burano's pockets.

His frown deepened, and she heard a low growl in his throat. She drew back. In his eyes, she was an enemy. Would he physically attack her?

Or worse, would he ask questions about Luca Manetti, and find out that the boy didn't exist?

Zaneta Lucia's earlier bravado evaporated. She wanted nothing more than to be back in her room with the door firmly closed.

Burano pulled his cloak over the papers. "I'm warning you to keep quiet." He shoved past her in the narrow stairwell, pushing her back against the wall.

The contact knocked the air out of her lungs. The light from Burano's candle disappeared down the stairs and Zaneta Lucia was plunged into darkness. It took a moment to catch her breath, and for her eyes to adjust to the dark.

A small sliver of moonlight shone through a tiny window at

the top of the stairwell. Zaneta Lucia used its light to feel for the door to the fifth floor and close it. She didn't want to leave Galileo's private rooms open to more intruders. Then she collapsed onto the top step.

Zaneta Lucia sat in the dark for some time. Her pulse finally slowed to a normal rate. She pulled herself to her feet and walked back to the fourth floor, turning over what had just occurred in her mind.

Burano was snooping in Galileo's apartments in the middle of the night. He had twice told her not to say anything, and threatened her if she did. Had he intentionally slammed into her when he left?

And what had he taken from Galileo's apartment?

Zaneta Lucia sat on her bed, cold fear gripping her heart, until the sun began to rise.

TWENTY-ONE

The sunlight peeked into Zaneta Lucia's room. She huddled in the corner of the bed, her knees pulled to her chest. Exhaustion fogged her thoughts. She was still shaken from her late-night confrontation with Burano.

Then, with a start, Zaneta Lucia remembered that today was her deadline. She was supposed to meet with the Inquisitor in the library.

She had no intention of hurting Galileo, especially not after Burano's trespassing.

Zaneta Lucia dropped her feet to the floor with a thud. What if she told the Inquisitor about Burano? Maybe she could set the Inquisition after the sneaking assistant rather than the professor.

She stood, stretching out her arms. Her whole body felt lighter. If she squinted, Zaneta Lucia could see a way out of two of her dilemmas. The Inquisition would stop following her, and Burano would be wrapped up in their investigation. And if she could solve the problem of Burano and the Inquisition in one swoop, then she could finally turn her attention back to the entrance exam.

It was only a few days away. Soon, she would find out whether she was smart enough to attend the University of Padua.

At midday, Zaneta Lucia set out for the library. She wore her hat, but she kept her head up. Her renewed confidence felt like a shield, protecting her from harm.

Then she saw a group crowded outside the library. Her curiosity pulled at her. Zaneta Lucia stepped forward to see what had caught the attention of so many students.

They were gathered around a broadsheet pasted to the side of the library. Zaneta Lucia almost didn't recognize it at first, but then she saw a large word printed at the bottom: ZORZI. Her eyes darted back to the sketch.

It was a likeness of her. She flashed back to the portrait her parents had commissioned the year before. Zaneta Lucia had stood in place for hours so that the artist could sketch her. When the painting was finished, her mother had declared it beautiful.

In the simple lines of the etching she looked happy, her eyes wide and her hair cascading over her shoulder. The engraver had not copied the lace dress she had worn in the original portrait, and he had left out the dangling jeweled earring. She almost choked on a laugh. Zaneta Lucia had never owned a pair of earrings. The painter had added it after her mother requested richer accessories.

Instead, the broadsheet etching focused on her face. Did she still look that young and innocent?

Zaneta Lucia's vision blurred. Her eyes darted left and right, feeling the press of the students around her. Panic rose in her chest.

She was about to race back to the boarding house when someone stepped up and ripped the sheet from the wall.

It was Paolo.

"Oh, Luca, I didn't see you there," he said with a grin.

Paolo had torn down the sign. Why would he do that? Did he know who she was? Was he trying to protect her?

She laughed nervously, and tried to keep herself from vomiting.

The crowd dispersed, a handful of students muttering curses

at Paolo for stealing their entertainment. Paolo shook his head, and returned his eyes to Zaneta Lucia. He lowered one of his eyebrows. "Are you okay?"

"Oh, yes." Her voice came out gruff and unrecognizable. She cleared her throat. "I was up late, studying."

"Of course, the exam is coming up," Paolo said, slapping the side of his head. "I'm sorry I canceled our tutoring sessions last week."

He thought she was mad at him. How could she be mad at Paolo?

She roused her brain, calling it to activity. Before she could open her mouth, Paolo spoke again.

He took a step closer and lowered his voice. "I've been meaning to ask you. Have you heard about the runaway girl? The one from Venice?"

She swallowed hard. Her eyes darted to the broadsheet still clutched in Paolo's hand.

He mistook her attention and unrolled the poster. "She's quite pretty if you ask me," he said, looking at the sketch.

A blush rose on Zaneta Lucia's cheeks. She dropped her eyes to the ground.

"You came from Venice around the same time, right?" Paolo asked, rolling up the broadsheet.

"I don't know. I mean, we weren't exactly in the same social circles, from what I've heard."

Paolo laughed, seeking out her eyes. "You're not a very good liar. Didn't I tell you that the first time we met?"

Her heart stopped beating.

"Luca, what's wrong?" Paolo slapped her on the shoulder.

She tried to shake off her terror. At least he was still calling her Luca.

"I . . . I know the family she was supposed to marry. I don't want them to know where I am." It was the first thing that came to her mind, but it had the benefit of being the truth. She prayed that Paolo would believe her.

Paolo nodded knowingly. "Is that it? Well don't worry, your secret is safe with me."

He winked at her.

Zaneta Lucia took a deep breath. They were standing in the middle of the street, the midday sun shining on them, in full view of hundreds of strangers. She could not faint, or cry, or scream and run away. She had to stay composed. She had to act how Luca Manetti would act.

Then she saw more broadsheets stuffed in Paolo's pocket. "Why are you taking down those posters?" The words flew out of her mouth without a second thought.

Paolo shifted his weight, one corner of his mouth rising in a grimace. "Well, she must have had a good reason to run. So who are we to uncover her secret?"

Zaneta Lucia's throat tightened, and she pretended to brush something from her eye to cover the tears that had welled up. She could not open her mouth. She did not trust her voice not to waver.

"Look, I'll see you around. I need to keep working." He waved goodbye and walked off. She saw him stop and pull something else off the wall.

How many of those posters were there?

The meeting with the Inquisitor had flown out of her thoughts. She had more pressing concerns now.

At least Paolo hadn't connected the dots between Luca and Zaneta Lucia. She was closer to Paolo than anyone else in Padua. He had helped her find a place to stay, sign up for the examination, and he introduced her to Galileo. He had been tutoring her for weeks, and she saw him nearly every day.

And yet she still hadn't told him about finding Burano in Galileo's private rooms. Nor had she confided in him about her encounter with the Inquisition. And, of course, she was lying to him about who she was.

Was she protecting Paolo? Or herself?

Either way, it didn't make a difference now. She could not stay in Padua. Not when her face was posted around town. Sooner or later someone would figure out that Luca Manetti was Zaneta Lucia Zorzi.

And when that happened, she would be trapped.

Her face crumpled. She turned away from the street, pulling her cap low over her eyes. She didn't want to leave. The exam was days away. She had been working so hard to enroll at the university. And what would Paolo, and Mazzeo, and Galileo think when they learned about her deception?

She blinked back tears and sucked in a gulp of air. Breaking down on the street was not an option. Throwing back her shoulders and pretending she had Paolo's easy confidence, Zaneta Lucia hurried home to the boarding house.

As she climbed the stairs, she nearly crashed into Burano, coming down from the second floor. He gave her a scowl and stepped aside to let her pass. Zaneta Lucia held back a ragged laugh. The man had not forgotten their encounter the previous night, but she had. Her entire being was focused on her secret identity. She did not have the time or the energy to care about Burano.

The sound of voices on the third floor slowed her footsteps. She could hear Mazzeo talking loudly about a girl he had met at a tavern the previous night. Ugolino was laughing about some prank he was planning. Zaneta Lucia raised a hand to the doorknob but dropped it as if burned. She could not afford to waste time on such frivolities, when her life hung in the balance.

It was time to face facts. She could not keep living as Luca Manetti. She would have to leave behind her new friends and the life she had dreamed about.

A voice startled her out of her thoughts. "Luca!"

It was Galileo, calling down from the fourth floor landing.

"Luca, is that you? I've been looking for you."

Zaneta Lucia's eyes widened. "You have?" Had Galileo noticed that she had been avoiding him? Was he angry that she had not been working her full hours in the workshop for the past week?

"Yes. There's a matter of some urgency I wish to discuss with you upstairs."

"Now?" she sputtered. What if Burano had accused her of trespassing in Galileo's rooms? How would she defend herself? Her stomach flipped, and she grabbed the rail to steady herself.

"Let's go upstairs," Galileo said, waving at her to follow him. She quietly trailed him up the steps. When they reached the fifth floor, Galileo pulled open the door and gestured for Zaneta Lucia to join him in his study. The room was just as messy as it had been during their last conversation, with stacks of paper covering nearly every inch of space. He sat at the desk, and she settled into the chair across from his.

Her eyes were drawn to something at the edge of the desk. It was a loose folio tied together, perhaps a book manuscript. Zaneta Lucia instantly forgot every thought running through her mind. Had Galileo written something new? She was overcome by the urge to grab the folio.

Galileo must have noticed her attention. "Would you like to read my manuscript?" He lifted it from the desk and placed it in her hands.

She grabbed it hungrily. But before she opened it to gaze inside, she looked up at Galileo, a question written across her face.

"Go ahead," he said. "I've already circulated it with several friends, but because of your interest in natural philosophy, I thought you might want to take a look."

She eased the front page off and read the title—*The Starry Messenger*.

Galileo raised a hand. "Wait. There's something we should talk about first."

She braced herself, her hand frozen on the cover of the manuscript. Would Galileo accuse her of snooping? He wouldn't hand over his book and then throw her out on the street for trespassing. Right?

"Your examination is later this week. Is that correct?"

"Yes. It's Thursday morning." Her mouth felt drier than a desert. Would she even still be in Padua by Thursday?

"You should take the rest of the week off," Galileo said with a broad smile. "I'm sure you have some last-minute studying to do. And hopefully we'll be celebrating your entrance to the university on Friday."

Zaneta Lucia looked up with wide eyes. Galileo wanted her to succeed. How could she let him down after everything he had done to help her? Zaneta Lucia couldn't vanish in the night. What would Galileo think? He'd conclude that she was a thief, or that she was afraid of the exam.

She had to find a way to stay in Padua until Thursday.

"Thank you so much, Ser Galileo. I appreciate it more than you know."

In her entire life as Zaneta Lucia Zorzi, no one had validated her academic pursuits. No one had encouraged her. But here, Paolo and Mazzeo spent hours tutoring her. And Galileo sat and talked with her about natural philosophy. If she passed the exam, Galileo would be there to celebrate with her, along with Ugolino, Nonni, Timeo, and everyone else from the boarding house.

She could not let them down. "Thank you," she whispered.

"Since you're interested in natural philosophy, I assume you will take my class when you become a student." He reached into his desk and pulled out a small object. "So I wanted to present you with this compass, made here in the workshop. It's useful for all sorts of mathematical calculations." He handed it to her, and she set it on top of the manuscript.

Tears rose to her eyes.

Before she knew what she was doing, her mouth flew open. "The Inquisition is investigating you!" Zaneta Lucia clapped her hands over her mouth. How had that slipped out? But she knew the answer. Galileo was being so kind to her, more than she deserved. She couldn't let him be blindsided by the Inquisition.

"I know."

Her jaw dropped. Questions raced through her mind. "But how?"

He gave her a wistful smile. "It is a sad era we live in, Luca, where the church sees natural philosophy as an enemy. Studying nature is simply another path to understanding God's greatness."

A wave of guilt washed over her. Now Galileo would know that she had not confided in him sooner. "Professor, I was approached by a member of the Inquisition. He wanted me to report on your activities," she confessed. "I didn't tell them anything, though."

Galileo's eyes drifted to the window and then returned to Zaneta Lucia. "Thank you for telling me, Luca. You must have been in a difficult position."

"There's more," she said, barely above a whisper.

"What?"

"Someone in the boarding house was snooping in your rooms. I confronted him last night, and he told me not to say anything. I was afraid to tell you, because he might blame me." With a sigh, she collapsed back in the seat. She had not told him everything—she would not reveal her true identity—but at least now her conscience was clean.

"It was Burano." It was unmistakably not a question.

"Yes," she gasped. "You already knew?"

"Burano has been spying on me for months, maybe years. He is working for the Inquisition. Luca, you are not the first person they asked to report on me. They opened a file on me years ago, because they think my work threatens the church."

"They've been watching you for years?" Her voice squeaked with surprise, and she cleared her throat. "And Burano was working for them. But why didn't you fire him?"

"It is better to know your enemy. If I let him go, they would simply replace him with someone else, and I would never know who to trust."

She bit her lip, weighing her response carefully. For an instant, she thought about confiding in Galileo, and revealing all her secrets—but he would never understand.

"Please, Luca, don't worry about me. I am confident that those problems are nearly behind me."

"But how can you avoid the Inquisition?" Her fingers curled around the manuscript, still sitting on her lap.

"I may be leaving the University of Padua soon."

Her face fell. "Leave the university? But where would you go?" She had risked so much to come here. Why would Galileo give up his position?

Galileo pointed to the manuscript. "Just look at the next page."

She flipped past the cover read the heading. "It's dedicated to the Grand Duke of Tuscany," she exclaimed. Her eyes jumped from the page to Galileo.

"I tutored him when he was just the heir to the Grand Duchy. I would never draw the comparison, because of my humility, but you might say we were somewhat like Aristotle and Alexander the Great. While I am no Aristotle, I do believe the Grand Duke may expand his realm like Alexander. One day he might rule a new Italian empire."

"And this book will help him?"

"Keep reading," Galileo prompted.

Under his watchful eye, Zaneta Lucia began to scan the manuscript pages, eager to see what they contained.

In the book, Galileo described his new invention. It was some sort of looking glass, or spyglass as he called it. He claimed that it could be used to make far-away objects seem near.

It sounded like magic rather than science. But if Galileo said it worked, she believed him.

Zaneta Lucia stopped reading. She nearly dropped the text. Her eyes were drawn to a leather tube resting on Galileo's desk. "Is that the spyglass?" she whispered.

"Yes," he said with a chuckle, reaching out to pick up the tube. "Would you like a look?"

The air rushed out of her lungs and she felt lightheaded. "Of course!"

He held out the leather tube and she took it gently with both hands. It was lighter than she had expected. As she turned it around, she saw that each end was capped by a lens of ground glass.

"Look out the window," Galileo suggested.

She quickly adjusted the tube so that the eyepiece was flush with her eye, and leveled the spyglass. She lifted it to her face. When she closed her right eye, and gazed through the tube, the buildings several streets away were suddenly right before her. Even though she had not doubted the instrument, she gasped.

"This will revolutionize science," she said quietly.

"You're exactly right. I've shown it to others who think only of its military applications. Tell me, Luca, how do you believe the spyglass will help us study nature?"

"The power to magnify can tell us so much about how the world operates. Does it enlarge all objects, or is it primarily useful for looking at far-away things?"

"It's mainly for observing things at a distance," Galileo said.

"It is very difficult to perfect the ground glass for the other sort of magnification, though I suspect it will be possible in the future."

"Then think of what you could learn about the universe," she said. "You could look at the sun, or at the planets. You could see the *primum mobile*, the crystal spheres that turn the heavens." The possibilities were overwhelming. Everything they knew about the universe might be upended by this new invention. "You could experiment on the universe itself!"

"And that's exactly what I did," Galileo said, reaching over to flip the pages forward in his book. "I turned my spyglass on the heavens as soon as I realized what it could do. And I suspect my enemies will not be happy with the results."

With the spyglass still clutched in one hand, Zaneta Lucia read for a feverish moment, trying to soak in all of the text. Her eyes jumped between drawings of the moon and Galileo's description of the celestial body. "It's not perfect? The moon is imperfect?"

"Yes, it is," Galileo said. "You can see the problem."

"It goes against Aristotle. It contradicts every classical authority. The heavens are supposed to be perfect and unchanging. What does it mean?"

Galileo didn't answer her question directly. "This spyglass will anger many people. I can prove that the heavens are not permanent. They are always changing. The surface of the moon is marred by craters and mountain ranges, much like the Earth.

"The moon cannot be like the Earth." Her mind struggled against a new view of the universe that clashed with everything she knew. The Earth was unique. It was a different material than the heavens.

Galileo continued, casually tearing down two thousand years of astronomy. "And moreover, I have discovered new planets which are rotating around Jupiter."

"But that should be impossible," she gasped. "The planets are held in place by the crystalline spheres. Nothing could rotate around a planet. It would shatter the spheres."

"Yes," Galileo replied. "Which is why I doubt the spheres exist."

Zaneta Lucia blinked, her thoughts scrambled. Although she believed in Galileo's observations, her world was turned upside down. Everything she believed was in doubt, because Galileo had turned his instrument on the heavens and seen the impossible. It was hard to put her thoughts into words. "Does it prove Copernicus right? Is the sun truly at the center of the universe?"

"Yes, this evidence fits with Copernicus' theory," Galileo said, shrugging his shoulders. "The Inquisition will not be happy about that."

Zaneta Lucia raised a hand to her brow. "The Inquisition will claim you've contradicted the Bible," she said quietly. She slowly closed the manuscript. "But then how can this text protect you?"

"The dedication," Galileo reminded her. "The Medici will accept me at their court, and put their name on my book. They will verify my results to the world." He held out a hand for the spyglass, and she reluctantly handed it back to him.

"Because of the dedication?"

"Because I am giving them the new stars."

"No one has their own stars," she murmured.

"Exactly. It is a gift greater than any man has ever given. Who can gift stars? Their names have been fixed for centuries. The Medici will be the first in living memory to have their fame written in the heavens."

"They would be fools to refuse."

"And once they accept, no one can question my findings. No one can say my spyglass distorts the heavens. If they deny my observations, they risk slandering the honor of the Medici family."

"You'll use the Medici to verify your experiments," Zaneta Lucia breathed. It was daring. She had never heard of anything like it. But then again, she had never heard of giving someone a star. And what could match that?

"Luca, you study natural philosophy and you're unsettled by my work. You look like you've just seen a ghost steal the pope's tiara." He chuckled, but his mood quickly turned serious. "This book will be controversial. People will be shocked when they read that the moon is not perfect, Venus had phases, the heavens are changing, and new stars appear before our eyes. Many will deny my findings. They will blame the instrument, or faulty eyesight. I could spend a lifetime traveling across Europe with my spyglass, proving to doubters one by one that it works. Or I can use the Medici to advance my science."

Zaneta Lucia heard the confidence in Galileo's voice, and saw it mirrored on his face. He was not worried about the Inquisition or Burano. No, instead he had invented a shield for himself. He would use the Medici for protection.

"Thank you for showing me your manuscript. It is an honor." She handed the bundle of papers to him.

"Luca, I should be thanking you. It took real courage to tell me about the Inquisition and Burano. You could have held your tongue, but you did not."

His compliment turned her cheeks red, and she ducked her head. "I want the world to learn of your experiments."

"So do I," he said, another chuckle shaking his body. Zaneta Lucia looked up at his face and saw a twinkle in his eyes. "Now, I'm sure you have other things to read."

She gripped the compass in one hand and stood. "Yes, Professor." She walked out the door, leaving him in his office holding the spyglass and looking at his manuscript.

TWENTY-TWO

The conversation with Galileo gave Zaneta Lucia a new sense of purpose. His invention would revolutionize the world. It would inscribe his name in history. If Galileo could do that with the Inquisition spying on him from inside his own house, then Zaneta Lucia could avoid her pursuers for a few more days and take the exam.

No matter what happened after Thursday, if she passed, she would know that her choice had not been in vain.

So Zaneta Lucia vowed to stay in her room until Thursday, reviewing her notes for the examination. In quiet moments, she could almost hear a large clock, ticking down the minutes until she would appear in front of the examination board.

Zaneta Lucia poured over a little notebook, which she had bought with her dwindling coins. Inside, she had scrawled notes on a range of topics, from poetry to history to natural philosophy. Zaneta Lucia read over the notes so often that the words began to run together in her mind. She anxiously imagined the most obscure topics the professors might raise in her exam, and tried to prepare for every possible question.

She was too nervous to eat, and too afraid to leave the boarding house. She avoided everyone, including Paolo.

Finally she lay down on her bed, eyes closed, and counted her breaths. The exam was the next day. Cramming at this point wouldn't make a difference.

A knock on her door startled Zaneta Lucia awake. She had fallen asleep, her face nestled against her notes on Aristotle's concept of the soul. The fog of the nap still lingered in her brain.

She pushed herself up, and took a few short steps to the door. Who could be knocking? When the door swung open, she saw Paolo standing in front of her.

"Luca!" he exclaimed. "You look terrible."

"Thanks," she replied, giving his shoulder a shove.

"Ouch!" He feigned an injury. At least, she assumed he was faking. "You must be hard at work preparing for the exam."

Zaneta Lucia looked over her shoulder at the mess of books scattered across her bed. "Yes." She stifled a yawn.

"Did you forget about the female humanist? Lucrezia Marinella?"

Her eyes widened, and she raised a hand to her forehead. Had she been so busy that she had missed the speech? She groaned.

"Luca, it's today! That's why I'm here."

"What?"

"You asked if I wanted to go with you. And I said yes." He spoke slowly, as if she were an imbecile.

Zaneta Lucia tried to shake the sleep from her mind. "Do I have time to get ready?" Before Paolo answered, she started piling up her books and looking for her hat.

"We'll make time. It looks like you've been wearing those breeches for weeks."

She blushed, thankful her back was to Paolo. He was right, but she only had two pairs of pants. "Can you give me a minute? I'll meet you out front once I change."

"If you want, I can help you clean." Paolo pulled an orange peel off the edge of her desk.

Her blood ran cold. He had to leave. She could not change

her clothes in front of him. "No, I don't need help. I'll be down in a minute, I swear."

"Where did you even get an orange? You're full of surprises."

Zaneta Lucia heard the door squeak shut behind her She was alone. Was Paolo surprised by the orange, or her modesty? She had not spent much on the orange, not really. She just needed a reward for all of her studying.

Zaneta Lucia combed out her hair with her hands, tying it back in the leather binding. She splashed water on her face, and pulled on her slightly cleaner set of clothes. It would have to do.

In the blink of an eye, she and Paolo were walking down the street. Paolo was telling her a story involving a monkey and a parrot, and she couldn't figure out if it was true. Like most of his stories.

"And so he trained the parrot to sit on the *monkey's* shoulder. Can you believe it? I'd pay to see that."

Zaneta Lucia interrupted his laughter. "Paolo, did you read that book I gave you?"

His eyes were trained on a crowd in the square ahead of them. "What? Yes, of course."

"What did you think?"

"It was interesting. Do you think that's what women really talk about when we're not around? All that stuff about wanting to live without men?"

She cleared her throat. "Probably not." Would he say more? She wondered if Paolo thought like Mazzeo and the other boys. Did he see women as simpleminded diversions and nothing more? Zaneta Lucia count not find a way to voice her fears without revealing her secret.

"Anyway, it made me go look up a book I've been meaning to read, one by Boccaccio."

"Oh?"

"It's about famous women in history, all the great things they've accomplished, that sort of thing. Want to borrow it?"

"Of course." She breathed a sigh of relief. That was a good sign, right?

"Look." Paolo pointed. "I think that's the stage."

The square was packed with people gathered around a wooden platform erected in front of the main building of the university, between two of the pillars holding up the portico. So many students were waiting to hear a woman speak. Zaneta Lucia smiled. At the edge of the square she also saw groups of women, standing in threes and fours. Some must have come over from the outdoor stalls selling sweets and novelties, and others looked like young wives, or maybe even the mothers of the students.

Paolo grabbed her arm and pulled her into the thick of the crowd. "Sorry . . . apologies . . . *scusi*," he said as he elbowed past the young men. When he stopped, they were nearly in front of the platform. He gave her a grin, and her heart beat faster. Was he here because he wanted to see the female humanist, or because he knew it was important to her?

Important to Luca Manetti, that is.

She could never forget that Paolo did not really know her, even though they had spent so much time together. Their friendship would dissolve faster than Alpine ice in a Po Valley summer if he found out she was a girl.

But she still grinned back at him. His smile was infectious. Then she turned her eyes to the stage.

A professor appeared, dressed in the university's black robes.

"He lectures on rhetoric," Paolo whispered as the man began to speak.

In a monotone introduction, the professor promised a unique experience for the students and assorted listeners. He said Lucrezia Marinella was one of the finest living female orators, and named a handful of her published works.

Zaneta Lucia only half-listened, her pulse pounding in her ears. What would the female humanist look like? Would she wear pants? Would the students applaud her, or would they boo?

The professor left the stage, and a petite brunette, perhaps in her late thirties, took his place. She wore a simple dress of dark blue, and her tightly curled locks pulled back from her face, a thin cloth covering the hair wrapped at the nape of her neck. She was married. What did her husband think of her writings?

The crowd was silent, waiting for the small woman to speak.

"Thank you, Padua, for welcoming me." Her voice carried through the square, powerful yet melodic. "I am humbled by the opportunity to speak here today. Your city, and your university, stand testament to the virtues of Paduan men. My father studied medicine here, and my husband has given lectures to the medical students. Truly, I am honored to receive such a warm welcome."

There was a smattering of applause. Lucrezia Marinella cut it off with a hand. "However, you will not see me in your classrooms, nor will my sisters walk the portico around the university. And that is a shame. For nothing more than the crime of being born a woman, I was not allowed to attend the university."

Zaneta Lucia's fists clenched. Had Marinella actually tried to enroll? Did they publicly reject her? A rumble through the crowd sharpened Zaneta Lucia's fears. Would the male students revolt at Marinella's indictment of the university?

Marinella raised her hands. "I speak provocatively because I assume you are open to new ideas. Otherwise, why study at the university? So hear me now." The murmurs from the crowd quieted. Zaneta Lucia marveled at Marinella's confidence. How could she stand, so exposed, in front of a crowd that might riot at her words?

"God created man and woman, as we read in the Bible.

Genesis tells us that man was made from clay, from the lifeless matter of the earth. Woman, in turn, was created from the rib of man. Many male commenters take this as proof that woman should be submissive to man. I disagree."

The rumbles began again. Zaneta Lucia saw a few young men walk away from the crowd. But to her astonishment, most of the listeners remained. Zaneta Lucia caught sight of Paolo's face. She could not read his blank expression, but he had made no move to leave.

"Consider this. Man was created from dirt. Aristotle teaches us that the matter of a living object will shape its nature. Man, then, carries with him a lowly origin, from a lifeless object. Woman, on the other hand, is built from a different sort of material. The matter of woman is an ensouled, living being."

"Let us, then, assume that the material nature of women is superior to men. It follows, from Aristotle, that women are more suited to matters of the intellect. That makes women better than men at learning the arts and sciences."

Zaneta Lucia's mouth gaped. Marinella was deploying Aristotle in a way that Zaneta Lucia had never imagined possible. She was using Aristotle to prove that women were smarter than men. And most of the men in the audience were listening to her ideas.

"Should, then, the university exclude the higher sex? I can only conclude that women should be welcomed with open arms—unless you men are afraid of being eclipsed by women?"

At that, the crowd laughed. Zaneta Lucia saw a woman on the edge of the square shake a broom at the man next to her. He smiled, putting up his hands.

Some of the boys were certainly laughing at the very idea of a woman surpassing the male students, but Zaneta Lucia saw the truth in Marinella's argument. After all, Marinella had shown herself to be craftier than Aristotle, by using his own words to argue in her favor. And wasn't Zaneta Lucia herself already better at natural philosophy than Paolo, and most of the other boys in the boarding house?

"Look over there," Paolo whispered in her ear, pointing to the left of the stage. She followed his gesture. Back in the arched portico of the university she saw Galileo standing with two girls. They looked to be a handful of years younger than her, still young enough that they could walk through the city without an escort.

"Who are they?" she whispered back.

"His daughters. Virginia and Livia."

"I didn't know he had daughters."

"They are his natural children," Paolo explained. "He isn't married."

Zaneta Lucia watched the dark-haired sisters, who stood quietly with their father. Both girls kept their eyes trained on Marinella, absorbing every word. Galileo rested a hand on each girl's shoulder, and nodded along to Marinella's argument.

Marinella had shifted topics. Now she was explaining how much doctors could learn from so-called "uneducated" midwives.

Zaneta Lucia's gaze lingered on Galileo and his daughters. What would it be like, she wondered, to have a father who wanted to educate his daughters? Lucrezia Marinella, too, must have grown up in a family that prized learning for daughters as well as sons.

But maybe it was easier for the daughters of doctors or professors. Galileo's natural daughters might never marry. Even if they did, they had no family name to carry on. And Zaneta Lucia had never heard of the Marinelli family. They were certainly not in Venice's Golden Book of patricians. So Marinella could write, and give speeches, but what of the daughters of patricians? Were they too valuable as economic commodities on the marriage market to "waste" with an education?

A wave of applause caught Zaneta Lucia by surprise, and she started. Her shoulder bumped into Paolo's in the tight quarters of the crowd, and she reached out to apologize. Had the speech already ended?

Paolo grabbed her hand and tugged her forward. She could not see where he was taking her.

"Excuse me! Excuse me, Signora Marinella!" Paolo called out. He waved toward the stage, pulling Zaneta Lucia behind him.

Zaneta Lucia tried to yank her hand away. Her face must be red as a beet. What could she possibly say to Lucrezia Marinella? But in an instant they were standing next to the stage, and Paolo was reaching out to shake Lucrezia Marinella's hand.

"I'm Paolo Serravalle and this is my friend Luca Manetti," Paolo explained. "You definitely shook things up out there."

"Thank you, Paolo," she said, nodding at them.

"Anyway, my friend wanted to meet you," Paolo said, shoving Zaneta Lucia toward Marinella. "He's studying for the entrance exam, and he's a big supporter of female humanists."

Her chest tightened as she came face-to-face with Lucrezia Marinella. Zaneta Lucia stammered for a moment, then swallowed hard. "I've never heard Aristotle used in quite that manner," she managed to say.

"There are always new ways to interpret old questions," Marinella said with a quick smile. Then she looked deeper into Zaneta Lucia's face, her eyes narrowing. "What was your name again?"

"Luca Manetti," she said, a shiver passing through her body. Could Marinella see through her disguise? It was not possible.

Marinella reached out a hand, and gave Zaneta Lucia a squeeze. "Good luck on you examination."

Then Marinella turned, whisked away by the professor who had introduced her. Zaneta Lucia's knees shook.

Paolo whooped beside her. "Luca, you really have a way with the older women!" he chortled. "But watch out—she's married!"

Zaneta Lucia could not find the words to answer. Paolo had completely misread the moment between herself and Marinella. There had been nothing romantic about their connection. Instead, it felt as though Marinella had looked into her very soul and measured her worth. Her disguise might have fooled everyone else in Padua, but Lucrezia Marinella had seen the truth.

But, Zaneta Lucia knew in her heart, the woman would never speak a word of it.

TWENTY-THREE

Lucrezia Marinella's speech had left Zaneta Lucia weak in the knees. But she was also optimistic for the first time in weeks. She no longer felt quite so alone. There were people in the world arguing for women's education.

Zaneta Lucia might still be in disguise, but Lucrezia Marinella had shown her another way of existing in the world, where she might some day be openly accepted for her intellect.

But only if she passed the examination.

That night, the night before the exam, Zaneta Lucia could not sleep. She tossed and turned in her narrow bed. Her mind wove fantastic tales of her future, as she imagined the examiners laughing at her, or dark figures cornering her on the way to the examination to throw her in jail.

And what if she failed? Her shame would be shared by Paolo, Mazzeo, and Galileo, who had worked so hard to prepare her for the test.

When the sun rose, Zaneta Lucia forced herself to unwrap a dry, hard roll that had been in her cabinet for days. Her mouth chewed out of habit, not even tasting the bread. Between bites, she watched her hands shake. She shivered with nerves.

In a few hours, she would either be accepted into the university, or rejected. Zaneta Lucia had been working toward that goal for months, and today was her judgment day. She had risked so much, abandoning her family and her life in Venice. Now, finally, she would know if it had been the right decision. For an instant, she heard the beans jumping in the soothsayer's cup, but she cast off the vision.

Zaneta Lucia sighed. What if she had made a terrible mistake? What if she failed? Her stomach flipped at the thought. Would she slink back to Venice, her tail between her legs?

She would be humiliated, and her virtue would be destroyed. No one would believe that she was still an honorable woman after two months of independence. She would never marry. If she was lucky, her family would take pity on her and pay the entrance fee so that she could join a convent.

Her family name would be an even bigger laughing stock. The Zorzi Affair would go down in history as the scandal of the century.

What a terrible life. People on the streets would point at her, and mothers would warn their daughters not to be disobedient like Zaneta Lucia Zorzi.

At best, she would be locked up in a convent where no one could laugh at her. She would never again be able to come and go as she wished. How did Aunt Ricciarda stand it? Shuttered away from the world, forgotten and cast off.

Zaneta Lucia could not live like that, especially not after her time in Padua. As Luca Manetti, she could do as she wished and act with total freedom. How could she go back to such a restricted existence?

Venice was not an option.

Then Bologna? Pisa? She could find another university where they had never heard the name Zaneta Lucia Zorzi. She could adopt a new identity, and change her name again.

She could keep studying.

Eventually she would pass an entrance exam, and then she could attend a different university.

Zaneta Lucia collapsed back on the bed, tears rushing to her eyes. Even if that happened, what about after she graduated? She could not live as a boy forever. Eventually her secret would come out.

Unless she locked herself in her house, never marrying, never venturing out. She could never have friends, she would never see her family again. It would be not so different from the convent.

Zaneta Lucia wiped tears from her eyes. If she couldn't go back to her family and she couldn't move forward as Luca Manetti, what else could she do?

What was the point of even taking the exam?

Would it really matter if she passed or failed?

The large clock attached to the university struck nine, and it was time to leave for the examination.

~ ~ ~

In the early morning hours of Luca's exam day, dark still cloaking the city, Paolo paced on a small street just off the Via del Santo. He could feel the five hundred ducats slipping through his fingers. He had put off Sorto at their last meeting, but the man was losing patience. Without a concrete lead, Paolo was doomed.

Paolo leaned against the cool brick wall and lifted the broadsheet again, trying to catch the flickering candlelight from a nearby window. The girl had an oval face, and her long hair was pulled over one of her shoulders. She gazed directly at the artist. Her eyes were piercing even in the etching, and her expression blended confidence and naiveté.

Maybe the girl had never made it to Padua. She looked sheltered, like most patrician girls. He had known several of that type in Rome, and they couldn't be very different in Venice.

Paolo squinted at the image, and tried to imagine the girl wearing a disguise. Had she colored her hair, or trimmed it? Worn it up instead of down, or under a bonnet? If she had cast off her noble dress and donned the clothes of a peasant wife or a merchant woman, she might conceal her true identity. He angled the paper again toward the light, but her beguiling face still hid her secrets.

Paolo's thoughts were interrupted by a jolt. Was the ground shaking?

No, someone had shoved him, hard.

Before he could catch himself, Paolo tumbled to the ground, losing his grip on the broadsheet. He barely had time to throw out his arms and break his fall, as he tried to roll into the shove.

It was not his first fight, but this one had caught him off guard. Paolo pushed up with his arms, ready to face his assailant. Before he could stand, he felt a sharp blow to his ribs. He collapsed to the ground again. Paolo yelped out a curse and rolled away from the kicks. He grabbed his knife from the inside pocket of his coat as he leaped to his feet.

Paolo spun around, his breath heavy and his ribs screaming with pain. He squinted in the dim light of the street, searching the shadows for his attacker.

"Burano?"

It was Galileo's assistant. The man scowled, keeping Paolo at arm's length.

Paolo's roiling anger distracted him from the sharp twinge in his side. "So you'll attack me when I'm not looking, but you run from a fair fight?"

Burano scowled and reached into his pocked, pulling out a knife of his own. The gold handle glittered in the light. But the man did not advance. They were frozen in place, mirror images of each other on the dark street.

Paolo's eyes darted toward the Via del Santo, only a few steps away, and returned to Burano's knife. He could not see a soul walking by on the Via del Santo. No one would interrupt their fight.

But why had Burano attacked him? Had Paolo's suspicions about the man finally reached his ears?

Still, that did not seem reason enough to threaten him with a weapon. His thoughts pounded in his head.

The street—no, really, it was more like an alley—was lit primarily by moonlight. It was not the best setting for a fight. And Paolo's ribs howled when he shifted his weight. He would have a bruise the next day. If he was lucky.

Instead of advancing, Paolo slowly lowered his knife. When fighting was too risky, talking sometimes worked. "What's this about?"

Burano feigned a step closer to Paolo in response. Paolo leapt back and slammed against the stone wall of a merchant house. This was a bad spot. He had to seize control of the situation, and soon.

"Is this because you're stealing from Galileo?"

Burano's face dropped, and he stopped in his tracks. "So he did tell you," the man muttered. "I figured that little rat couldn't keep his mouth shut."

Rat? Paolo shook off Burano's cryptic answer. He had to focus all of his attention on the knife pointed at him. "You thought no one would notice? You aren't a very good thief."

A growl rose in Burano's throat. Paolo grimaced, gripping his knife's handle in his fist. His words were only fueling Burano's rage. Paolo had to change his approach.

"You can't run away from your crimes. I'm not the only one who knows," Paolo lied.

For an instant, Burano's attention wavered. Paolo saw him flinch at the words, and the large man's eyes jumped to the Via del Santo. This might be his only chance.

Paolo propelled himself forward, shoving the full weight of his body into Burano's right arm, which held the knife. The gold handle, flashy but not practical, slipped in the man's grip and he dropped it. In one smooth motion, Paolo kicked the knife out of Burano's reach.

Burano jumped back, recovering from the skirmish. Paolo still clutched his own knife in his hand, but his opponent was at least five stone heavier than Paolo, and the loss of his knife hadn't cowed Burano.

In a flash, Burano lurched at Paolo, and nearly caught him off balance. Paolo dodged, and as the man sailed past him, he shoved Burano's shoulder. With a crack, Burano's head connected with the stone wall behind them, and the oaf fell to the street.

Paolo stared for a moment, half expecting Burano to leap back up and continue his assault. But instead, his body lay motionless.

Paolo wasn't going to wait around to see what would happen when the man woke up. He shoved his knife back into his pocket, and for good measure he picked up the gold blade on his way out of the alley. He let out a breath of air once he was back on the Via del Santo, and quickly began walking toward the boarding house.

Paolo glanced over his shoulder.

Were there more assailants hiding in the shadows?

He still wasn't sure why Burano had attacked him. Was it simply because Paolo suspected the man of stealing? And who was Burano calling a little rat?

Paolo stopped in his tracks. He stood in front of a wall of broadsheets posted near the university. His eyes were drawn to the face of the runaway girl, with its sparkling eyes and mysterious upturned mouth.

And it hit him. Everything clicked into place.

Luca. It was Luca.

Paolo's heart pounded out of his chest and he broke into a run. The earliest pale light of morning was just breaking into the blue sky. Here, in a cluster of inns, he finally saw a handful of people walking through the streets. Paolo ignored their looks of surprise as he raced past.

He was thinking only of the reward.

But when he reached Anna's inn, the door was firmly closed. It was not even six o'clock in the morning, and most inns did not open their common rooms that early. He sank onto a low stone wall outside the inn, and raised a hand to his aching head.

Luca was the runaway girl from Venice. How was it possible? But it had to be true. Everything lined up—the timing of his encounter with Luca, who was fleeing from Venice. The boy's desire to attend the university. The shifty eyes and jumpy behavior. Luca had to be the girl, Zaneta Lucia Zorzi.

Paolo shook his head, suddenly exhausted. Why would a girl try to enroll at the university? He groaned, thinking of the hours he had spent tutoring her.

Why hadn't he noticed sooner?

TWENTY-FOUR

Zaneta Lucia walked on unsteady legs through the streets of Padua, each step taking her closer to the exam.

She didn't recognize anyone on the short walk to the administrative building where she would take the exam, and for that she was grateful. She had waited until the stairwell was quiet to leave the boarding house. Her stomach flipped as she imagined running into Burano, now that she knew he was a spy for the Inquisition. And she didn't want to talk to anyone else. If she opened her mouth, she might vomit.

Soon she was standing outside the tall, imposing building. Zaneta Lucia paused, her eyes searching the façade as if it were a text she could absorb in the last minutes before her test. With a sigh, she forced herself to take a step toward the building, and then another. She could not put off the examination any longer.

The large wooden door squeaked as she pulled it open, and she skittered toward the stairs like a frightened mouse, not wanting to make a sound. Her mouth was parched, and she silently cursed herself for not bringing a waterskin.

Finally she was standing outside the examination office.

Pretending a confidence that she did not feel, Zaneta Lucia walked through the door and gave her name at the desk—well, not her name, but Luca Manetti. In truth, it was feeling easier each day to fall into her new identity and forget her past.

The man behind the desk pointed her toward a small room with a table and four chairs. It looked nothing like the cavernous lecture hall she had imagined in her anxious dreams about this day.

The table was a long slab of wood, thick and imposing. Three chairs sat on one side, while a single lonely seat faced them from the far side of the table. Did she have to sit there all alone while she was interrogated?

Zaneta Lucia slipped around the table and into the chair, tapping her foot nervously on the floor.

The minutes stretched by, and her clammy hands began to shake. She gripped the arms of the chair and began counting in her mind. When that became dull, she added, subtracted, and multiplied figures in her head. Finally her hands were still.

The loud scrape of the door opening made Zaneta Lucia jump in her seat. She scolded herself for acting like a frightened dove. Her eyes were locked on the door, where three professors appeared in their doctoral robes. It was time for the exam to begin.

As the professors filed in, she noticed with a start that she recognized one of them. It was the professor who had given the lecture in Venice, a lifetime ago.

"Luca Manetti?" he asked, and she nodded, not trusting herself to speak. "You're here to take the examination." She nodded again. "Have we met? You look familiar."

She swallowed her fear and spoke, her voice shaking. "Yes, Professor Cornaro. I attended your lecture in Venice a few months ago. The one on Aristotelian mechanics?"

He smiled, and relief flooded Zaneta Lucia's body. "I recall. I look forward to discussing Aristotle with you during the examination."

Zaneta Lucia froze. Mazzeo had warned her not to bring up natural philosophy, for fear of angering the old-fashioned professors. But she knew Professor Cornaro was open to Galileo's ideas because of his lecture. She released a shaky breath and forced herself to smile at the other two professors.

The three examiners spoke in low voices for a moment and then sat behind the table, across from her. The tall, dark-haired professor sitting in the middle of the three seats looked down at a stack of papers, and then up at her. She felt small in the imposing wooden chair. "Luca Manetti. We will be testing you today for admission to the University of Padua, the oldest and most illustrious university in the world."

The rounder, white-haired professor to his right spoke next. "The examination will consist of three parts. First, I will examine you on classical subjects, including literature, poetry, and history. Then my colleague," he said, gesturing to the dark-haired man, "will ask you about music, grammar, and rhetoric."

"Finally," Professor Cornaro interjected, "We will discuss natural philosophy, geometry, and mathematics."

The white-haired man took over again. "The examination is not meant to be comprehensive, and we do not expect you to know the answer to every question. We are looking for a demonstration of sufficient knowledge in these areas to gain admission to the university, where you will be allowed to select your own course of study."

Zaneta Lucia nodded, her eyes jumping between the three professors. She swallowed. Would she be able to impress them? Or at least not embarrass herself?

She would have to fight against her fears if she wanted to succeed.

The professors leaned in and spoke to each other in quiet tones. When they settled back in their seats, the white-haired professor began to ask about Virgil and Terrance, and then about the last days of the Roman Republic.

For a second, her mind went blank. But she forced herself to focus on his words. She found, to her surprise, that she knew the answers. In fact, Paolo had prepared her for these very questions. He said the professors always asked about Roman poets and classical history, so she had rehearsed those topics endlessly during their tutoring sessions.

Zaneta Lucia answered smoothly and evenly. She took a moment to plan her answers, and avoided rushing through the material. She heard a whisper of Paolo's voice, encouraging her to give polished responses. He had made her practice again and again, firmly declaring that how she answered was nearly as important as what she said.

Thinking about Paolo calmed Zaneta Lucia, and she fell into a familiar cadence, poised and easy. " . . . and Octavian took the name Augustus in part to symbolize his transformation into *princeps*," she heard herself saying. "As well as to honor his adoptive father Julius Caesar."

The white-haired man nodded. Did that mean he approved of her answers?

She could not afford to second-guess herself during the exam. And anyway, the professor had already moved on to questions about the Greeks. She was shakier on the Greeks, but fortunately he focused on Athens during the period of their empire, and she had read her Thucydides. She spoke about Pericles, and the Peloponnesian War, and dropped in a reference to Socrates. Her confidence grew, and she leaned forward. To her surprise, she was actually enjoying the conversation.

The professor's last question was on Homer—which she had read several years ago. She grimaced silently. Her copy had been published specifically for female readers, so it highlighted the love stories and removed some of the bloodier scenes, deemed inappropriate for her sex. But she managed to stumble her way through an answer, and the white-haired man nodded when she finished speaking.

"I am satisfied," he said to Zaneta Lucia. "However, I am not saying that you have passed this section of the examination. We will confer at the conclusion of the test and decide whether you have passed in full." He gestured to his thin colleague to take over the questioning.

The younger man's style was very different. Speaking with the white-haired professor had felt like a conversation, which allowed Zaneta Lucia to relax. But this professor began peppering her with questions, and she had to follow closely to avoid missing anything. His questions were long, thought-out discourses, and they were often open-ended.

Zaneta Lucia frowned as she listened. How could she address every area he raised? She gulped a breath of air, and tried to focus on the positive. His long questions gave her time to think.

He began by asking her to compare the rhetorical techniques of Petrarch and Bruni, but in the middle of his question he launched randomly into the mathematical laws behind minor chords. She did her best to keep up with him. With a staccato rhythm, he would jump into the next question before she had fully answered the previous one.

"In Latin grammar, please explain the use of reflexive pronouns in the genitive," he asked, and as she stumbled through a response, he interrupted her. "Now tell me about philology, specifically as promoted by the humanist Lorenzo Valla."

His style flustered her. She tried to give complete answers, and speak clearly, but it felt like she was caught up in a whirlwind.

After a short time, the professor said, "I'm satisfied," and sank back into his chair.

Zaneta Lucia had no idea if she had done well or not, but at least it was over. She tried to shake off the unsteady feeling, and drew in a deep breath.

She had made it through two rounds of questioning, and now the finish line was in sight.

Her eyes turned to Professor Cornaro. He gave her a quick nod, and began. "Let's start with an explanation for the Aristotelian effect of an arrow's path when falling to the earth."

She instantly had the answers at her fingertips, and began relating how Aristotelian elements behaved in nature. She explained Aristotle's idea that an arrow created a vacuum behind it so that it would be pushed forward by the air rushing around the arrow to fill the vacuum.

When she finished, she looked at the examiner. He was nudging her on with his eyes, challenging her to contradict Aristotle. But she remained silent, remembering Mazzeo's warning to avoid provocative arguments, especially since the first two examiners seemed committed to the classics and Aristotle's authority.

"Is there anything else you'd like to add?" Professor Cornaro pushed.

Zaneta Lucia planted her feet firmly on the floor. This was her one chance to show her intellect. She would rather answer truthfully than pretend ignorance. It might cost her the exam, but her education was not simply about passing tests, it was about enriching her mind.

She cleared her throat and began cautiously. "Some have challenged Aristotle on this point." The other two examiners leaned forward in their seats, and she faltered. She took a moment to compose herself, and continued. "Galileo, for one, an esteemed professor of this university, has argued vacuums, as they don't exist in nature, cannot explain this phenomenon. He also uses a different method to explain the motion of an arrow. Although the arrow's movement seems unnatural from our perspective, particularly after the force of the bow is no longer acting upon it, it can be explained mathematically."

She fell silent, trying to read the faces of the three professors. They were as blank as marble statues, even Professor Cornaro. Had she said something wrong?

The professor changed the subject to less controversial topics. He quizzed her on several different mathematical equations, and asked a question on architectural geometry that nearly stumped her until she realized that her church in Venice, topped by a dome, could serve as an example.

Professor Cornaro didn't bring up Aristotle or Galileo again. Was that because Zaneta Lucia's answer had gone over well, or because he didn't want her to dig a deeper hole for herself?

Her mind raced, one compartment trying to assess her standing while the other wrestled with questions on quadratic equations developed by medieval Saracens.

During a pause between questions, the white-haired professor interrupted. "I think we've heard enough."

Her heart sank. Had her answers been so terrible? Did they always cut off examinations in the middle of questions?

Professor Cornaro seemed to read her fallen face. He gave her a reassuring nod. "We need a moment to confer."

The white-haired professor asked her to wait outside while they discussed her candidacy. Zaneta Lucia stood, her legs shaking.

She thanked the panel and walked to the door.

Zaneta Lucia had no idea if she had passed or failed. But as she stood in the hallway, her hands cold, she smiled. The examination proved how hard she had worked in the last two months. It showed how much she had learned. The panel had not asked a single question that she was unable to answer. She stood taller, and balled her fists.

She had done it. No matter what the professors decided, in her own mind she had succeeded.

Yet her breath was still shallow while she waited to learn her fate. Her knees felt weak, as if her body was betraying the confidence of her mind.

Zaneta Lucia leaned against the wall, and pretended that she had not a care in the world. She tried to ignore the faint sounds of muffled voices coming from behind the door.

Finally the door swung open, and her eyes jumped to Professor Cornaro. He was gesturing for her to return to her seat.

Before she did, a movement in the corner of her eye caught her attention. She swung her head to the right, and looked down the long, empty hall. At the very end, a man had just reached the top of the stairs.

With a start, she realized the man was pointing down the hallway, directly at where she stood.

Her heart pounded, and she slipped into the room, firmly shutting the door behind her. The crack of the door made her jump. Was the stranger pointing at her? Who could he be?

"Please sit, Luca," the dark-haired man said. She swallowed hard and returned to her seat.

Professor Cornaro smiled at her. "We have reached an agreement. Our decision does not need to be unanimous, but you must receive the votes of two examiners in order to enroll at the university."

Her eyes darted between the three men, reading their faces for clues and praying that Cornaro would speak faster.

"We carefully discussed your candidacy, as well as your examination, and it is the ruling of this faculty committee that you should be allowed to enroll at the University of Padua."

Zaneta Lucia felt faint, and she blinked several times. She had passed! A wave of excitement flowed through her body and a grin broke out on her face. She wanted to jump out of the chair and shout with joy, but all three sets of eyes were still locked on her.

So instead, she acknowledged each of the professors with a nod and said, "Thank you." She was suddenly hit with the monumental nature of her achievement. As far as she knew, Zaneta Lucia Zorzi was the first woman to pass a university entrance exam—but of course, they would never know she was a girl.

"I am honored, and I look forward to joining the students of the University of Padua." Suddenly the worries and fears from the past month were forgotten, and she was thrilled to realize she was a university student.

Then the door opened.

TWENTY-FIVE

A tall, thin man with graying hair stood in the doorway. He had a sour face, as though he had just bitten into a lemon.

Zaneta Lucia's stomach clenched. The man from the hall had followed her.

"Excuse me." He spoke to the professors, completely ignoring Zaneta Lucia. "My name is Leonardo Sorto. I must insist on speaking with you immediately."

Zaneta Lucia's forehead broke out in a cool sweat. She was cornered. All four men stood between her and the door. A shiver ran up her spine.

The white-haired professor frowned at the newcomer. "Is this university business? This is highly irregular."

"It is university business, because the University of Padua has an honor code. And this person has lied to you." Sorto finally turned his attention on Zaneta Lucia with a cold grin. "*She* is not Luca Manetti."

The silence echoed through the room. Zaneta Lucia could almost hear her pulse pounding through her body.

Professor Cornaro lowered an eyebrow at the stranger. "What are you saying?"

"This *person* has been masquerading as a boy." His voice dripped with distain. "She is making a mockery of you by trying to enroll at the university as a cross-dressing abomination."

"That's not true!" Zaneta Lucia burst out. Her voice reverberated in the small space. "That isn't true," she repeated quietly.

"Which part?" The white-haired professor's voice had turned grave.

"I just wanted to get an education," she whispered. "I just wanted a chance to study at the best university in the world."

But she saw their faces. She saw their heads shaking.

They must agree with the stranger. They believed she was an abomination.

"So you admit that you are a woman?" the white-haired professor pressed.

Her eyes darted around the room, hoping for a reassuring look or gesture. Instead she found only cold silence. "Yes," she confessed.

The tall professor gasped, and Sorto's smile widened.

"But I never meant to cause any harm, I just wanted to study at the university!"

Zaneta Lucia was ashamed to hear the pleading tone in her voice. She wanted to prove that she was just as capable as the male students, but if she burst into tears they would dismiss her without a second thought.

The white-haired professor shook his head, setting his jaw firmly. "Under the circumstances we will have to withdraw your offer of admission. I'm sure you understand."

A fire rose up in Zaneta Lucia's belly, surprising her with its strength. "No. I passed the examination. It should not matter if I'm a man or a woman. You all just agreed that I am qualified to attend the university."

The white-haired professor raised a hand, cutting her off. "Think of the scandal. Think of what the faculty would say. Who would want a *girl* in his classes? The medical faculty would be too ashamed to mention natural facets of the body, and the historians would have to abandon all talk of war."

"*You* asked me about war within the past hour!"

"But that was before I knew you were a member of the weaker sex. It would not be proper for you to attend the university."

Zaneta Lucia shook with rage. But what had she expected? She knew how society treated women. She had witnessed it first-hand while disguised as Luca Manetti. Men bragged that women were only good for sex and male heirs. Disrespectful words blossomed in men's mouths. They barely saw women as human.

Still, it was deeply humiliating. She had wanted so badly to do something different from her mother, and her mother, and her mother before her. She had been so proud of her own intellectual capacity.

But now it was all crumbling around her, and there was nothing she could do about it.

Zaneta Lucia wanted to scream, and cry, and throw things. But she held back her anger, and her deep sadness, and all the other emotions coursing through her body.

She could not change the world by herself.

Caught up in her thoughts, Zaneta Lucia barely heard the tall professor lean over and whisper to the white-haired professor. "See, this is why we can't enroll women. They get so emotional. Women have no control over their higher faculties of reason."

His words shot ice through her veins. A cool, marble-like discipline descended over her mind.

Zaneta Lucia picked up her notebook, her face blank. She squared her shoulders and gazed at the committee. In a chilly voice that she barely recognized, Zaneta Lucia said, "Thank you for your consideration. I regret that I will be unable to enroll at your university. I apologize for wasting your time."

She did not wait for a response. Instead, she turned her back on the committee, pushed her way past Sorto, and left the room.

No one stopped her.

Once she was in the hall, Zaneta Lucia walked steadily and quietly to the stairwell.

"Wait!" a voice called out from behind her.

It was Sorto. The sneer had vanished from his face. "I apologize for my theatrics. Your parents hired me. You will be returning to Venice with me."

Zaneta Lucia spun around to face him, already several steps down the staircase. "I don't know who you are, but I have no obligation to you. You are nothing to me."

He gave his head a little shake. "I have already written to your father, who is worried about you. Your family will receive the letter by tomorrow, and I promised that we would arrive the next day. You will come with me."

Fatigue swept over Zaneta Lucia. She had been fighting for so long, and it had come to nothing. She had failed. "Fine. But I will not leave until tomorrow. Come to my boarding house at nine o'clock and I'll go with you."

She watched Sorto's face compress into a grimace.

"Your parents will not be pleased if they discover that I allowed you an unsupervised night before returning to Venice. They will not be pleased at all."

She locked eyes with Sorto, her earlier fire returning. "Then they do not need to know about it."

Sorto broke their eye contact, clearing his throat. "There will be consequences for this," he predicted. "And not just for you. For Galileo and your friend Paolo as well."

But Zaneta Lucia turned away from Sorto before he had finished speaking, and walked down the stairs. She only had a few more hours of freedom before she would be returned to the watchful eyes of her family home. She was not going to waste them arguing with Sorto.

Outside, it was a clear, crisp fall day. Zaneta Lucia could

smell cinnamon in the air, wafting from the stalls in Piazza del Erbe. Students crossed the open square in front of the university, laughing and complaining about their classes.

Zaneta Lucia felt suddenly exposed, as though she glowed with a halo of infamy. Were people looking at her? Had Sorto somehow announced her crimes to the entire city before destroying her chance to attend the university? She hurried back to the boarding house, and kept her head down.

Zaneta Lucia managed to run upstairs to her room before the stream of tears fell from her eyes. She threw herself on the bed, melancholy gripping her soul.

Her adventure was over, and now she would be forced back to Venice. Sorto would drag her back to her family regardless of what she wanted. And in Venice, she would be seen as a shameful, fallen woman, a black mark on the Zorzi name.

But Zaneta Lucia was tired of fighting. She was tired of hiding.

She pulled her hair out of the leather binding and shook it out. It fell at her shoulders, much too short for any respectable woman—but then again, she wasn't a respectable woman any more. It would take months, or years, before it would grow out. And until then, she would not be able to leave her house without people pointing.

Zaneta Lucia slapped her hands over her forehead. Had Sorto said something about Paolo? How did he know Paolo?

She frowned, remembering the posters with her picture. The ones that Paolo had ripped down. Zaneta Lucia had hoped that Paolo was trying to protect her—but now she saw that was the wishful thinking of a little girl.

How could she have been so blind?

Paolo must have been after the reward all along.

He had betrayed her. He had told Sorto about the exam. How else would the man have known to show up in that room at that exact time? Paolo knew how important the examination was to her, but he only cared about the money.

He didn't care about her.

A rap on the door interrupted her thoughts. Her heart skipped a beat. Had Sorto changed his mind? Was he here to drag her, kicking and screaming, out of the boarding house and past all her former friends?

She buried her face in her pillow, and ignored the knock.

Zaneta Lucia heard the scrape of wood on the doorframe. She jumped up from the bed, ready to shout away any intruder.

Paolo stood before her, his clothes disheveled as though he had slept in them.

Had he come to gloat? Or to brag about his reward? She lifted a hand to straighten her hair, loose and unkempt. But what did it matter? He already knew her secret.   She scowled at him. At that moment, she didn't care about her red-rimmed eyes and tear-stained face. "What do you want?"

"Can I come in?"

"It looks like you already did."

"Luca—I mean, Zaneta Lucia . . ." His voice trailed off. He stepped inside the room and closed the door behind him. "I heard what happened at the university."

"Who told you?"

"Leonardo Sorto."

She took a step backward, her lip curling in disgust. "You need to leave."

Her voice sounded strong, but inside she was unmoored. Some part of her had wished that Paolo could explain everything. That he was on her side and still her best friend. That her secret hadn't changed anything between them.

But he was no different than everyone else. They all divided up the world into neat little boxes. When anyone challenged the system, they were cast aside as a heretic, or a madman, or a witch.

She would not cry in front of Paolo. She blinked, keeping her eyes trained out the small window. Her composure would crumble if she looked at Paolo.

But he stood there, not moving. Did she have to push him out the door?

"Please, listen to me," Paolo pleaded.

"I don't want to hear your justifications. I just hope the reward was worth it."

Instead of leaving, he stepped toward her. He grabbed her by the shoulder and pulled her eyes to his. "It's not what you think. I am not the one who told Leonardo Sorto about your secret."

Zaneta Lucia's heart beat faster. "You didn't? Then how did you know?"

His eyes searched her face, and she cringed as she imagined what he saw. But instead of recoiling, or pushing her away, Paolo continued to hold her shoulders gently in his hands.

"I only realized last night. Burano attacked me in an alley, and he said something about a little rat. He thinks you were telling people that he was stealing from Galileo."

Zaneta Lucia's mind went blank. Then the words tumbled out. "Burano attacked you? Are you alright? Did he hurt you?" Burano had confronted Paolo because of her—because of their encounter in the stairwell. If Paolo had been seriously hurt, or killed, it would be her fault.

"I'm fine, but it knocked a few things loose in my mind. I realized that you were the girl in the posters." He stopped, his gaze falling to the floor. "And you're right. At first, I wanted the reward. That money would change my life. I could travel, or start my own business. I wouldn't have to study law just to impress my father. But that was before I knew it was you."

Her throat tightened.

Paolo continued. "I was confused. But I didn't tell Sorto, I swear."

"But if it wasn't you, who turned me in? You don't think it was Burano, do you?"

"I know who it was," Paolo said quietly. "But you aren't going to like it."

"I need to know," she said. "Please tell me."

"I ran into Sorto this morning. He was already on his way to the exam. I tried to stop him, but he refused to listen to reason. He told me who turned you in." Paolo paused. "It was Mazzeo."

"Mazzeo?" she repeated, her mind trying to process what Paolo had said. "Why would he do that? He was so supportive of my studies."

But she had a sinking feeling. She remembered their conversation about female humanists, and the flash of anger Mazzeo had tried to hide. He had encouraged her when he thought she was Luca Manetti, but maybe he felt uncomfortable with a girl studying mathematics. Maybe, like Marinella said, he could not stand to be eclipsed by a woman.

He had never been a true friend, not like Paolo.

"Paolo?" she asked quietly, searching his eyes. She could not read them. "Why didn't you turn me in?"

His answer came quickly, as though it was a reflex. "I didn't want to hurt you."

His eyes softened and she saw a smile touch his eyes before it reached the rest of his face. One of his hands moved up from her shoulder to her jaw. His fingers brushed her face gently, and a shiver went up her spine.

"Zaneta Lucia, you're brilliant. I wish you could attend the university. You're worth a hundred of the students who mindlessly parrot what the professor says, or what their fathers say, or what they read in some ancient text. I can't imagine what you've been through in the past few months, hiding who you are. Your happiness is worth so much more than money. And I never want to hurt you."

She reached out to him, and without thinking, she pulled him into a kiss. At first when their lips met she could sense him pulling back, almost instinctually, but soon he gave in and wrapped her in his arms. The kiss deepened, and Zaneta Lucia felt the tug of desire in her chest.

Paolo stepped back, a lopsided grin on his face. "I, uh, forgot for a moment that you're a woman," he admitted bashfully.

She giggled, and he began to laugh, too. It broke the tension in the room. Her shoulders loosened, and she caught Paolo's eye again.

Their kiss had taught her something—her independence as Luca Manetti was not true freedom at all. She had been playing a part, and concealing who she really was. She had let one part of her, the intellect, dominate.

Even as Luca, she had been conforming to all the unspoken rules about how men and women should behave. She had been an actor, reciting lines.

She had never challenged the rules, she had simply hidden herself in a world of pretend.

She gazed into Paolo's eyes. "Stay here with me."

"Are you sure?"

"I have to go back to Venice in the morning. But tonight, I want you to stay."

He wrapped his arms around her, and she rested her head on his chest, melting into his embrace.

In Paolo's arms, she saw another option. She could be herself, and not just play a role. Paolo knew her secrets, and he still wanted her.

And she could make her own choices, based on what she

wanted, not what others expected of her.

In the morning she would become Zaneta Lucia, the disgraced and fallen woman. But she wouldn't let that label define her. She would be herself, no matter what.

TWENTY-SIX

Light seeped through the cracks of the shutters that Zaneta Lucia had drawn the night before. A ray of sun touched Zaneta Lucia's face. She slowly opened her eyes, squinting against the light, and smiled. Paolo's arms were wrapped around her. The narrow bed was not meant for two people, but she had not slept so well in weeks.

Zaneta Lucia drew in a deep breath. She did not want to rise from the bed and face the day. Dawn signaled the return of reality, which she had worked so hard to ignore last night. Sorto would be outside soon, ready to cart her back to Venice.

She could not stay in Padua, where everyone who knew Luca Manetti would be furious like Mazzeo. And she could not keep running, always worrying about the next time Sorto would find her.

Paolo began to stir next to her. He stretched, resettled himself, and pulled her back into the crevice between his chest and his arm.

She sighed, and sank back into the bed. She just wanted another few minutes to ignore the outside world.

Paolo brushed her shoulder softly with his fingertips. "Zaneta Lucia?" he whispered.

"Hmm?" She refused to open her eyes and see the morning light creeping across her walls.

"Come away with me." Paolo put a hand on her cheek and gently turned her face so that he was gazing into her eyes. Zaneta Lucia wanted to pull back, but she saw the sorrow written across his face. "We don't have to live by your parents' rules, or my parents' rules, or anyone's rules. We can do as we please. We could travel the world together."

She shook her head, and a tear rolled down her cheek. Breaking rules didn't erase their consequences. Today, she would go back to Venice with Sorto. She would beg her family to place her in the convent with her Aunt Ricciarda. At least her aunt would understand what she had done.

Paolo would not like it, but it was her choice, not his.

And anyway, his idea was a fantasy. She had been hiding for weeks, constantly trailed by stress and anxiety. Paolo had no clue what that life would be like.

"Your father would disown you if you dropped out of school to run off with a disgraced girl."

"I don't care."

"Then what about your family? You could never see them again. You would not be a Serravalle."

She saw his resolve crack. He bit his lower lip. "I don't want to lose you. I'm just getting to know you."

"You've only known Zaneta Lucia for a day." She placed a hand on his chest to soften her words. "You can't throw your life away because of one day."

"You're wrong," Paolo said, gripping her hand in his. He locked eyes with her, and she saw the fire in his gaze. "I know you, Zaneta Lucia Zorzi, Luca Manetti, whatever you call yourself. You are the bravest person I have ever met. You're awkward, and endearing, and curious, and I love you."

Something in her broke, and she buried her face in his chest so he wouldn't see her tears.

Paolo held her close, his hand brushing her hair. He

whispered in her ear. "I will come with you to Venice. I will stand outside your palazzo until your father agrees to speak with me. I will ask for your hand in marriage, and we will spend our lives together."

She wanted to live in Paolo's dream, but her mother would never allow it. Bartolomea Zorzi still carried a grudge against her sister for shaming the family. If she knew that marrying Paolo would make Zaneta Lucia happy, she would throw her daughter into a convent without a second thought.

Zaneta Lucia swallowed her feelings and sat on the edge of the bed, her back turned toward Paolo. She could not face him as she spoke, or he would see her heart breaking. "I wish it could be. But we cannot ignore reality forever. I have to return to Venice, and you should continue working toward your degree."

"I cannot force you to do anything." He sighed. "I will have to live with whatever you decide."

Tears clouded her vision. "You know I would rather stay here in Padua, or run off with you, but I can't steal you away from your family and your future. I'm not that selfish."

Paolo rested a hand on her shoulder. She did not want to push him away, but she had no choice.

Zaneta Lucia stood, and began looking around the room for clothes. "I have to get ready. I suppose I can't wear pants." For some reason, that simple thought struck her as one of the saddest things she'd ever heard.

She rooted under the dresser, reaching behind a loose panel for the dress and necklace she had been wearing when she fled from her parents' house. "I suppose this is as good a dress as any to wear back to Venice." She pulled it over her head, chafing against the uncomfortable tightness around her waist.

Paolo caught her from behind in a tight embrace. She turned to face him.

They clung to each other like sailors gripping the mast in a storm. He wrapped a hand around her head, his fingers running through her hair to pull her closer.

"This is the first time I've seen you in a dress," he said.

Zaneta Lucia could hear the wobble in his voice.

Finally they broke from each other's arms, and Zaneta Lucia gathered the small number of things she would carry back to her old life. She would bring a stack of books, even if her mother might throw them into the canal.

This room had been her home, her sanctuary, for nearly two months, and now she had to leave.

As she looked around the room, her eyes landed on Paolo. It felt like her heart was ripping in two. She had found independence, and a man who loved and respected her. And already, she was being forced to leave it all behind.

Zaneta Lucia could crumble, but she walled off her emotions and vowed not to cry. She would go back to Venice with her head held high.

The bells tolled nine o'clock. Zaneta Lucia pulled Paolo into one last embrace, their lips meeting for the final time. He seemed to sense the ending of a chapter that had only just begun, and held on to her even as she pulled back.

But she would not linger. It would only make parting harder.

She brushed off her cheeks and picked up her small bag. Paolo followed her out the door, and down the hall to the stairs.

As they walked past the common area, she saw Ugolino and Timeo, staring with their mouths open.

She had forgotten that she was wearing a dress. And Paolo clutched her hand as though it were a protective talisman. Zaneta Lucia gave the boys a flippant grin, and kept walking down the stairs. She might not change their minds about women, but at least they would think twice before they openly joked about silly, ignorant girls.

Zaneta Lucia stopped in front of the closed door of the

boarding house. What would she face outside? Would Sorto bring an angry mob to force her into a wagon or carriage? Would people come to stare, or jeer at her?

Paolo gave her hand a squeeze.

She took a deep breath and pushed the door open.

In the bright light of a brilliant fall day, she saw a crowd gathering outside the boarding house. A murmur rose from the group as she stepped out of the building.

But she didn't see Sorto. Instead, the man at the center of attention was Galileo.

"Thank you!" he called out, his voice booming off the surrounding buildings. "If not for the city of Padua, and the university, I would not be receiving this great honor."

The crowd cheered, and Zaneta Lucia shook her head. What was happening?

Galileo waved to the crowd and lifted something over his head. It was the spyglass he had shown her in his office only a few days earlier.

Galileo turned back toward the boarding house. His eyebrows raised as he saw Zaneta Lucia and Paolo.

As he walked over, several people stopped to offer him congratulations and handshakes.

"Ah, Luca . . . or should I call you Zaneta Lucia?" Galileo said.

A hot flash of shame erupted in her body. Galileo had given her a place to live and shown her his manuscript and his invention. And she had deceived him. Her eyes fell to the ground.

"I am so sorry, Professor, for lying to you," she began.

But before she could continue Galileo interrupted her.

"I can understand why you did it. I saw you at the Marinella lecture. I can't begin to describe the look on your face as you watched her. I don't hold your deception against you. It was the only way to achieve your goal."

A wave of relief flooded through Zaneta Lucia.

"Let me explain something to you," Galileo continued. "It's something of a thought experiment, which I know you enjoy."

Zaneta Lucia nodded and listened, her worries fading into the background.

"Imagine a boat, sailing on the sea. It's traveling very quickly and a strong wind pushes its sails. Can you picture it? Now imagine a room, filled with butterflies. They are wafting through the air, every color in the rainbow. The room is still, without a breeze. The butterflies are floating completely naturally. You follow?"

The image devoured her mind, consuming her. She could almost feel the gusts of air from the butterfly wings. "Yes."

"But what if the room of butterflies is inside the boat? The ship is cutting through the water, moving so swiftly. What happens to the butterflies?"

The two visions collided in her mind.

Galileo continued his monologue. "The butterflies will float, untouched by the boat's speed. Their movement is not affected by the ship's motion." He lowered his voice, leaning in so only Zaneta Lucia could hear his next words. "To me, this proves that Copernicus is right. The earth is traveling around the sun, even if we don't feel the wind. The butterflies cannot tell they are crossing an ocean. They have no idea that they are on a ship. And yet they are moving, even though they are unaware of their motion."

Zaneta Lucia was rendered speechless. Galileo's words contained more truth than many of the books she had read. And yet, he had to whisper, for fear of triggering retribution. How could the nature of the universe be so dangerous?

She found her voice. "Ser Galileo, I'm convinced."

He gave her a wink. "Then imagine that you are one of those

butterflies. You go about your business, acting in accordance with your nature, unaware of the systems around you. They do not affect you. They do not even touch you." He paused for a moment. "I have two daughters, you know."

"Yes, I know." She pictured them standing next to Galileo during Lucrezia Marinella's lecture.

"I would be proud if one of my daughters grew up to show an interest in mathematics and natural philosophy. What I'm saying, Zaneta Lucia, is that you should be like the butterfly. Be yourself, and ignore the systems moving around you. They might affect you in ways you do not realize, but you should be free to act as you wish within that enclosed system."

Her throat tightened. His words were a gift. They would carry her through the difficult next days of her life. For a second, she closed her eyes and imagined herself surrounded by butterflies. Zaneta Lucia dropped her eyes to the ground as tears began to cloud her vision. She tried to find words to respond to Galileo, but found none.

"Galileo," Paolo said. "She plans to return to Venice."

"I'm sorry to hear that," Galileo said. "Because I, myself, am going to Florence. As you know, Zaneta Lucia, I dedicated my work on the spyglass to the Medici. I have negotiated a position at their court, working and demonstrating natural philosophical principles."

"Congratulations." Zaneta Lucia kept the sadness out of her voice. She truly was happy for Galileo, who was moving to one of the most important courts in Europe. She wanted him to escape the Inquisition's spying. And his fame and status would surely rise from his association with such a noble family.

Galileo smiled at her. "I would be honored if you would join me."

"What?" Zaneta Lucia wondered if she had heard him incorrectly. "You want *me* to come to Florence?"

"I will need an assistant, and the court would certainly be impressed with your knowledge of natural philosophy. Women at court are often interested in studying the world and nature. And my daughters will be traveling with me. They could use a tutor."

Zaneta Lucia's mouth hung open. Galileo was offering to take her to Florence, where she could avoid the shame of returning to Venice a fallen woman. She could start a new life for herself in Tuscany. And at the court of the Medici! It was more than she could ever have imagined.

"The honor would be mine," she managed to stammer.

Paolo whooped and clapped her on the back.

"I should also let you know that I spoke with my colleague, Professor Cornaro."

Zaneta Lucia froze. What had the man reported about her exam? Had he catalogued her shortcomings to Galileo, or told the story of Sorto unmasking her secret?

"Cornaro was quite impressed with your exam, and he believes you would have made an excellent student at the University of Padua. Based on his recommendation and my own, you might be able to take courses at the University of Pisa once we move to Tuscany."

"Thank you, Ser Galileo!" she cried. Her throat tightened. She wanted to make a grand speech worthy of Lucrezia Marinella, but her mind was a jumble of thoughts and emotions.

"Don't thank me yet," he said with a smile. "It will be hard work, assisting my experiments, tutoring my daughters, and taking classes."

"Of course, but—"

At that moment, Leonardo Sorto appeared, walking toward the boarding house. His face was contorted into a grimace.

"Let's go," he said brusquely to Zaneta Lucia. He smirked at Paolo, still standing at her side. "Say goodbye to your little paramour."

"She's not going anywhere with you," Paolo said, stepping toward Sorto.

Zaneta Lucia put an arm on his shoulder and gently pushed him back. "Let me take care of this." Turning to Sorto, she drew herself up to her full height. "I will not be traveling back to Venice with you. I will be accompanying Ser Galileo to Florence, to work at the court of the Medici. If you have a problem with that, take it up with Grand Duke Cosimo de Medici."

Sorto's eyebrows folded together. "Stop telling tales. Your parents expect you to return home tomorrow."

Her heart pounded, but she refused to show any weakness. "No. Tell my parents I will write to them, and hopefully some day I can visit. But I won't be returning to Venice today."

In an instant, Sorto darted toward her, his hands striking fast as a viper. He tried to grab her arm. Zaneta Lucia jumped back, narrowly avoiding his grip.

How far would Sorto go? Would he try to carry her back to Venice against her will?

Luckily she did not have to find out.

"Stop this right now!" Galileo bellowed in his most authoritative voice.

Sorto froze. Zaneta Lucia took another step back, well out of the man's reach.

"You should be ashamed of yourself," Galileo said to Sorto. "This woman is under my protection as the Philosopher and Mathematician to the Grand Duke of Tuscany."

Sorto shrank under Galileo's scrutiny. "Signore, I thought the girl was lying," he began.

Zaneta Lucia fumed. "Perhaps you should listen more closely, then." She was grateful for Galileo's intervention, but this was her fight. "I will be going to Tuscany, not Venice."

"But my commission!" Sorto pleaded, still speaking to Galileo instead of addressing Zaneta Lucia directly.

She held up a hand. "I don't care about your commission. Go back to Venice and take it up with my parents." Zaneta Lucia turned her back on Sorto. He slinked off into the crowd that was now watching closely.

Galileo raised an eyebrow at her. "I doubt he'll be back after that. Now, we have plans to make. I will leave for Florence in two weeks, and I could use your help packing up the workshop and preparing my scientific instruments for the move. Shall we get started this afternoon?"

Zaneta Lucia nodded. Her mind reeled, struggling to comprehend the past twenty minutes.

"See you then," Galileo said with a nod of his head. He went into the boarding house, and the door slammed behind him.

Zaneta Lucia released a breath of air, her knees suddenly weak. Paolo reached out a hand to steady her. "I can't believe I'm really going to Florence with Galileo," she said.

"I'm so happy for you," Paolo said.

And even though they were on the street he pulled her into his arms.

"Paolo," she sighed. Would she always have to choose between what her mind wanted and what her heart wanted? She was afraid to admit it, but she did love Paolo.

They had become friends, and love had been the last thing on her mind while she was hiding as Luca Manetti. And yet here she was, enthralled by the boy she had met on the dusty road to Padua.

He released her. "Zaneta Lucia, I meant it when I said I would follow you to Venice. Why would that change now that you're going to Florence? I only have another year of classes, and I can finish them in Pisa just as easily as here. And then you can come down to Rome with me, to meet my family. This is just the beginning."

Zaneta Lucia beamed so hard she thought her face might

shine like the sun. "Are you sure?"

"Of course I am," he said, and folded her into his arms once again.

The tension melted from Zaneta Lucia's body. For weeks, she had run from her troubles. She had fled from Mario Barbaro, fearful that her life would be over if she stayed in Venice. She had watched her dreams evaporate, and had tried to reconstruct them as Luca Manetti. And that, too, was only a temporary escape.

But now, she was standing at the dawn of a new phase of her life, one where she could learn about the world with Paolo at her side. Paolo was right—it wasn't the end, it was just the beginning.

The End

AUTHOR'S NOTE

This novel is grounded in the history of seventeenth-century Italy, but I have taken some liberties with historical facts. Yes, Venetians really did cast beans to predict the future—it was the Venetian version of reading tea leaves. But Zaneta Lucia Zorzi, as well as Paolo Serravalle, are imagined characters, though Zaneta Lucia's family was prominent in Renaissance Venice, and you can still see her palazzo in the Castello neighborhood.

Galileo, of course, is real. He did, in fact, run a boarding house in Padua, where he manufactured and sold instruments to his students. The Inquisition did keep a file on Galileo, and they did have an informant living in his house. And Galileo's telescopic discoveries did gain him a position with the Medici. Over two decades later, Galileo was put on trial for heresy because he promoted a heliocentric universe. However, the trial largely focused on obedience rather than scientific principles. Many in the Catholic Church, especially the Jesuits, accepted Galileo's findings. Yet the Church reserved its right to interpret Scripture, and resented Galileo's assertion that nature was a more reliable source on God's creation than scriptural interpretation. Galileo was found guilty and sentenced to house arrest, near his oldest daughter who had taken religious orders in Tuscany.

The novel accurately depicts science in the early seventeenth century, which was embroiled in turmoil. Englishman Francis

Bacon argued that natural knowledge had been built on a faulty framework. Bacon promoted tearing everything down and starting anew. This provided opportunities for men like Galileo, who challenged Aristotelian knowledge, but it also engendered strong opposition. Galileo successfully tied his astronomical findings to the authority of the Medici family, a strategy that many, including the Royal Society in London, would copy.

At its heart, this novel is about women in the Renaissance. These women are too frequently ignored in the history books. Many were treated like pawns in dynasty-building families, useful for marriage alliances but treated as financial burdens. Most Renaissance women were forced into marriage or the convent. This was especially true in Venice. The republic created the *Libro d'Oro*, or Golden Book, in 1297. It named the patrician families who would hold political power in Venice, and membership was restricted to those listed in the *Libro d'Oro*. Patricians had to marry their daughters into Golden Book families, but dowry inflation and a shrinking patrician class meant that many were unable to find suitable partners. By the late sixteenth century, 60% of patrician daughters were placed in convents, the majority against their will.

Many, like Zaneta Lucia, wanted to escape that fate. Seventeenth-century nun Arcangela Tarabotti called the convents a "living hell" for women enclosed against their will, writing that Dante's message over the gates of Inferno, "abandon all hope, ye who enter here," should be inscribed above convent doors.

Tarabotti was one of a number of published female authors in late Renaissance Venice. Lucrezia Marinella and the other female humanists mentioned in *The Zorzi Affair* are real, and did argue that women were equal, or perhaps superior, to men. I included their story to emphasize that women did fight against their assumed inferiority. These women were often educated by mothers and fathers who prioritized learning. However, university education was still restricted to men. That would change, but it took centuries. Although Zaneta Lucia was not able to attend the University of Padua, the school would award the first diploma to a woman, the Venetian mathematician Elena Lucrezia Cornaro Piscopia, in 1678. By comparison, Oxford University did not grant a diploma to a woman until 1920!

In the Renaissance, many women found a way to build meaningful lives in spite of the restrictions they faced. I like to imagine that Zaneta Lucia made a splash in Tuscany, and lived a long and happy life studying nature in whatever manner she desired.

ACKNOWLEDGEMENTS

Thank you for reading *The Zorzi Affair*. And thank you in advance to all the readers willing to share their opinions by writing a review—reviews from people like you help other readers find *The Zorzi Affair*.

If you enjoyed *The Zorzi Affair*, check out the prequel series, the Palazzo Galileo Mysteries. In the first book, *A Matter of Glass*, Paolo Serravalle agrees to run errands for the eccentric professor Galileo. But when he comes face-to-face with assassins, Paolo quickly learns that the trouble might not be worth the discount in rent.

I would also like to thank my family for their support. This book is for my daughters.

For more, visit http://www.sylviaprincebooks.com

email: SylviaPrinceBooks@gmail.com
Twitter: @SPrinceBooks
Facebook: facebook.com/SylviaPrinceBooks

ALSO BY SYLVIA PRINCE

BARRETT BRIDES TRILOGY

The Barrett family have fallen on hard times.
Can Elinor, Livia, and Arabella find love as scandal threatens to tear their family apart?

ENGAGED TO AN EARL (BOOK ONE)

Driven by duty, Elinor Barrett agrees to marry a stranger. When a handsome printer catches her eye, will Elinor abandon duty to follow her heart?

SEDUCED BY A SURGEON (BOOK TWO)

A passion for machines animates Livia Barrett.
When a Scottish surgeon romances her, how far will Livia go to run from love?

ROMANCED BY A RAKE (BOOK THREE)

Shunned by society, Arabella Barrett longs for love.
When a dashing rake suggests a fake engagement, can Arabella deny her feelings?

BELLADONNA'S KISS TRILOGY

The Belladonna are Renaissance Florence's best-kept secret.
An elite guild of female assassins, the Belladonna patrol Florence
to protect women from wealthy and powerful men.
But who's really pulling the strings?

BELLADONNA'S KISS (BOOK ONE)

Serena Fortuna might be an orphan, but she found her family in
the Belladonna. Until her best friend goes missing and a mission
with the Medici puts her life in danger.
Now, Serena will have to choose between the Belladonna and
her life.

BELLADONNA'S EMBRACE (BOOK TWO)

Serena takes a job with the Borgias in Rome to unravel a mystery
about the Belladonna. And Tessa Forte vanished from
Florence—only to find herself working for Caterina Sforza.

BELLADONNA'S REVENGE (BOOK THREE)

Serena, Tessa, and Matteo have to work together to save the
Belladonna—or die trying.
Assassins don't get a happily ever after—or do they?

THE STOLEN CROWN TRILOGY

Denying your birthright can be deadly.
Caterina de' Medici, the youngest daughter of Europe's richest family, and Scottish orphan James Stewart must learn to trust each other—or lose everything.

THE MEDICI PRIZE (BOOK ONE)

When a failed kidnapping attempt strands Caterina de' Medici in the Tuscan woods with her mysterious Scottish guard, she must confront her enemies to save their lives.

THE BROKEN BLADE (BOOK TWO)

The past can't stay hidden forever. Caterina and James must uncover a kingdom-sized secret before it destroys them both. But will they discover the truth before their enemies strike?

THE STOLEN CROWN (BOOK THREE)

A lethal secret threatens Europe's most powerful families. In the shocking conclusion to the Stolen Crown Trilogy, Caterina and James must choose between a crown or their lives.

THE LION AND THE FOX

When a mysterious letter sends Niccolo Machiavelli to investigate the murder of a Medici, he stumbles into a dangerous world of rich young patricians, mysterious prostitutes, and shocking violence. Niccolo thinks he can play the fox to outwit his enemies—but has he underestimated the lion?

SALEM MEAN GIRLS

Cavie Lucas came to Salem hoping to make friends.
She never dreamed it would be so deadly.
It all started with Ann Putnam—blonde, flawless, and leader of
the Glass Girls, the most popular clique in the colonies. At first,
Ann seemed perfect. Until she started calling people witches.

The Salem witch trials meets *Mean Girls* in this dark, wickedly
funny, and explosive book.

PALAZZO GALILEO MYSTERIES

Can you trust your senses?
When your landlord is Galileo, you should question everything.

A MATTER OF GLASS
(Book One of the Palazzo Galileo Mysteries)

When Paolo Serravalle travels to Venice to pick up a mysterious
package for his landlord Galileo, he quickly realizes that the man
harbors dark secrets. Is it really worth risking his life just for a
discount on rent?

ABOUT THE AUTHOR

Sylvia Prince writes intense, page-turning novels that bring the past to life. She specializes in historical fiction and young adult. Sylvia holds a PhD in history—and loves the bizarre but true stories she has encountered over the years working as a historian. Did you know, for example, that in 1492 the pope received a blood transfusion by literally drinking the blood of three young boys? (It didn't work—the pope and the boys all died.) Sylvia lives in the Pacific Northwest with her husband and two daughters. She and her sister, bestselling author of historical romance Emma Prince, love comparing notes and picking each other's brains about all things historical.

For more, and to sign up for Sylvia Prince's newsletter, visit http://www.sylviaprincebooks.com.

email: SylviaPrinceBooks@gmail.com
Twitter: @SPrinceBooks
Facebook: facebook.com/SylviaPrinceBooks

Made in United States
North Haven, CT
15 December 2021